THE MIRROR IN THE RIVER

DALE LOVIN

ILLUMIFY MEDIA GLOBAL
Littleton, Colorado

The Mirror in the River
Copyright © 2019 by Dale Lovin

The views and opinions expressed in this book are those of the author and do not necessarily reflect the official policy or position of Illumify Media Global.

Published by
Illumify Media Global
www.IllumifyMedia.com
"Write. Publish. Market. *SELL!*"

Library of Congress Control Number: 2019911974

Paperback ISBN: 978-1-949021-60-8
eBook ISBN: 978-1-949021-61-5

Cover design by Debbie Lewis

Printed in the United States of America

DEDICATION

To the memory of my parents, Wanda and Buddie Lovin

MONDAY, AUGUST 27

He had done this before. How many times, he couldn't guess, but it seemed like a million. What he did know was that each visit was becoming more difficult, practically unbearable. As Senator Bertram Russert contemplated the awful experience that was only minutes away, the familiar symptoms gnawed at him. His stomach was queasy, and he had difficulty breathing, as if he were within a vice. Worst of all, the senator recognized that his own hand controlled the jaws.

Making matters even worse was the insufferable weather. Washington, DC withered under a brutal heat wave and there was no relief in sight. An oppressive atmosphere and clogged traffic created a pall of stagnation. Russert stared through the window of his vehicle, anguish in his eyes reflected in the darkened glass. Russert could feel the stop and start of the automobile as it clawed its way through the gridlock. Inch by inch, his grim destiny drew closer; the destiny that he had created.

Russert had held office as a United States Senator for twenty years and was regarded as one of the most powerful men in Washington. Life in the national spotlight had become routine, and he was comfortable with the elite status to which he had risen. He was an intuitive maestro in the ageless symphony of government, wealth, and power. On this torrid morning, however, the maestro found himself before an orchestra with no score. Twenty years of political ascendancy meant nothing as he faced the next twenty minutes.

Russert shifted his attention back to the world within the limousine. He absent-mindedly flicked imagined particles from his suit and straightened the cuffs of a crisp, white shirt. The vehicle's air-conditioned sanctuary was nothing more than momentary respite from the wretched heat and the awful moments that lay ahead. Russert knew his sanctuary was almost to end.

How many of these meetings had he endured? He envisaged the ordeal that lay before him and the humiliation that it would deliver. He longed for the occasions when these matters could be handled on the telephone; such conversations were no problem, they were easy. All he had to do was to exchange a few pleasantries, discuss the business at hand and conclude with a crisp farewell, the entire experience could be void of personal contact. It was the face-to-face episodes that he so dreaded. They had become more than he could bear.

The limousine finally made it through the bustle of Washington's endless throngs of tourists, government buildings and museums. The driver, a seasoned veteran to Washington's traffic madness, eased the vehicle into a no parking zone adjacent to the office building that was Russert's destination.

"We're here, sir," he said reluctantly, as he glanced in the rearview mirror.

Russert sat in silence, evaluating what was about to take place and contemplating the irony of his situation. It was nothing for him to appear on a Sunday morning television news show and articulate national policy to millions. He could dine with dignitaries, cabinet secretaries, the First Lady, and even the President. Almost daily, he exchanged intellectual banter with members of the press and national leaders. Russert knew he was regarded as a master in the delivery of sophisticated jokes. He could laugh with an admiring audience as they approved his wit and endorsed his intellect with knowing smiles and raised cocktail glasses.

Dropping his head with his hands over his face, he pressed hard on his brow. There sure as hell was nothing sophisticated or intellectual in what he was about to do. "How, in the name of God, have I allowed myself to get to this point?" Russert breathed the words into his hands. How could it be that every day the world came to him, yet here he was, preparing to grovel like a pariah before a man he detested?

Unable to prevent a quiver in his voice, Russert spoke to his driver, "I should be no more than twenty minutes."

"Yes, Senator. I'll be waiting right here."

Russert lifted his face and sucked hard, holding breath within his lungs for a final moment of introspection. It was time. The door opened, and he lifted himself out of the car and into the suffocating air. Brushing past the mass of bodies that filled the sidewalk, he made his way through a revolving door and stepped into a cool lobby adorned with waterfalls and tropical plants. People rushed about in a blur of business suits and tailored skirts. An aroma of coffee filled the air. Conversations and laughter reverberated off the cavernous walls, the throb of the business of life. Russert ignored it all.

Russert moved quickly; his eyes laser-focused on a bank of elevators. Without breaking stride, he stepped into an awaiting glass capsule and ascended to his rendezvous. Upon reaching the fourth level, he walked a corridor of polished marble and, with a silent prayer and sickening dread, United States Senator Bertram Russert entered the law offices of Whitman, Markham, and Schultz.

"Good morning, Senator." A receptionist smiled her words. "Mr. Whitman is expecting you. Please go on back."

"Thank you, nice to see you." Russert dispatched a robotic smile as he started down the hallway that led past the law library and cluttered offices of attorneys and staff. At the end of the corridor, Russert paused. After taking a deep breath, he uttered a silent prayer before entering the office of Mark Whitman.

Whitman's office was immaculate. The windows offered a spectacular panorama of Washington, DC. Haze lay trapped over the heat-stricken city, creating the impression of a surreal, three-dimensional mural suspended outside Whitman's office. Heavy windows stifled the clamor of traffic and construction. Whitman's office was cool and eerily silent.

Mark Whitman sat behind a massive wood desk and was engaged on the telephone. The lawyer silently motioned for his visitor to take a seat. Russert nodded his head in greeting, closed the door behind him, and situated himself in a high-backed chair. As he waited, his gaze drifted about the office that had become much too familiar. Framed diplomas, elegant bookcases, and photographs of Whitman in the company of athletes, politicians and dignitaries, were a testimony to the people of power to whom Mark Whitman had access.

Russert had often noted that Whitman's office held no photographs of a wife or children. Nowhere were there any images of a family enjoying a vacation on the beach or a mountain ski resort. Shortly after they first met, Whitman had told Russert that he was married with children. But Russert couldn't find any evidence of that. There was nothing that indicated a human heart or love for another person.

Concluding his conversation, Whitman muttered goodbye and hung up the telephone. He did not stand to greet the senator or even extend his hand. Instead, he practically glared at him.

"Thanks for stopping by." Whitman's voice was curt.

"Not at all." Russert nodded as he spoke.

"Would you care for something to drink?"

Russert desperately wanted this ordeal to terminate as quickly as possible, but he doubted his ability to carry on without at least a sip of water. His throat felt like parchment. He had to remind himself to breathe.

"I would love some cold water if you don't mind. It's brutal outside."

Without breaking his penetrating stare, Whitman pressed a button on his desk console. "Water please, Janet."

Uncomfortable silence followed. Russert felt himself being stripped naked under Whitman's merciless stare. In years of public life, Russert had refined the art of presenting a flawless image of senatorial dignity. He maintained a slender physique with perfectly groomed silver hair. He was poised, appropriately tanned, and always immaculately dressed. But Russert knew that Mark Whitman looked straight through this veneer and could see with crystal clarity the loathsome truth buried behind the public image of Senator Bertram Russert.

Russert grew hot. *Oh, my God, how has this happened? How did I ever allow myself to come to this?* He attempted to break the awkward moment with a nod of his head and a weak smile. Whitman responded with an unblinking, cold stare.

Momentary relief was blissfully granted when a middle-aged woman entered the office carrying bottles of water. With a wave of his fingers, Whitman silently indicated that the water was for the senator. The woman removed the lid from a single bottle and handed it to Russert.

"Thank you," Russert said, receiving the water and taking a sip to sooth his throat. Whitman's secretary made her exit and cumbersome silence again descended. Russert set the water bottle on the floor beside his chair and resolved to end the nightmare. He reached into his briefcase and extracted a bundle of legal-sized papers.

Leaning forward, he placed the documents on Whitman's desk. "This is the information you requested from Sherri concerning the shopping mall in Richmond. She said if you need anything more, feel free to call."

Whitman glanced at his desk and said, "I'll have someone handle it." His eyes shifted back to Russert. "Sherri's doing well, I hope."

"Fine, thank you. She sends her regards."

Whitman, not interested in small talk, merely nodded. Sherri Stone, Russert's wife of thirty years, was a part of the Stone family that owned shopping malls, sports arenas, office buildings, casinos and hotels around the world. Mark Whitman represented the legal interests of Stone Enterprises and understood perfectly the relationship between Sherri Stone and Senator Russert. Any semblance of love had long disappeared from their marriage that was held together by shared political and social demands. The expected duties of their public life were executed with pleasantness and respect.

Russert took another sip of water and again reached into his briefcase. He retrieved an oversized, plain brown envelope. Clear tape sealed the edges to ensure the safety of its contents. Without a word,

Russert placed two hundred thousand dollars in cash on Whitman's desk. He then leaned back in his chair grateful the ordeal was almost over.

Whitman let silence permeate the air like toxic gas.

Finally, Whitman spoke. "Thank you."

Lips pressed tightly closed, Russert nodded slightly as he rose to leave. Whitman remained seated; his mouth now turned into a sardonic grin. Russert stood in awkward silence, feeling like an embarrassed schoolboy searching for courage to speak. When his words finally came, they were a choked whisper: "I'll be fishing in Colorado next week. The judge will be with me."

Whitman cocked his head slightly, his eyes drilling into Russert's face. "I'll let Maria know."

"Yes, please do," Russert spoke again, scarcely more than a whisper. "The particulars are in the envelope."

Russert stood motionless as Whitman eased his chair backward, entwining his fingers together beneath his chin, obviously delighting in the moment. Russert had no choice but to endure the torment.

After a long, deliberate pause, Whitman brought his body forward and spoke in a brusque, dismissive tone. "I'm sure it's nothing that we haven't done many times previously. Consider it handled. See you next time."

"Yes, yes, next time," Russert breathed as he turned, silently praying that his legs would not fail. Bertram Russert walked out of Whitman's office and made his way down the hallway, a corridor that seemed to extend into eternity.

Whitman watched the doorway and wondered what was going through Russert's mind as he was forced to pass by the offices and walk the gauntlet. Whitman contemplated the minutes that had just transpired, recalling Russert's quivering voice and the pathetic weakness in his eyes. But it was more than that. What exactly was it? As Whitman reflected, he began to grasp the entirety of Russert's reticent demeanor. It was everything the man had done from the moment he had stepped into the office. His body language. As animals detect an earthquake minutes before the seismic rumblings, Whitman could sense that Russert was a man teetering on the brink of collapse.

Whitman pressed the button on his desk console. "Janet, call Felix Gomez. I want him in my office at six o'clock this evening."

————

EVENING'S RUSH hour traffic choked the blistering streets. Within the air-conditioned respite of Whitman's law firm, attorneys concluded their day. Many gathered in offices to discuss cases or the latest sports news. Laughter and tinkling of ice cubes in cocktail glasses filled the halls. It was a welcomed ritual to conclude another rigorous day.

Mark Whitman sat in his office alone. This had become a common occurrence in recent months. He was aware that other members in the firm were discretely commenting about his behavior. He knew they talked about how he was spending less and less time practicing law and handling matters for the firm. They talked about how he passed hours alone in his office with his door closed. Yes, people were talking. They said he had changed, that he rarely spoke anymore, and was rude.

Whitman swiveled his chair away from his desk. He didn't care what the hell people were saying. *Let them talk*, he thought. He looked about his office, recalling the endless hours he had spent within the confines of these walls. How many times had he toiled alone into the wee hours of the night? Had he made a decent living? Yes, of course. But did he have a fraction of the wealth that most of his prominent clients enjoyed? No fucking way. Whitman smiled slightly, obviously comfortable with his decision. They could all go to attorney hell. His business was now with Felix Gomez, not a bunch of suspender-wearing, limp dick, overgrown Boy Scouts who happened to have law degrees. Whitman's smile widened. His world was about to change.

He heard Felix Gomez in the hallway. Whitman gathered the envelope he had prepared and quickly placed it inside his desk. He was prepared to greet his visitor.

Gomez entered Whitman's office dragging a handkerchief over his brow and neck, managing only to smear the accumulated grime from the sweltering, smoggy outdoors. With a final swipe beneath the black ponytail that hung to his shoulders, Felix closed the door behind him and collapsed into a chair. Luxuriating in the refrigerated air, he paused for a moment before speaking. "God, what an awful day. I tried to get here in a cab, but traffic was not moving, so I gave up and walked. Who in hell was the genius who made this place the capital of your country anyway?"

Whitman grinned as he evaluated the well-dressed man whose slight accent added to his dignified persona. "You can always go back to Mexico, Felix."

Felix flashed a quick smile and shook his head. "I'm way too smart to even think of something that crazy," he said. "Those were hard times. I have no desire to return to those days."

"You know, Felix," Whitman said in a tone that implied the two of them shared a special secret. "I am probably the only person in Washington who understands the road you have traveled. I consider it both our good fortunes that the road led you here."

Sensing that Whitman expected a response, Gomez deliberately appeared thoughtful, taking care not to give any hint that might betray his true feelings. Gomez had long considered Whitman nothing more than a spoiled, rich bastard who wouldn't last a day outside of his air-conditioned, privileged life as a lawyer. Gomez masked his face and spoke with sincerity. "I agree. Things have worked out very well for us." He absentmindedly lifted his arm to stroke his ponytail and remained silent, allowing Whitman to direct the conversation.

"I can only imagine what your life has been," Whitman said as though he had intimate knowledge of Gomez's life.

Gomez felt like vomiting at the phony benevolence in Whitman's voice. Controlling his impulse, Felix was thoughtfully quiet as memories of his life flashed in his mind, knowing that a man such as Whitman could never begin to understand what he had been through:

Filthy streets where he learned to survive by his wits. His mother's sacrifice of mattress politics so that her son could escape to a life as a low-level assistant with a consulting firm in Washington, DC. His street instincts had quickly developed into polished and articulate speech, lending an air of refinement. With an uncanny ability to be in the right place at the right time with the right people, Felix soon moved within the social scene of Washington's affluent. Strikingly handsome, many women found him irresistible, and men paid vast sums of money for his services. Felix blinked a final moment of introspection. Yes, he had done well in America. But he would never forget where he had been, what he had seen and done. Felix Gomez knew the ruthlessness of street life. The lawyer seated before him had no idea.

With a forced smile, Gomez spoke. "Yes, I agree. We have seen many changes over the years. I hope our arrangement will last for a long time."

Whitman threw his head back and expelled a hard laugh. "Changes? That's an understatement. You began with me by handling small, chickenshit stuff. Now look where we are. We are on the brink of millions."

Distasteful as it was, Felix admitted to himself that Whitman did indeed hold the keys to his future, at least for short while longer. Crossing his legs and reaching to stroke his ponytail again, Felix assumed a business tone. "I'm sure you had a reason for calling me here today. What do you need me to do?"

"Yes, Felix, I do have something for you to handle." Whitman leaned over his desk and dropped his eyes for a moment before continuing. "The good senator was here today. He and the judge will be in Colorado again next week. I need for you to get in touch with Maria. Give her the details and ensure that everything is taken care of. It should be a pretty routine drill, a bit more bizarre than usual but still the same old stuff," Whitman said with a grin that resembled more of a sneer than a smile.

"Not a problem, I'll handle it."

"Fine, with that out of the way, now we need to discuss the other matter." Whitman smiled. "The one that is going to make us wealthy men."

Gomez felt his body involuntarily tense. "I'm listening."

Whitman tapped his fingers on his desk as he formulated his thoughts. After a few seconds he said, "Felix, we are going to have to make our move quickly. My gut tells me that our window of opportunity may not be as large as we initially thought. Early September is our time. The other dates are too far out. That's the way it has to be, so plan accordingly."

Gomez nodded thoughtfully, acknowledging Whitman's words. "That's very soon. Any particular problems?" he asked.

"I'm not sure how to answer that, Felix, but yes, I think we may have a problem. It's nothing that I can specifically put my finger on. Over the years, I've learned to trust my instincts, and after meeting with the senator today my gut is sure as hell talking to me and I intend to listen." Whitman seemed to look straight through Felix, as though he were speaking to himself. "There is something about how Russert handled himself today," he said. Whitman seemed lost in thought for a moment before focusing back on Gomez. He then spoke in a commanding tone. "We've been planning this for months, Felix. Every detail has been discussed a hundred times. It's time to move."

"If September is our best opportunity, that's when we will make it happen. I'm sure I can handle any problems that come up."

The air in the room instantly electrified. Whitman's eyes narrowed as he leaned over the desk and hissed, "I do not pay you to handle problems, Felix. I pay you so we don't have fucking problems!"

Felix remained motionless and silent. He had experienced these outbursts before and knew to let a few seconds pass before responding. His face registered the reprimand. Finally, he said, "Absolutely sir. I understand. No problems. No problems."

"Very well," Whitman said, easing back into his chair and relaxing. "Plan on September. October is pushing it for the weather anyway. Lots of things about September are better. Unless we get something totally unexpected thrown at us, we're going in September."

"I'll be ready, you can count on it," Felix replied, acknowledging

Whitman's authority, but he struggled to maintain his composure. It took every ounce of his resolve to conceal the hatred he felt for the man.

As Whitman looked down to open the top drawer of his desk, he spoke, "First things first. Just make certain that next week goes well with the senator and the judge."

"I'll get on it immediately," Felix replied.

"It should be routine. We'll be speaking again soon to keep everything in motion for the big job," Whitman said in a tone that indicated that the conversation was over. He retrieved an envelope from his desk and shoved it toward Felix.

They had done this before. Felix knew that he was receiving seventy-five thousand dollars and written instructions. Placing the envelope into his pocket, he stood. "Thank you. I'll stay in touch." He turned to walk from Whitman's office.

"Oh, Felix," Whitman called out just as Gomez reached the doorway.

Felix turned and faced the lawyer.

Whitman sat behind his desk, and with a look of contempt on his face said, "You will not fucking believe what you are going to read." He paused, then raised his voice to a near shout. "A princess! A goddamned princess! A crown and fucking jewels! Holy Christ!"

Felix Gomez stood in the doorway, void of expression. *What could this man possibly know about what I would believe?*

Giving only a slight nod in response, Felix walked away.

THE LATE MORNING sky sagged over Arlington, Virginia. It was going to be another day of heat and gritty haze. Maria could faintly make out Washington's skyline through the thick air as she looked out her apartment windows while recalling her earlier telephone conversation with Felix. When Felix called, he had been insistent that they meet today. This was not unusual, but in recent weeks when he exhibited urgency, she couldn't help feeling nervous. Ever since Whitman had told them of his big idea, conducting routine business had seemed trivial. Felix was perpetually on edge and had become withdrawn. This was not what she was accustomed to, and she didn't like it.

Without realizing it, Maria shook her head in determination. Her decision was final. Whitman's plan was the opportunity of a lifetime, and she would not let it slip past. She hoped that Felix's commitment was just as strong. Gathering her purse and sunglasses, and with a quick glance about her apartment, she left to meet Felix for their lunch in Washington. They had much to talk about and Maria welcomed a chance to talk face to face. Words were not important. It was his eyes that were important. Felix's eyes would tell her all that she needed to know.

Arriving at their usual restaurant, Maria spotted Felix at a table in the back. He loved this place. He found it ironically humorous to handle business among suited executives and government officials who always filled the tables around them. Felix wore summer slacks and a brightly colored Caribbean shirt that directed attention to his dark ponytail.

As usual, Maria felt admiring eyes track her movements as she crossed the floor. When she reached his table, she could feel the eyes diverting to Felix. Men were envious of the man who was meeting a woman of such beauty. Maria slid her body into a chair across the table from Felix. "Thank you," she said softly, acknowledging that he had already ordered her favorite summer drink, iced tea with lime and strawberries. Felix greeted her with a forced smile that did little to disguise his inner tension.

Maria offered her own smile, hoping to take control and set a light mood for their talk. "Why is it, my dear man, that the only time you offer to buy me lunch is after you have had a talk with Whitman?"

"Why is it that my relationship with that *pendejo* sets me on fire?" Felix replied with no attempt to return the friendliness of her demeanor.

Maria lifted her glass, held it toward Felix in a toast, and smiled again. "Well, I say we drink to each other and to the wonderful days that lie ahead for both of us."

Felix's face held its scowl as he halfheartedly lifted his glass but offered no response.

Deciding to forgo further attempts to brighten his mood, Maria sighed as she spoke. "You know, Felix, I've been thinking a lot recently. I've thought about all kinds of things, but mostly I've thought about when we were young. We were like brother and sister. Do you ever think of those days, Felix?"

Felix held Maria's gaze; he wondered where she was going with this.

"We were only teenagers when Mother moved me away to California. I will never forget the day we left, leaving you and Auntie to stay behind in Mexico. Remember how frightened we all were to be separated? We each felt so alone. I've been thinking about those days, Felix."

For the first time, a smile appeared on Felix's face. "Come on, Maria, of course I remember. I remember like it was yesterday. It doesn't seem possible that almost twenty years have passed."

"That's exactly what I've been thinking. How quickly time has passed and how hard we have worked to get to where we are today. And looking back, Felix, we didn't let that move drive us apart. In fact, it brought us closer together. Because of our separation, each of us has learned how to survive on our own, whether we were in Mexico or the United States. That's what really started us off as a team. Don't you agree?"

Felix nodded as he reflected on how far he and his cousin had come.

"I can't help but think about these things, Felix. It was those days that brought us to where we are today. Without those tough times, we would not be here right now and looking to make millions."

Felix's eyes narrowed as he nodded again.

"Tell me, Felix," Maria continued, "how many times did we mule drugs for some *cabrón* who cared nothing for us? Most of those people would have thrown us away in an instant if necessary. How many times did we cross the border, everything on the line, for someone who paid us hardly anything and didn't care if we were caught or killed? We worked all those years hoping to find a big chance, the right person. We were looking for the one perfect opportunity. Even though we didn't realize it at the time, we were looking for a person just like Whitman. We did it, Felix, we've found the perfect person."

Felix looked hard at Maria. "Of course, I think about these things, Maria," he said. "Those days are a part of who we are."

"We have risked so much to find an opportunity like this." Maria said with a mixture of confidence and pleading in her tone. "So even though what we are doing right now is not what we expected or what we wanted, and no matter how horrible it is to work with *him*, we're about to make it really big. We can't let this slip away." She scrutinized his face. "But Felix, I don't know what you're thinking. I can't read you."

Felix sat stoically. His face revealed nothing of the thoughts inside his head.

Looking directly into his eyes, trying to see inside him, Maria wondered if Felix was showing signs of running. Was he in this to the end? She had to know. There was a time when he had depended on her physical beauty to open their doors. But things had changed. They were operating in the big leagues now, and it was Felix, through Whitman, who opened their doors. Times had definitely changed. Maria silently acknowledged that she needed Felix far more than he needed her.

"Felix," Maria said softly, "do you remember how close we came to losing everything when we were arrested in Phoenix?"

"Of course I do. I thought we were going down."

"I thought so too. But we didn't give up. We had to pay a fortune for our lawyer, but we made it."

Felix smiled as he said, "Yeah, the lawyer helped, but convincing the witnesses that anyone who testified against us would end up dead was the real reason the charges were dismissed." Felix laughed and continued, "The lawyer just made everything look pretty."

"The reason really isn't what's important now. What's important now is that we did get a second chance. Your mother got you to this city of money, power, and beautiful people. Nobody from our world gets chances like this. Nobody. Yet, here we are. You and me; we've done it. Just think of the opportunity we are looking at. This is amazing!"

Felix was silent for a moment before he leaned over the table, his eyes drilling into Maria's face. "Listen to me, Maria. Let me tell you what is amazing. Yesterday was just like every time in the past when I've had to sit in Whitman's office. I had to look at him. I had to listen to that asshole. I swallowed his shit, Maria. I swallowed it piece by piece as he sat behind his fancy desk and talked down to me like I was some peasant boy. *Chingadero!*" Felix paused as his anger built. "Yes, Maria, I think of you and me a lot. I think of us every time I go into that bastard's office, every time I sit with him in a car or a restaurant. Every time I look at his arrogant, sneering face I think of us. I think of everything you have just talked about, Maria. Yes, I know how far we have come, of course I do!" He paused and leaned even closer. "But let me tell you," he said softly. "Sometimes I think I liked life better when we were on the streets. We didn't have money, we didn't have much, but at least we were in control. We directed our own lives. We didn't take orders from that scum." Felix eased away, fury burning in his eyes.

Maria reached across the table and grasped Felix's hands and held them in a tight grip. Both were silent, each reflecting on what had been said. Maria whispered, "I can't argue with anything you say. I could never be alone with that man and you do it regularly. I don't know how you have done it."

Maria's understanding seemed to soften Felix's anger. "You know something, Maria?" he asked in a softer tone. "I knew right away after coming to Washington that all the rich people I saw everyday were just the same as those I had left behind. They were the same people on the inside as the street people you and I had dealt with all our lives. Nothing was different. The new, beautiful people were the same selfish people we've always known. Sure they dressed nicer, had faster cars, and were willing to pay a hell of a lot more money for their drugs and sex, but they were just the same. They all wanted just drugs and sex."

"Yes, Felix, yes," Maria replied passionately. "But don't you see? Your instincts were right. You saw the opportunities and all we did was simply open the door. Could any of the people we used to work with have done what we have done? Could they have traveled from dirt to where we are now? No, Felix, no way at all. Not a person from our old world is as smooth as you, able to move in the streets of a ghetto one day, then sip wine with lawyers and big shots the next. That's how you met Whitman, by being able to act as though you were raised with these rich fools. And Felix, all I need is a sexy evening gown and I can have the keys to this city. We've done it, Felix, and we can do it just a while longer. We are almost there. We can put Whitman behind us, and we will be in control again. All we have to do is just get through this one last job, and we're set for life."

Maria crossed her arms and leaned back in her chair. She had said what she had to say and now she scrutinized Felix's face for clues of what lay behind his eyes. Maria hoped that her own face did not betray the doubt she felt.

A genuine smile appeared as Felix spoke. "You're worried about me, aren't you?" he asked. "You're thinking that I may walk away from this whole deal just because I want to castrate Whitman every time I see him." His smile broadened and a twinkle appeared in his eyes. "Come on, Maria. What are you really worried about, my ability to continue with Whitman or the future of your pretty little face?" he asked with a laugh. "I think your real concern is what will happen to Maria if I decide not to go through with Whitman's crazy plan."

"Well, maybe you're right. I have had some worries, but I promise you, my worries are about both of us." She leaned over the table, her face only inches from Felix's, and whispered, "I don't care if you castrate Whitman. Take his *cojones* and his *chorizo*. In fact, I want you to. I want to watch. I just want you to wait until we get through this. If you'll do that for me, I'll give you the knife, a really dull one."

They laughed together for the first time.

Felix handed Maria an envelope. "The senator and judge are making another trip to Colorado next week. Here are the instructions. Make it happen just like always. And don't worry, Maria, I'm with you. I'm with you to the end. This is it. There's no turning back now."

Maria breathed deeply and looked at Felix gratefully. Her doubts were erased. Everything would be fine. She flashed a wide smile. Her white teeth were a beautiful contrast to her copper-colored skin. "I'm starved. Order me something wonderful. Surprise me."

While Felix spoke to the waiter, Maria considered all she had to do. She was so thankful that she could fly to Denver. When they had first begun, there had been no choice but to drive and handle transportation. Now everything was set and in place. Other people handled details. She and Felix handled only the most important clients now. People like the senator and the judge.

MONDAY, SEPTEMBER 3

AFTERNOON SUNLIGHT FILTERED through the forest in shafts of light and dust. Bertram Russert and his companion, retired Federal District Judge William Holloway, stopped their rented SUV beside the small gatehouse at the entrance to Elk Run Fly Fishing Resort. A middle-aged man in blue jeans and a baseball cap stepped out of the building and approached the driver's side of the vehicle.

"Hello, senator, good to see you." The attendant leaned down and looked at the passenger. "Hello, judge," he said. "Nice to see you back in Colorado again."

Both men smiled. Russert extended his arm through the window, shaking hands with the friendly man who always welcomed him to the resort. Russert grinned and said, "Great to see you again. You sure as hell haven't gotten any prettier since I last saw you!"

"I'll get pretty the day you learn to fish," the man fired back.

The men bantered. Fishing was great only if one knew how to fish, which surely meant that Russert and Holloway would be skunked as they floundered about in the river. Between laughs and insults, Russert accepted an electronic card key that controlled the gate and granted access to the resort.

Silent hinges opened the way and Russert guided the vehicle over a gravel road that curved past granite outcroppings and ponderosa pines. The road wound through the woods for two secluded miles before breaking out into an alpine meadow that was sprinkled with near-uniform log cabins.

Serving as the focal point of this postcard scene, the main lodge of Elk Run held a commanding vista of surrounding mountains and the South Platte River. Flowers shimmered in beautiful gardens that welcomed visitors into a land of enchantment where men and women talked of reclusive brown trout or the exquisite splendor of a rainbow trout's body arching from the water.

Russert and Holloway passed behind the lodge. They planned to join the other guests in the dining room later in the evening. Though they were frequent visitors to the resort, Russert and Holloway never stayed more than a day or two. They simply paid an outrageous daily fee and departed.

Upon arrival at their cabin, the most secluded on the resort, they were met by a polite young man in starched blue jeans and a cowboy hat. "Good afternoon, gents," he spoke in a southern drawl that seemed the perfect condiment to the relaxed atmosphere of the resort. "I hope you're ready for some Colorado blue skies and wild, feisty trout."

"We sure as hell are," boomed Holloway. "It's always good to be here. Even my associate, the esteemed senator, seems to loosen his asshole a bit when we visit here." Holloway laughed as though his comment was worthy of a late-night comedy routine. He continued with obscenity-laced small talk while their luggage was carried from the SUV to the cabin. The young man filled the ice buckets and wished them a pleasant stay before departing.

Russert could take no more. He felt himself about to explode. Stepping outside, he walked to the tree line just yards from the cabin. He shut his eyes and took in the dry, cool air, the gift of a forest standing eight thousand feet above the sea. Washington, DC, seemed a distant nightmare, and he craved solitude. Judge Holloway had joined him early that morning at Dulles Airport. As usual, Russert had grown weary of the man long before they landed in Denver. The drive from the airport to their destination should have been beautiful and relaxing. Instead, his companion's incessant, self-serving brashness and vulgar jokes were unbearably grating.

Russert walked away from the cabin and into the trees and boulders that were his cathedral. He sat on the ground and covered his face with trembling hands. Darkness sealed his world. He sat for a moment rocking back and forth as his tormented mind seemed to swell within his skull. Was there a God to help him? Why did he have to come to such a beautiful place only to violate and destroy?

He knew exactly why he was here. Time after time he returned to this very place, sometimes alone, sometimes with the judge. He came because of the cravings, thoughts of the dreaded episodes refused to leave him and always left him wanting more. When the horrible yearnings invaded, he felt like he was suffocating, as though tantalizing tongues, moist and slick, licked his skin. The desires intensified and then the voices, only a slight murmur at first, then soft euphoric fantasies. But the whispers always grew louder, escalating into screaming, vulgar ecstasy.

In the beginning, Russert had tried to resist the cravings. Now he simply succumbed. There was nothing left in him, no strength remained to fight.

Opening his eyes, Russert forced himself to breathe slowly. He tried to stand, but his legs felt weak, almost trembling. He could hear his own heart pounding. Shuffling cautiously, Russert made his way back to the cabin. Thankfully, he found it empty. The judge was gone, undoubtedly to the lodge for drinks before dinner. He slumped his weakened body into a chair. He tried to see the beauty that evening brought to the mountain valley and its winding river, but it was no use. The cravings would not leave him. Cursing the demons that infested his body, worming like parasites, he gulped a swallow of scotch. It was his only hope for respite, at least for a while.

———

AFTER DINNER the guests enjoyed brandy to warm their spirits before heading back to their cabins. The evening held a chill. The first hints of autumn at nine thousand feet could be seen with each exhale, as breath floated into starlight.

A mellow glow of pathway lanterns guided Russert and Holloway across the meadow as they walked. Holloway puffed a cigar, its embers glowed orange in the night. As usual, his breath soon became labored. Even though Holloway blamed the altitude for his breathing difficulties, Russert was confident that Holloway's protruding stomach and a lifetime of smoking were the true culprits. Walking through the night without conversation, their silence became a flimsy barrier against the charged atmosphere both men felt.

Reaching the end of the pathway, a small porch granted entry to their cabin. Hinges creaked in protest under the strain of a solid pine door. Dim lamps giving the look of candlelight welcomed the men into their guest home. Holloway walked to the backside of the cabin. Stopping at the bathroom door, he turned to Russert and for a lingering moment the two men faced each other. The air in the cabin was on the verge of igniting. "Make the goddamned phone call," Holloway's command was a rude grunt.

Barely able to control the shaking in his hands, Russert pulled a paper from his pocket and read the numbers aloud as he pressed them into his telephone. After three rings he heard the familiar, soft voice.

"Yes."

"Hello, Maria. We're ready. I'll meet you at the gate."

Leaving Holloway alone, Russert drove to the resort's main gate. Maria was waiting. Russert turned his car around and pressed the gate remote. The metal frame swung open. Maria drove behind Russert as he retraced a way over the empty road. Both vehicles circled slowly and quietly to the rear of Russert's cabin where they were hidden among the trees. They turned off their engines, and with the headlights extinguished, silence descended sealing them in isolation and darkness. The night was black, stars looked down in silent observance. A coyote's sorrowful howl creased the night, a vile presence recognized. The air stirred. For a billionth of a second the cosmos blinked as a celestial teardrop veiled the heavens.

Russert approached Maria sitting in the driver's seat of her car. "The judge first" were his only words.

Quietly entering the back door of the dimly lit cabin, Russert filled a glass with scotch before lowering himself into a reclining chair. He closed his eyes closed and felt his pulse quicken with anticipation. He savored the burning liquid as it seeped through his body. It was the icy fire he so desperately sought to cool the inferno that raged within.

Maria entered the cabin. Her eyes drifted about the dimly lit room; it was a scene she knew well. She gave a slight nod. Russert remained silent.

"Are you ready?" Maria's voice was a whisper.

"Yes, we are ready," he choked in reply.

Maria turned toward the door she had just entered and made a gesture. A young boy came and stood next to Maria. He wore white sneakers, faded blue jeans, and a red T-shirt embossed with a bright yellow image of the sun's happy face. He was thin and looked to be no more than eleven years old with straight brown hair and dark, empty eyes that were void of expression or movement. The boy stared directly at Russert, but he saw nothing, comprehending no more than did the glowing sun face that smiled from his red T-shirt.

"Judge, it's time," Maria softly called.

The door to a back bedroom opened and harsh light spilled into the cabin. A completely nude Judge Holloway stepped into the threshold. His legs were slightly spread, and he held a can of beer. His presence loomed, filling the room. His eyes were red with the shroud of alcohol. Holloway fixed his gaze upon the boy.

Maria turned away.

Holloway raised the can, draining its contents into his mouth. Then, in a deliberately prolonged motion, he lifted the can above his head as if it were a ceremonial torch. The corners of his mouth crept up as his fingers opened, dropping the emptied can onto the wood floor. A hollow twang shattered the air, followed by foreboding quiet like the haunting silence that lingers in the wake of a single rifle shot.

The naked man scrutinized the boy standing before him as if he were a mere object. As he made his way closer, the man's arousal was clearly visible beneath a bulging stomach. Standing before the boy, Holloway placed his hand under the child's delicate chin. Tilting the young face upward, he evaluated his prize. Vacant eyes returned his scrutiny.

Holloway pressed on the boy's shoulders, forcing him to his knees. He closed his eyes, and his breath quickened. For a moment there was quiet. Then suddenly Holloway roughly grasped the boy's hair, pulling him to a standing position. Clumsily he reached to the boy's jeans, fumbling to unbutton the soft material. His smile turned into a sneer as he forced the child to turn. The boy was programmed for obedience.

As Holloway began, breathing accelerated from his twisted mouth. For the first time, expression registered on the boy's face, a grimace, as he closed his eyes tightly. The bright yellow sun from his red T-shirt continued to smile.

Russert remained reclined in his chair. His eyes were glassy, dilated with ecstasy. Oblivious to Maria in the corner, he was surprised when she ushered someone to him. A girl no older than thirteen years knelt beside him. Dressed in a yellow satin gown, red lipstick glossed her mouth. On her small head was a cheap plastic crown, bejeweled with glass beads and tawdry sparkles. A band of dime-store pearls encircled her slender neck.

Diverting his eyes from the shameful degradation on display before him, Russert looked at the girl and his lips parted in a smile. "Hello, little princess," he said softly. "Be a good princess now." His voice remained soft. "Oh yes, you are such a good princess."

In a darkened corner of the cabin Maria stood in silence, her face turned away and eyes closed. She refused to look.

TUESDAY, SEPTEMBER 4

AFTERNOON GRUDGINGLY SURRENDERED TO EVENING. Brad Walker took solace leaning against a boulder he had befriended long ago. The perfectly placed rock was perched on the crest of a rolling hill, and the rare visitors to this place were rewarded with breathtaking views of Colorado's snow-capped mountains to the west and Stone Creek ambling below. For years, Brad had fished the stream and brought his family for hikes along its serene banks. He and his wife, Elizabeth, had spent countless hours embraced by the boulder, savoring their secluded paradise.

However, today was Brad's first visit in almost two years. His extended absence was not because he had lost his love for this place. He had never forgotten the tranquility it held. Brad had considered coming back several times but simply had not been able to summon the courage. Each time he had considered a return, fear gnawed within. He could not imagine what it would feel like without her. One year ago this month, Elizabeth had died. Could this one-time sanctuary ever again be a place of solace or would it now haunt him?

Earlier in the day, Brad reached for his treasured fly rod, perfectly balanced in his hand, for the first time since Elizabeth's death. Tossing his gear into his fishing rig, Brad headed west. He passed over Gore

Pass at ten thousand feet and then descended into an expanse of meadows laced with small creeks. He marveled at the sight. Century after century, the valley waltzed with timid streams, urging them to their inevitable union with the Colorado River.

After so many months, Brad felt like an outsider when he parked his car near the banks of Stone Creek. He loved rivers, felt their coursing waters to be simultaneously wild but peaceful. For Brad, rivers delivered a sense of reassurance. They were alive and eloquent, the essence of Mother Earth carried within their mercurial flows.

He tried to fish. But after his long absence, the cold water of Stone Creek felt strangely alien. Silt and stone shifting beneath his feet were disconcerting, a sense of balance elusive. The fraternity he sought refused to come. Even worse, there was no rhythm in his casting. Like a brute, he flung the delicate fly and wads of translucent filament with no trace of subtlety. Two small trout had been foolish enough to investigate in spite of his clumsiness. He snapped his rod with ferocity, launching the fly like a feathered missile. It was worse than amateurish.

Finally, Brad admitted to himself the true reason he had decided to make this journey. He stashed his gear into his truck and began a hike to the hill's summit. It was the place he yearned to be yet dreaded. It was like a risky rendezvous with an old lover.

Now settled within the familiar embrace of the boulder that Elizabeth and he had always called "Their Rock," Brad took in the scene below. The beauty was stunning. Evening sun cast a violet and orange hue across the sky and danced magically in the stream below. Brad remembered watching a sunset with his son, Cody, so many years ago. The little boy exclaimed with wonder, "Look, Dad. God took his markers and painted the sky."

Oh, how life had changed. Cody was now in the Navy, serving in the Persian Gulf. Brad's two younger children were also grown and away in college.

While resting against the rock, Brad determined to make his peace with why he had finally returned to this place. *OK, I'm here,* he thought. *Think about her while sitting right here. Face the demon.* He shut his eyes. His heart hurt. The last year of the life they shared was a fog of antiseptic hospital wards and contemplative physicians. Finally, they returned home to face their inexorable destiny. Each day held some laughter. They both made certain of that. Each day held tears. Neither of them could help that. Hours passed with Brad simply sitting beside her bed, each of them in silent reflection of their past and a pensive clairvoyance of the threshold ahead.

Brad had been an FBI Agent for over twenty years when Elizabeth was diagnosed. He immediately retired when they found out. It was an easy decision. There was no choice but to spend every possible moment with Elizabeth.

Sitting against the boulder, Brad considered for the thousandth time the tidal wave of changes he had experienced the past several months. He remembered how he had sat in stunned silence when a man in a white coat told him that his wife's life would soon end. The words had seemed a dream at the time and now, months later, reality still had yet to settle.

Brad pondered the river below. As he observed its serpentine wandering, it occurred to him that in so many ways, rivers were like life. Sometimes they meandered gently; other times they roared and crashed with terror. Rivers and life both etch a journey through time. When a river moves through soft, pliable meadows, it cuts its own banks and masters the landscape. But when it falls through steep terrain, it crashes, consuming everything within its banks. Rivers are always changing. Tributaries mature its personality; landscape molds its character. Gravity, relentless gravity, powers a river into the next soft meadow or into the next crashing canyon.

Nestling his chin in both hands as he sat, Brad allowed his thoughts to flow. He recalled a family vacation when they had rafted a river together. As they drifted on calm water, they had time to enjoy the passing scenery. They talked and laughed and splashed one another. But without warning, the water had transformed. An unseen force energized the current into undulating swells that seemed to hurl their frail craft past jagged boulders in a dizzying blur. Screams of delight and fear were muffled by the deafening roar of the raging water. Then it was all over. The water calmed and Brad and his family once again drifted. Drenched and gasping, their hearts slowed in the tranquility of a meandering river.

There simply was no better analogy to life. Meandering in calm water, years of marriage, children, and careers pass. But out-of-control times of crashing are inevitable. Brad shook his head. Since Elizabeth's diagnosis, it had been all crashing. The months that he watched his wife die had not been a time of meandering. The vibrancy of his life had been ripped from his soul. Was there calm water ahead? Would he ever again meander?

Darkness loomed before Brad reluctantly began his hike back down the hill. He contemplated his afternoon, sorting out his feelings as he maneuvered over the trail. He felt he had handled the day pretty well. He had faced his memories and was still standing. The only part of the day that had been a total disaster was his miserable attempt at fishing. He grinned at the thought. He offered silent thanks that no one had witnessed his efforts and he swore to try again soon. The South Platte River was an option. He knew a place just upstream from a super exclusive resort called Elk Run Fly Fishing Resort. Occasionally, a big rainbow abandoned its coddled life in private water and trespassed into an adjoining section of river open to the public, giving the common man a shot at a trophy.

Reaching his truck, Brad decided to return home by way of twelve thousand-foot Berthoud Pass. He would stop in Winter Park for a coffee under the stars. It was a new moon so the sky would be spectacular. It would also be a good time to enjoy Sarah Brightman or Michael Crawford. Maybe some Willie Nelson also. They were always good companions.

Breathing deeply, Brad started his engine.

God, I miss Elizabeth.

———

A WISP of smoke and a squeal of tires announced the arrival of Christine Reynolds's private jet. The sole passenger on the luxurious craft, Christine peered out the window. She loved mountains and the contrast they offered to the desert landscape of her home in Phoenix. Craving something other than scorching sun, Christine was ready for the cool of Aspen, Colorado.

Christine was disappointed that her husband was not with her. She savored the times when she and Brandon traveled together, escaping their hectic routines. But he was in New York City for business, leaving her to travel alone. It was probably for the best since this trip was going to be one of the colossal social affairs that he utterly despised.

Bill and Emily Cotter, family friends for years, were throwing an open house extravaganza to celebrate their new home in Aspen. Christine thought the party was ridiculous since the Cotters had just hosted a similar open house bash for a new home in Hawaii. Christine knew it was a good bet that Brandon had purposely arranged his business obligations just to avoid having to deal with this entire episode. She smiled to herself. She did love him.

Within moments of setting foot inside the terminal, Christine spotted the white hair and ruddy cheeks of Howard, her driver. His face lit up like a neon sign when she walked straight to him, put down her purse, and gave him a genuine hug. "Hello, Howard. How's my favorite person in the great state of Colorado?"

"I'm fine, Mrs. Reynolds. It's so nice to see you again. How's life been for you and your family?"

"Everything is wonderful, Howard. My children are monsters and Brandon, that spoiled, rotten husband of mine, is totally out of control. However, I accept my fate with resolve." Christine's face fell in mock despair, but her eyes sparkled.

Howard had met dozens of wealthy people in this terminal. He was one of the most favored drivers for the rich and famous who floated in and out of the exclusive mountain valley. In his opinion, they were pretty much all the same: aloof, detached, superficial, and full of shit.

Mrs. Reynolds was different, though. She was drop-dead beautiful no matter what—evening gown or jeans, make up or natural. But it was much more than that. When Christine Reynolds smiled, he knew she meant it because her eyes smiled too. She always asked about him, his wife, and his children. She actually cared about his life. They joked together and when she laughed, it was from deep down inside, not phony nasal twitter. They laughed together, and quite often Christine laughed at herself.

"Well, young lady, are you sure Aspen is ready for you?" Howard asked with a smile as he lifted her luggage into the BMW he had arranged.

"Aspen had better be ready," Christine fired back, "because I'm not leaving until you sing like Frank Sinatra or I'm elected mayor."

"Okay! Sounds like you'll be here till the end of the week. You can leave right after my concert." Laughter filled the BMW as they began their drive.

"Are you sure you won't need me to drive you around while you're here?" Howard asked. "You know there is nothing that I would rather do."

"Thank you so much, Howard. It just seems that life gets crazier all the time. I really do want some time alone to try and get uncrazy. I may never leave the hotel. I may walk and shop or I may take a drive through the mountains. I'm not sure. I have so little time and part of it will be at a party I have to attend tomorrow evening." Christine paused thoughtfully. "That's it! Could you put on a dress and go to the party for me? Just pretend you're me?"

They laughed again.

"Now, wouldn't I be a knockout?" Howard's smile filled his face. "My gorgeous, squatty, sixty-two-year-old body with a crooked potato nose and hairy legs. Absolutely! No one will know the difference. We can send photographs to all the local gossip columns."

"Why don't you take a date?" Christine intoned with an exaggerated aristocratic air. "Such affairs are sooo much more meaningful when shared with someone special, don't you agree, darling?"

They were still laughing as her bags were taken into the hotel. Howard passed the BMW keys to valet, grasped Christine's hand, and spoke in a fatherly tone. "I really don't like you running around by yourself, Mrs. Reynolds. I wish you would let me take care of you. But, if you're sure that some time alone is what you want, then go have a ball."

"Thank you, Howard, but this Aspen, Colorado, not New York City. I'll be fine, I promise. But I'll tell you what, if I should change my mind, you will be the first person I call. That is, of course, unless you're busy driving some other bimbo through the slums of Aspen."

Howard looked at Christine in absolute seriousness. "Mrs. Reynolds, you call me any time. If I was scheduled to drive the President, I'd tell him to hitchhike if you called."

Christine placed her arms around Howard's neck, hugged him tightly, and pecked his cheek. "I know you would, sweetie. I know you would." Stepping back, she announced, "You know, Brandon and I do plan to spend a few days here in about a month. If you can put up with us, we'll give you a call. We'd be thrilled if you would drive us. We love the mountains in autumn, but it's a sure cinch I won't ride in a car if Brandon is driving. He's worse than a blind teenager who's been drinking! If Colorado only had one tree, he would hit it, square on at full speed, no doubt."

They both laughed.

"You can plan on it, Mrs. Reynolds. I look forward to it. Remember now, when you leave, just park the car at the airport; same routine as always. I'll handle everything for you."

"Got it, Captain," Christine replied standing at attention and saluting smartly. Her brown eyes were mischievous but always smiling.

"Bye, Howard. See you soon."

Christine had it planned. First, she would take a walk about town and choose a quiet restaurant for dinner. Then she would go to bed early. Tomorrow was all hers until the party. Time would fly, and she would be returning home before she knew it. She smiled to herself. *What a wonderful break*, she thought. *The only way things could be better is if Brandon were here.*

WEDNESDAY, SEPTEMBER 5

Thankful for a cushion of pine needles and some shade, Felix Gomez settled into a stand of trees. The walk from the trailhead was less than a mile, but it was steep. He had made the hike before and each time it was a strain. This was not his world. Felix preferred to be in a city.

The scene below had become familiar. A magnificent home, constructed of stone and logs, dominated the center of the property. Close by was an equally striking but smaller guesthouse. Beyond the houses, a horse barn linked the space between indoor and outdoor riding arenas. At the tree line, a tennis court and swimming pool completed the landscape. From his elevated vantage point, Felix had an unobstructed view of the entire complex. He could also observe the paved county road leading away, straight as an arrow for about a mile, before it curved out of sight on its way to Aspen.

With practiced precision, Felix arranged his two-way radio, cell phone, tripod and spotting scope. Gazing through the scope, he marveled at the beauty and extravagance of the house and all that surrounded it. Felix shook his head in amazement mingled with disgust. He didn't know the value of the property, but a spread of this magnitude, only minutes from the charm of Aspen had to be worth many millions. He recalled his days in Mexico when his mother struggled just to survive and the harsh streets where he and Maria had been raised. *What a different world these spoiled people have*, he thought. He also thought of Whitman and how this night was going to change his life forever. He whispered softly, "Okay, you rich people, it's my turn."

Focusing his scope on the field adjacent to the outdoor riding arena, Felix was prepared. After dark, the area would be filled with cars and he had to see it clearly. Felix's body tingled with excitement and, he had to admit, a touch of fear.

———

THE BEAUTIFUL EVENING light had a narcotic effect on Christine Reynolds. She loved it here. The silver BMW felt a part of her body as she cruised past towering cliffs of red stone that seemed to glow in the magic of a setting sun.

Christine had passed the day lounging beside her hotel's pool after a walk through Aspen and the decadence of a strawberry ice cream cone—two scoops even!

"What a wonderful day!" she said out loud, happy to hear the sound of her own voice. She laughed, not caring in the least if another person should see her talking to herself.

Christine treasured her life and the people in it. Even so, an occasional break surely was a welcome respite. Only a few people on the planet came close to holding the immense wealth that she and Brandon had accumulated, but they knew life was more than a golf game at a country club. They took seriously the notion that their fortune offered a unique opportunity to make a difference on a global scale. It was an opportunity they did not intend to squander.

Brandon was now back in their Arizona home and Christine felt a hint of guilt for being away. In her mind, she justified her indulgence knowing she would be home by noon the next day. Christine considered that after so many years of marriage, they were still pretty darned good at making up for nights spent apart. She blushed at the thought.

Unable to think of a good reason to rush to the madness of the celebration, Christine drove slowly. She considered how she could graciously handle the evening without having to stay too long. Once back in her hotel, she would curl up with a book. Then tomorrow she would return home to Brandon. Perfect!

Finally, at the house, Christine turned the BMW onto the long drive that served as the regal entrance to the Cotter's estate. As she approached, she could see that a number of guests had already arrived and were ambling about the grounds. The drive ultimately circled a massive fountain with a majestic water display of changing patterns and colors. A young man greeted her, offering to park her vehicle. With a smile, Christine thanked him, entered the residence and immediately embraced Emily Cotter. It was time. Let the festivities begin.

———

THIS WAS IT. A critical moment had arrived. Felix strained his eye as he peered through the spotting scope. He caught only a glimpse of Christine Reynolds as she stepped from her vehicle, but she was of no concern to him. His focus was the BMW. He watched as a parking attendant moved the car across the property. Holding his breath, Felix tracked the BMW until it was parked directly beneath the lights of the outdoor riding arena. "Thank you, thank you," Felix breathed. This was perfect. Even without his scope, the vehicle could easily be seen.

Felix had feared Reynolds might show up with a driver who would simply wait for her. Whitman told Felix that Reynolds' husband would not be with her, but the issue of whether or not she would have a driver had been an unknown. That she was alone, and the car was in the open caused him to relax. So far everything had gone as planned. Felix smiled. *This is perfect.*

With time to kill, Felix wondered about Whitman and how he knew so much about Christine Reynolds. There obviously was someone on the inside providing detailed information. Whoever it was, they were worth their weight in gold. At least there had been no surprises yet.

Relaxing against a tree, Felix contemplated the rest of the evening. If anything developed that didn't feel right, it was his call to cancel the entire operation. He smiled slightly, savoring the fact that he was now in control. Whitman could screw himself. The risk was now on Maria and him, not on Whitman in his office a thousand miles away. Felix took a deep breath and told himself not to worry. He was in charge tonight. Everything would work out fine.

———

EXHAUSTED AFTER A RIGOROUS WORKOUT, Brad Walker left his gym. Elizabeth's illness had brought an abrupt halt to his fitness program. Even after she died, he had found it difficult to resume his lifelong routine. But that was changing, and he was working himself back into old habits. He could definitely feel his body improving.

The sun was setting, and Brad looked to the Continental Divide. At eight thousand feet above sea level, evenings cooled rapidly. With his sweat-soaked shirt, Brad felt a chill as he entered his truck.

A herd of grazing elk lingered under pink alpenglow alongside the road. More quickly than he could realize, Brad's brain played a cruel trick by speaking to his heart as had happened a thousand times before: *What a perfect night for a walk with Elizabeth.*

Bam! The pain of a sledgehammer hit his chest.

This had happened before, and Brad was learning how to handle such moments by forcing his mind to look ahead and think of other things. He had to get his mind off Elizabeth. He told himself that he should try fishing again. He recalled his pathetic performance at Stone Creek, thinking that he needed to redeem himself. But Brad knew it was more than fishing. He desperately wanted to find his way back into calm water, to bring some balance back into his life.

He again thought of the spot on the South Platte River, the one joining Elk Run Fly Fishing Resort. Brad made a deal with himself. If the weather held, tomorrow evening he would make it happen. A drive to the canyon and hike to the river was what he needed.

Brad pulled into his garage and entered an empty house.

———

SHADOWS EDGED out twilight and cool air settled into the valley. Wrapping his jacket more tightly around his shoulders, Felix kept vigil. People strolled about the property below, appearing as ants moving in slow motion. Even from his distant observation point, he could hear the outdoor sound system delivering the crooning of Celine Dion and Rod Stewart.

Night's falling temperatures proved too severe for the guests' chic summer clothing, and they began moving indoors. Within minutes, only parking attendants remained outside. The sound of the outdoor stereo was replaced by a live band inside the residence. Even from within the mansion's walls, Felix could hear a raucous throb escalate by the minute. He shivered from somewhere deep inside and tried to convince himself that it was because of the temperature. But in his heart, he recognized the silent truth. It was actually going to happen. The shiver excited every nerve in his body.

Felix checked his watch. Almost ten o'clock.

———

THE OPPORTUNITY for a graceful escape presented itself. The band pounded a clamor that held no recognizable melody and, to compete with the cacophony, conversations had amplified to shouting. Any sense of intimacy that the party may have held had disappeared. Christine could slip away and very few would even notice she had left. After saying farewell to the Cotters, Christine stepped outside. Within minutes the valet delivered her BMW, and Christine pressed a twenty-dollar bill into the young man's hand. She had made it. She was free.

Pulling away from the residence, Christine opened the windows of the car, longing for cold air over her face. As the lights of the sprawling estate faded in her mirror, so did the prattle of the party. Once she turned from the drive onto the main road, she felt at peace. She closed the windows and tuned soft jazz onto the radio. Christine basked in an illusion of gliding as the luxury car seemed to float soundlessly through the night.

———

FELIX'S BODY tensed as he watched Christine Reynolds drive away from the house. Everything seemed surreal, like the world moved in slow motion as he spoke into his cell phone. He gathered his gear and began the walk back to the trailhead. Felix fought the urge to run and deliberately restrained his pace to a brisk walk. His small flashlight cast just enough light on the rugged path to show where to place his feet.

His heart threatened to blow completely through his chest. Felix told himself to watch his step and be careful. Now was not the time for a fall.

———

CHRISTINE REYNOLDS DRIFTED on a current of bliss. She had survived the party, even had fun at times. But now the evening was hers to really enjoy. Her plans were to get to her hotel room, call Brandon, and then fall asleep after relaxing with a good book. She felt exhilaration at the responsiveness of the superbly engineered automobile as she cruised over the deserted mountain road. The dim glow of her instrument panel and the radio's soft music wrapped about her like a warm blanket.

Christine recalled that the road was straight for some distance before beginning a winding descent into Aspen. She drove slowly, relishing the serenity of an alpine valley under the magic of night. Cautiously scanning the roadside for the eyes of grazing deer or the flash of a darting fox, a beautiful woman drove beneath the canopy of heaven, unaware that heaven held its breath.

As Christine rounded a curve, a billowing cloud of steam filled the road. It took less a second for the accident to register. A pick-up truck, crusted in mud, appeared to have hit a tree head on. Christine's eyes and mind became momentarily paralyzed as she tried to make sense of the scene before her.

A woman was on her knees beside the road.

Christine blinked.

Blood was on the woman's clothing, terror was on her face.

Pressing her brakes, Christine stopped hard.

Blink.

The woman outside her window was crying for help.

Blink.

In a nanosecond, Christine Reynolds made the mistake of her life. She put the car in park and pressed the button to lower the window. The protected and enclosed world of Christine Reynolds dissolved. She heard the woman's pitiful cry: "My husband..."

Unaware that a hooded man had crept from behind, a gloved hand closed over Christine's mouth. Her door flew open as she felt her body being lifted out of the car. Pain jolted her limbs, as her arms were wrenched from the steering wheel. Was it a rope that bound her? An abrasive, foul smelling cloth burned into her face. Her mouth sucked a coarse material that scratched her tongue and tore like sandpaper across her face. Lungs burning, Christine gasped, her constricting throat desperate for air. The last thing she saw before her world turned black was the woman from the road standing over her.

The hooded man half dragged, half carried Christine across the hard ground and then tossed her like a discarded pouch onto the floorboard of the pickup truck.

The woman slid behind the wheel of Christine's BMW and drove away.

In rushed calmness, the hooded man removed a fog machine from the ground and tossed it into the truck's rear bed. In a quick maneuver he backed the pick-up truck away from the tree and departed.

Minutes later, the pick-up truck came to a stop. Felix pitched his pack into the rear and climbed in the passenger door.

He placed his boots on Christine Reynolds' body as if she were a rolled carpet.

The truck disappeared into the night. No other vehicles were on the road. No one saw what had happened. No moon illuminated the night.

Stars, tiny dots of frozen blue, dangled from a silent and stunned sky.

THURSDAY, SEPTEMBER 6

It was past midnight when Maria drove Christine's BMW through the deserted the streets of Aspen. She was now dressed in a trim skirt, silk blouse and a pearl necklace. Make-up had been applied and her hair was pulled back. Parking directly across the street from Christine's hotel, Maria sat quietly. She needed a few moments to simply breathe. Finally, after a quick glance into the mirror, she opened her door and crossed the roadway to the hotel entrance.

The silence of the lobby was unnerving. Without the bustle of day, Maria noticed the elegance of the hotel in a new way. It was truly striking. Polished stone floors and elaborate chandeliers set the stage for bronzed sculptures of wild horses and rugged cowboys, poised in frozen re-enactment of the glory of the Old West. Massive floral arrangements complimented exquisite walls of rich woods and sophisticated art. Genteel dignity imbued the atmosphere of the hotel.

Hours earlier, when Maria had stood in this exact location as she watched Christine, the rush of the hotel's activity had insured anonymity. She had felt invisible as she mingled with guests and hotel staff. Such luxury was not to be enjoyed at this hour. Each click of her heels on the stone floor conspicuously announced her presence. On one side of the lobby she saw a middle-aged couple sitting in silence, studying her every move as if they were charged to prepare a written report on hotel activity after midnight. On the opposite side of the lobby, a younger couple was half seated and half lying on a couch. Immersed in passion, the couple was apparently oblivious to the convenience of dozens of hotel rooms only feet away. As Maria crossed the polished floor, the couple separated and scrutinized Maria's every step.

Maria suppressed her urge to scream at the voyeurs. Instead, she calmly crossed the lobby looking like a beautiful woman returning from a night of entertainment. She reached the elevators and entered a waiting car. Once the door closed, Maria shut her eyes and gulped air as she ascended. When the doors opened, she stepped into a hallway that was thankfully void of people and walked briskly to Christine's room. With the card key taken from Christine's purse, she entered. The door closed behind her.

Within the privacy of the palatial suite, Maria's emotions finally ruptured. She collapsed into an oversized chair, desperate for a bit of time to calm herself. Pressing her hands over her face, Maria recounted the events of the past few hours. Had it really happened? Was she living in a dream or was this real? Maria opened her eyes and looked about the hotel room. Yes, this was real! So far, everything had gone perfectly. It had finally happened.

The silence of the room was a haven. Maria allowed herself to enjoy the luxury for just a few moments. The hard part was over. They had actually pulled it off. Only a few details remained. She stood up, removed gloves from her purse, pulled them over her hands, and went to work on the details.

Using the telephone in Christine's room, Maria placed a call to Las Vegas. She tossed the covers off the bed, ruffled the sheets, and threw pillows onto the floor. She dampened some bathroom towels and left them in a pile. She smudged a drop of toothpaste in the sink and scattered soaps and body lotions about the marbled vanity. Maria collected every personal item that Christine had left in the bathroom and the few items of clothing that hung in the closet. She gathered a book and some magazines that had been left lying about and packed everything into Christine's luggage.

It was two thirty in the morning. Maria stepped into the hallway with Christine's luggage, closed the door, and walked away. The hotel room was empty. Only hints of Christine Reynolds remained.

———

At eight o'clock on a September morning, the streets of Aspen are just waking up, still groggy. Maria had never felt more awake in her life. Still driving Christine's BMW, she drove to a coffee shop located only blocks from Christine's hotel. She entered the café, ordered two lattes with pastries, and handed the young girl behind the counter Christine Reynold's credit card. Easy, no signature required. Carrying her purchase to the BMW, she dialed another call to Las Vegas, this time using Christine's cell phone.

In less than ten minutes Maria arrived at the airport. After parking in an area reserved for passengers flying on private aircraft, she crossed the lot where she entered a waiting car and, with a smile, handed Felix Gomez a croissant and steaming latte.

———

Mark Whitman swiveled back and forth in his chair, staring at the ceiling of his office. *Felix should be calling any minute.* He had been waiting for what seemed like hours. Whitman hated waiting but he grudgingly accepted that this was a time in which he had no choice.

Unable to sit any longer, he stood and moved to his office window. Mark Whitman then did something that he had not done in a very long time. He actually looked out over the architectural grandeur and botanical splendor of Washington, DC. His eyes drifted over the monuments honoring the founders of his nation. People gathered about memorials, remembering a child or to honor a parent. They prayed silently, pleading for a compassionate God to know that they grieved for more than a mere name etched onto a wall. Whitman's gaze left the memorials, sweeping across the vista of the city. He focused on the dome of United States Capitol where the nation's flag undulated in the morning breeze. After a few moments, Whitman returned to his chair and swung his feet up onto his desk. In barely a whisper he spoke. "Who gives a shit."

Finally, the telephone rang. "Yes," he barked.

"Good morning. Everything went perfectly, exactly as planned."

"Did she give you any trouble?"

"No chance for trouble. It happened way too fast; over in a flash."

Whitman exhaled in relief. "Very well."

"I don't see how it could have gone any more smoothly." Felix spoke with confidence.

"This is exactly what I expected," Whitman replied. "But all the same, I'm relieved to hear from you. Is she in the motel?"

"Yeah, she's there. Tonight, we move to the cabin as planned but that arrangement won't work for very long. Let me know as soon as possible about when you plan to proceed."

"Don't worry, I will. But you have to remember it's going to take a little time for me to get a handle on her husband, to know for sure how he's going to react and how the police will respond. As soon as I learn what I need to know, I'll get straight back to you."

Felix spoke in a clipped manner, "OK, that's important. I'll wait to hear from you." He then exclaimed, "Jesus, you weren't lying when you said she wore a big diamond. I've never seen anything so damned huge. I've already shipped it to you. You'll have it soon."

"That diamond is nothing my friend, absolutely nothing. You should see their house and all that goes with it," Whitman said gently rocking in his chair. Closing his eyes, he recalled the night he had been invited into the Reynolds' home. It had been a unique opportunity to see the rich bastards and their billions up close. Whitman again spoke, "Felix, remember when I told you she was rich? I've been inside their house. It was a big social and political deal. Believe me, what those rich fuckers call home is nothing less than a damned museum and a theme park all in one."

"It must be something."

"Holy Jesus, you can't imagine. Every wall is covered with fancy art by some faggot artist who they call a master. God only knows how many millions simply hang on their walls. The rugs where they walk and laugh when their dog takes an occasional shit are all from European castles or palaces. The damned things are worth more than most people's entire homes."

"I can believe it."

"Swimming pools, yes more than one, fitness rooms, a movie theatre, tennis courts and putting greens. Holy Jesus, it went on forever." Whitman paused. "Let me tell you, Felix," he continued. "I've seen some amazing homes in my time, but that broad's estate is in a league all by itself. Listen to this. Those fuckers have their own yacht. It looks like a floating palace. They have a helicopter and a big-assed jet just for funzies!" Whitman's laugh was sour. " Everyone needs a private helicopter to whisk them away to their private yacht to float them to a private island in the middle of their own private fucking ocean!" Whitman was shouting into the telephone.

"Unbelievable." Felix spoke softly.

Whitman leaned into the telephone, contempt filling his voice. "Felix, my friend, believe me when I tell you that the millions you and I will soon make out of this deal is not even a ripple to the Reynolds. Not even a ripple in their fucking swimming pool."

"Oh, I believe you. The place where she went to her party before we grabbed her was something out of a damned fairy tale."

"Yes, I'm sure that's true. Birds of a feather I suppose."

Felix jovially retorted, "Whatever kind of bird, it's fair to say that the nests she will occupy in the motel and the cabin are a considerable step down from what she's been accustomed to. And she sure as hell won't just spread her wings and fly away whenever she chooses. We have our bird in the bush."

"Alright, Felix, stay in touch. I'll call you as soon as I learn what's happening inside the Reynolds' house. I want a smooth operation, no problems."

"No problems, no problems. I'll speak to you later."

Whitman now felt at ease. It was a waiting game now. A few hours, a day or two, he wasn't sure. That would depend on what he learned from inside the Reynolds' house, how Brandon Reynolds would respond to all of this. A satisfied smile spread over his face. His secret source gave him eyes and ears inside the mansion walls of the Reynold's mansion. The tough part was over. The rest was going to be fun.

Whitman stood from his desk and made a decision. He didn't need this crap. Today would not be spent with kids fresh out of law school worried about their careers and legal bullshit. Today marked the beginning of his new life, and it was a perfect day for a visit to the club. A steam and massage, maybe a martini with lunch. Hell, he might even call to see if that long-legged red head he fucked last week was available. God, she was sweet! If she happened not to be on today's menu, no big deal, another would do just fine. He really didn't care.

Ignoring the staff of people with whom he had worked for years, Mark Whitman followed the corridor from his office and spoke to no one. Very soon this place would be a distant memory. He felt great. It was his turn now. His turn for the good life.

While waiting for an elevator, Whitman thought of Christine and Brandon Reynolds. Fifty million ransom for little baby doll? Chump change. If old man Reynolds did balk, what the hell, it wouldn't be a problem. He would simply tell Felix Gomez to have some fun and fuck her a few times. Take some photos. Now, that would be something for Brandon Reynolds to enjoy with his morning coffee and *Wall Street Journal*!

Whitman stepped into the elevator. *What a great day!*

THE MORNING HAD DELIVERED a spectacular Colorado blue sky and perfect temperature. However, the afternoon threatened storms as Brad loaded a fly rod and gear into his truck. Clouds were building like smoky shadows over the mountains to the west. The weather forecast called for nasty stuff to move in, but Brad had learned long ago to ignore stockbrokers, politicians, and weathermen. He knew that the best way to ensure good weather was simply to prepare for bad weather. A rain jacket went into his pack.

After fueling his rig, Brad headed to Colorado Highway 285, the back way to Breckenridge ski resort. The winding, two-lane road was one of his favorites since it cut right through the heart of outstanding trout territory. For the millionth time, Brad fell in love with Colorado. Purple-grey mountains surrounded the open ranges he drove through as he sipped cold water and listened to Willie Nelson's "Mommas Don't Let Your Babies Grow Up To Be Cowboys."

By the time Brad reached the trailhead that would lead him to the South Platte River, he began to consider the weather people may have gotten lucky for once. There was no blue left in the sky as grey clouds billowed above the mountains. He could smell the sweet fragrance of dampness in the air. It was heavy, holding a seductive promise of rain for the thirsty mountains. But he couldn't be sure. So often these so-called storms rumbled and threatened only to slide past without a drop. Brad considered it Mother Nature's way of teasing just a bit. He looked to the heavens trying to feel what the sky might hold. The clouds rolled, but there was no lightning or wind. With a shrug of his shoulders, he whispered, "What the hell." Brad made the call. It was a go. With his pack secured, he began the hike.

Initially, the trail was a straight shot with only gradual incline. He followed a path well-worn from the boots of countless anglers, all in search of grandeur, solitude, and trout. Brad knew that grandeur was a guarantee and solitude was probable. Landing a trout, however, was never more than hope.

With bad weather threatening, the river would likely be all his. That was what mattered most. He just wanted some time with the river.

After hiking for almost a mile, he came upon a fork in the trail. To the left was an easy trek, mostly downhill leading to river access very quickly. The right fork was a different scenario. It was a steep climb to the top of a ridge. Because of its difficulty, this particular trail was seldom used. Brad knew that if he chose this route, he would top out within a stone's throw of the Elk Run Fly Fishing Resort and from there, he would face a steep descent to the river. Brad turned right. A tough hike awaited but the reward would be greater.

By the time Brad crested the ridge, he was breathing hard. He leaned against a tree to catch his breath and to soak in the surrounding beauty. The gate into Elk Run Fly Fishing Resort stood before him. It was closed and the check-in cabin beside it was vacant. On either side of the gate a three-strand wire fence stretched through the forest, delineating the boundary of the resort. Each fifty-yard interval held a sign prominently mounted onto the twisted strands of metal. Bold letters proclaimed a stern message:

POSTED

PRIVATE PROPERTY

ELK RUN GUESTS ONLY

NO TRESPASSING HUNTING FISHING

VIOLATORS WILL BE PROSECUTED

BRAD THOUGHT ABOUT THE SIGN. Knowing the obscene amount of money required to enjoy the resort, it seemed a more appropriate message would be:

WELCOME

PRESIDENTS AND ROYALTY

SPOILED CHILDREN AND FAT BUSINESSMEN

ALL OTHERS

KEEP YOUR ASS OUT

BEYOND THE GATE, Brad could see the road that led to the fly-fishing mecca. He had actually had the rare privilege of touring the exclusive ranch on a few occasions. His old friend, Clayton Price, a biologist with the Colorado Department of Wildlife, had been responsible for periodic, state-mandated, health checks on the river that passed through this stretch of private land. Clayton sometimes let Brad hook a ride when he performed the inspections.

Clayton Price was now retired and living in Florida so the pleasant days of exploring the exclusive ranch and this private segment of the river were in the past. Brad was glad he had taken the opportunity to visit the resort. It had been a chance to glimpse the lifestyle of a few, very wealthy people.

After catching his breath, Brad began the final portion of his hike. He passed only about one hundred yards from the gate of Elk Run before he came upon a group of small, dilapidated cabins standing just within the fenced property of the resort. The long-abandoned cabins were crumbling in neglect.

Clayton Price had related to Brad the story behind these old structures and how they had come to such a sad fate. Years ago, a previous landowner erected the cabins in hopes of running a summer retreat. The poor soul had been a terrible businessman and was financially ruined in short order. Good-ole-boys with oil connections and deep pockets came along to buy the land for back taxes and Elk Run Fly Fishing Resort was the final chapter. Out of sight to all but the few who hiked this trail, these original cabins had been deserted, left to fade away like the dreams of the hopeful man who built them so many years ago. In the silence of an empty forest, Brad surveyed the sagging roofs and window frames that were boarded over. The walls of bleached pine timbers were held together by nothing more than rusting nails and tightly woven birds' nests.

As he studied the old buildings, Brad was struck by how much these forsaken cabins resembled a structure in northern New Mexico that he had once visited with his mother. Mom and he had taken a day together to visit the old home place, a two-room house where she had been born and where she had lived the early years of her life. Her childhood home was virtually the same size as these cabins; there was hardly room to turn around.

While looking at the structures, it dawned on him. Even though these cabins were almost identical to his mother's old house, they were worlds apart. The cabins before him had been designed as a summer retreat, nothing more than a weekend get-away for persons of wealth. The place he visited with his mother was a home where a family had lived, babies were born, suppers were cooked, and children were reared.

Brad stood quietly remembering that special day he had spent with his mother in what had been the kitchen of her tiny home. In the silence of the deserted house, his mother had remembered a farmer and his wife with seven children scratching out a living during the Dust Bowl of the 1930s. They walked what at one time had been fields surrounding the old home place. His mother reminisced of the hard times they had endured. She also spoke about how grass-covered prairies had been home to herds of buffalo and nomadic Indian tribes. Then came different kinds of herds: farmers with steel plows, gouging the land without discretion or mercy. Skies refused to rain, and the wounded earth convulsed, retching the life-giving soil into the winds that carried it far away. Mom spoke softly as she told stories of monstrous storms that darkened the noontime skies to midnight black, of oceans of dust, of the damp rags they used to cover their faces just to be able to breathe. She remembered the endless grit in their beds, eyes, ears, and food. There was no relief and no money. Each day was like the day before. Yet, a prayer of thanks was offered before each meager meal. Brad recalled the strength of his mother's eighty-year-old hand that day as her fingers squeezed his own. With moist eyes she whispered, "Life was hard, but we were so happy."

Mom was gone now. Brad looked at the cabins, transfixed in another place and time. He spoke to the empty forest and the crumbling cabins, "Mom, I wish we could do it again. I'd give anything to talk with you just once more."

Bittersweet memories lingered as Brad moved on, walking cautiously down the steep trail. He heard the river before it came into view. Stopping at an overlook, Brad paused to admire the scene. When compared to Stone Creek, this was a large river. Boulders the size of cars diverted the water this way and that, creating riffles, white foaming runs, and quiet still pools that were deep and icy cold. The river adorned the canyon floor like a silver ribbon wrapped around a special gift too beautiful to disturb. This was what he had come for. Brad wanted to see, to hear, and to feel the river. He was in awe of its elegance and marveled at its power. Even from this distance, Brad felt serenity. Nothing else was like it. Not even close.

Brad thought of Elizabeth.

The final descent to the river was the most treacherous. He eased his way, never taking his eyes from the path. Then it hit. In a matter of seconds, the calm evening air transformed into a raging wind, ripping through the canyon like a tsunami onto an unsuspecting beach. Hardly able to stand in the powerful wind, Brad quickly evaluated his options. He sure as heck wasn't going to fish in these conditions. He could continue down to the canyon's bottom and follow the river until it intersected with the trail back to his truck. Or, he could retrace his steps back up the steeper but much shorter trail. He chose the latter. Wrestling with his disappointment over the change in weather, Brad leaned into the furor and began a hurried retreat back up the trail.

The first blast of lightning streaked across the sky directly over his head. He wasn't sure where it hit, but judging from the terrifying roar that followed, he sure as heck knew it was close—and that he was in trouble.

Frantically, Brad searched the hillside for protection. The gods were with him. On the upslope side of the trail, about fifty yards in front of him, stood a massive formation of rock in which he spotted several fissures and crannies that looked promising. He hustled the distance and easily found a nook that receded about six feet into the mountainside. He peaked inside to make sure he was not about to interrupt moments of intimacy between bears or mountain lions, and thankfully crawled into the small cave.

The storm's initial fury was a dazzling display of electrical explosions and furious wind. Giant raindrops spewed from the sky, smashing into the earth like millions of water-filled meteorites. The mayhem soon passed but a steady rain continued. Crooked fingers of lightning zigzagged across the sky in displays of exquisite beauty. Brad zipped his rain jacket and settled in. The storm had a hefty feel, and he knew it was going to be awhile before he resumed his hike. Darkness was not far away, but Brad wasn't worried. He always carried a flashlight in his pack. Nothing was happening that he had not encountered plenty of times before. Content within the security of his cave and mesmerized by the lullaby of rain, Brad allowed his eyes to close and his mind to relax.

When Brad awoke, darkness had fallen, and a damp chill was in the air. He poked his head outside for a better look at the sky. The rain was letting up. It was really nothing more than a slow drizzle now. Lightning continued to flash but it was not nearly so close, and the thunder was only a distant rumble. Brad was confident that shortly he would be walking again.

Night skies were one of Brad's favorite things, especially after a cleansing storm. Hiking out was something he would thoroughly enjoy, shooting stars and distant galaxies for companionship.

If only Elizabeth were with me.

When the headlights first appeared, Brad could not understand how an automobile had managed to get so deep into the forest. Then he remembered the private road that led to the entrance gate of Elk Run. He watched the vehicle, expecting it to drive through the gate and continue on to the resort. But the car did not move. Moments passed, and it continued to sit outside the closed gate.

Years of experience and love of wildlife had taught Brad to carry a small monocular in his fishing vest. He retrieved the instrument and placed it to his eye. The glare from the headlights through the lingering rain made it hard to tell what he was seeing. He strained his eyes but could see no movement.

Then he saw movement in his peripheral vision. Another vehicle was approaching the gate from inside the resort property. As it neared the gate Brad could tell it was a pickup truck. When the truck reached the gate, it turned around and stopped. Someone got out and the metal barricade swung open, allowing the waiting vehicle to pass through. Both vehicles then drove together.

What followed was absolutely bewildering. Brad watched as both vehicles veered from the road and cut a path across the rocky terrain. This was absolutely crazy. *What the hell could they possibly be doing?* Brad wondered as headlights bobbed in erratic gyrations, appearing to float through the forest. *Was it a resort guest or a worker? Was it someone seeking seclusion for a sexual encounter or some sort of drug deal? What motivation could possibly prompt two cars to leave a perfectly good road to drive through mud and rocks in total darkness?*

The vehicles inched through the night, moving straight toward Brad. Then, both cars abruptly turned, their headlights now illuminating one of the dilapidated cabins that he had seen earlier. The drivers of the vehicles seemed to act in unison as they simultaneously turned off their engines and extinguished their headlights, plunging the scene into blackness. Brad struggled to see through the small monocular. He could make out the general shapes of the two vehicles but nothing else. He heard car doors open and close as a flicker of distant lightning illuminated the area for a split second. He was almost certain he saw three people. Brad held his breath, trying to hear what they were saying through the gentle rain. The hushed voices and movement were too faint. A dim light appeared as the trunk of the car opened. It wasn't much but was enough to confirm that he had been right about the number of people; three silhouettes stood over the opened trunk. Two figures were obviously larger than the third. It had to be two men and a woman. Brad watched as the men leaned into the trunk and appeared to struggle to lift something out. He could see only that whatever they hoisted was long and awkward to handle. The woman turned on a flashlight. She directed the beam for the men carrying the bundle. Brad followed the shaft of light as all three people walked toward the cabin, floundering with the long object that had been removed from the trunk.

Brad prayed for more lightning, but he was given only darkness.

Voices reached his ears, slightly louder than before. He thought he heard swearing but couldn't be certain. Finally, a powerful bolt lit up the sky. The effect lasted for only an instant, but it froze the scene with compelling clarity. Brad was able to capture the image as if it were a portrait on canvas: an elongated bundle of blankets, a strong masculine jaw line, and a ponytail extending below the base of a man's neck. He saw no more.

From within his small den, Brad's eyes remained glued on the black outline of the cabin. *What in hell is going on here? What are those people doing inside that cabin?* Brad waited and listened. It was so dark. After several minutes, he again sensed movement from the direction of the cabin, indecipherable sounds drifted through the air. The flashlight appeared again; three people came out but no long bundle. Then Brad heard the sound of automobile doors slamming shut. Headlights pierced the night, illuminating the walls of the cabin before both vehicles slowly turned away and began a retreat back toward the gate. Brad could easily see when the gate swung open. The automobiles passed through and dissolved into darkness.

The night suddenly seemed empty. Brad continued to stare, his eyes never moving from the gate that he could no longer see. He tried, but he just couldn't wrap his mind around what he had just observed. Every nerve in his body told him that something was wrong. But what? He slowly exhaled. "Why do I feel like I just witnessed an escape?" Even though he had whispered the words, they seemed to echo within the cave.

Brad crawled from his retreat and looked up to the sky. It was no longer raining. All that remained of the angry storm clouds were mere billows of drifting vapor, evaporating away, unfurling the magnificence of a Colorado night sky.

CHRISTINE REYNOLDS WAS ALONE. Her hands and feet remained tied and her eyes covered, but her senses told her that she was lying on old wood, a floor crusted in dust, barely covered by her thin blanket. Christine tried to cry but no tears remained. She wanted to scream but the gag over her mouth was bound too tightly. She was cold. Her body trembled.

The haunting silence that remained after her captors abandoned her in darkness was more terrifying than when she had been dragged from her car. Since those awful seconds that had begun her ordeal, she had felt a mixture of fear and loathing for the people who would do this to her. But now it was even worse. Until now she had not been alone. Until this moment there had at least been human voices, the sound of a door closing, footsteps on the floor, an occasional touch. Now, there was only silence, blackness, and loneliness, a loneliness she could never have imagined.

Oh, God, where am I? Please, let someone come. Please, God, let someone be with me. Christine's silent prayer was not heard.

———

IN THE QUIET NIGHT, reflecting on the bizarre events he had just witnessed, Brad stretched his cramped body. He again looked to the stars. *Unbelievable.*

Brad moved slowly, remaining silent as he gathered his gear. He wasn't sure why, but he felt like he needed to be careful not to disturb anything or make any noise. He couldn't define the feeling hanging over him. Was it a premonition or just apprehension? He moved toward the trail without turning on his light. For some reason it seemed sacrilege to violate the night with such a paltry beam. In spite of the darkness, it was easy to know when he reached the trail as the feel of the earth changed beneath his feet. Brad turned in the direction to return to his truck, but he did not move. An invisible force seemed to control his body, forcing him to turn to face the cabin. His eyes strained. He could barely discern the outline of the building. He swallowed. Like a black ghost, it seemed to move, gliding through the trees. Brad tried to feel, to hear. *What or who is talking to me? What is inside that old place? What have I just seen? Do I slide under the fence, trespass, look inside?*

Sensations from his past life stirred. He felt the exciting but terrifying feelings he had experienced just before a dangerous room entry or high-risk arrest. His heart was racing, and he had difficulty swallowing. After standing in the darkness for lingering seconds, Brad leaned his rod and pack against a tree and quietly crawled under the fence. As he inched closer, the cabin seemed to recognize an intruder. Its walls seemed to be alive and on guard, as though hidden eyes were watching him. Brad felt goose bumps.

God, it's dark! he thought. *What is it about this place?*

Creeping to the corner of the cabin, Brad searched for the doorway. Even without a flashlight, it was easy to see. The silvery gleam of a new padlock stood out against the splintered old door. *Why would there be a heavy-duty lock on a decrepit old door?*

Brad stood only feet from the door. He closed his eyes seeking the sixth sense he had always relied on. But it eluded him, hovering just beyond his grasp. Brad tried to convince himself that this was nothing more than resort employees using the cabin as a storage building, but his instincts screamed dissent. Something more was involved.

Why does the cabin seem to whisper? It's like I can hear it breathing.
God, it's dark.
What is it about this place?

Answers refused to come as he thought about what he should do. Did what he had seen give him the right to violate another person's property? Brad thought about his lack of legal authority to even be standing on this private land. He sure as hell no longer had a badge and the power of the law behind it to justify going through that door. Thinking again of all he had seen, he wondered if he should listen to his heart or his brain?

After a few moments, and with his heart wrenching, Brad turned from the cabin.

It's not like someone's life is at stake.

Back on the trail, Brad stood quietly for a few moments. With a sigh of self-doubt, he turned on his light and began the hike to his truck.

———

CHRISTINE REYNOLDS SHIVERED, whether from the cold, horrible silence or simple fear, she didn't know. She had no idea if she been there for minutes or hours. It seemed like eternity. How long did she hear the sounds before she realized that the silence was broken? If only her heart would not beat so loudly. Again, she heard it: scratching, scurrying. It was so dark. Again. Closer. More sounds.

Softness brushed her leg. The sound of dried leaves moved past her face; warmth touched her cheek.

Mice!

God had forsaken her.

Her brain cruelly contrived visions of rats with protruding teeth and evil red eyes.

Christine felt a release of warmth in her loins as she wet herself, the second time in twenty-four hours.

———

BRAD HAD JUST enough light from his small flashlight to traverse the narrow vein of a trail. Reaching a clearing, he stopped, turned off his light and gazed to heaven. The beauty was certainly there, just what he had looked forward to. But things weren't right. What he had felt while in the presence of the cabin still haunted him. He yearned for the serenity that a night sky would usually bring. The forest was absolutely silent. There was nothing but stars, delicate ornaments in endless indigo. Brad listened to his senses. His bones felt an omen, not serenity. He continued the walk to his truck.

A chill seeped through Brad's jacket by the time he reached his truck. Thankfully, he had coffee in his thermos, which warmed his body as he began the lonely drive home. Images of what he had witnessed played over and over in his mind.

Music was always an effective diversion when Brad felt unsettled, so he selected one of his favorites. The clear voice of Sarah Brightman filled his truck, "Think of Me." This song held huge meaning for Brad. Every year on Father's Day his daughter, Meghan, sang this song to him as her special gift. "Think of Me" was one of Brad's favorites. Sarah Brightman's music always evoked great memories of his daughter. Meghan was now in college, swept away in her love of musical theatre and certain that the world was her stage to play as she may choose. Elizabeth and he had adopted Meghan, bringing her home when she was three days old. His love for her could not be measured.

It was midnight by the time Brad reached his home. He rummaged through the refrigerator, finding only a slice of stale pizza but plenty of cold Moosehead. He didn't care that the pizza was stale since it was the Moosehead he really craved.

Brad slumped into a chair that was close to his favorite photograph of Elizabeth. He treasured this particular portrait, and heaven only knew how many times a day he sought its company. He thought of her life as a prosecuting attorney and how her magical smile enchanted all who knew her. But Brad loved this photograph for a special reason. It was her eyes. Ever since Elizabeth's death, something inexplicable happened when Brad was in the presence of the photograph and looked into her eyes. He could not possibly speak with anyone about this, but he knew that her eyes talked to him. They always sparkled. Sometimes they cautioned him; sometimes they admonished him; other times they seemed to laugh, but they always sparkled. Elizabeth loved him with her eyes. This photograph was the closest Brad could come to being with Elizabeth. It brought her back in the only way he could ever have her again.

Brad settled with his Moosehead, going over in his mind the events of the evening. As he thought about all that he had seen, his gaze drifted to Elizabeth. What he saw jolted him as if live wires touched him. She had never looked this way before, not even close. Brad sat straight and looked closer. There was no sparkle in her eyes, no smile, none at all. Instead, she had a look of pure desperation, piercing like daggers. Brad locked his gaze with hers. Everything in her face was different. Her eyes were penetrating, and her presence filled the room. Brad felt his skin prickle. Seconds passed. Brad tried to decipher his feelings, but he could not hear or feel what was coming from Elizabeth. He just could not grasp what he was feeling or what she was trying to convey.

Touching her face with his fingers, Brad whispered, "I'm trying, sweetheart. I'm trying." Elizabeth's eyes did not relent.

Finishing his Moosehead, Brad walked away but the power of her eyes continued to fill the room. They wouldn't leave him. He returned to the photograph and stared in silence for a few moments, but still nothing came to him. Nothing that he could understand.

Another Moosehead in hand, Brad went to his bed and lay down across the top without undressing. In spite of his exhaustion, sleep did not come quickly. Too much was inside his head. When finally he did drift off, his mind did not rest but was tormented by a nightmare. He dreamed of a roiling, muddy river. He had waded too far with his rod, and the water was deep, suddenly swift, too late to turn back. As if falling, the river's bottom left his feet. A surging torrent engulfed his body, hurling him past jagged boulders. His rod shattered and icy water flooded his waders. Tentacles of an unseen creature entwined his legs. Unable to float, unable to breathe and lungs on fire, there was one last chance.

Clutching a low hanging branch, he pulled his exhausted body onto the river's bank.

Choking on water and vomit, he lay on the ground, shivering violently. *Where am I? What happened to the sun? Why is it suddenly so dark?* There, directly in front of him was the cabin, a phantom appearing in the blackness. But weren't the windows supposed to be boarded over? Then why could he see dim light glowing from within. Squeezing his eyes and breathing deeply, he looked again. He had seen correctly. There was an image in the window. It was his mother. She waved, pleading for him to enter.

FRIDAY, SEPTEMBER 7

Brad always rose before the sun. He needed to feel the dawn, greet the new day head-on, not looking back over his shoulder. The rare times that Brad had slept through a sunrise, the rest of his day seemed to be a step behind, out of sync. "What the hell," he muttered as he glanced out the window and looked at the rose tint of first light and then rolled from his bed. After splashing cold water on his face and starting coffee, Brad looked about his house. Remnants of stale pizza and an empty Moosehead stared back. Remembering his nightmare with a shudder, he vowed that next time he would skip the pizza and stick with Moosehead.

Stepping outside with his coffee, Brad wrapped his hands about the warm mug and, as he had done practically every morning of his life, cast his eyes upward to check the sky: clear and beautiful. Hoping that caffeine and cold morning air would clear the ache that throbbed in his head, Brad stood for a moment enjoying the morning's quiet.

The small table situated in his flower garden beckoned. Settling into a chair, he recalled the countless hours he and Elizabeth spent in this very spot. They had loved mornings here with newspaper and coffee. More often than not, the newspaper went unread, and they just talked.

Months of neglect in the garden were apparent. Without water and persistent attention, the once lush plot now supported only a few meager flowers with lusterless petals. Brad gazed about the garden that had played such a role in their lives. Maybe he should try it again. He could pull weeds and get his hands dirty. Brad was convinced that in order for a flower garden to thrive, hands must touch the soil. Brad had taught his family that flowers are delicate and intuitive, able to sense the difference between a metal spade and human touch.

A bellflower struggled in the toughened soil. Brad recalled how Elizabeth had loved the plant's delicate bells. The garden had been her private cathedral and the bellflower her favorite. The flower now drooped, begging for attention. Brad breathed deeply. Maybe next spring things could be different.

Coffee and fresh air worked their magic as the pain in his head was easing. But things still did not seem right. Why was last night bothering him so much? What was so sinister about what he had observed? He analyzed the evening's events and tried to make the pieces fit. It didn't work. Something was wrong. Why would anyone risk the terrible conditions of the storm to visit a dilapidated old cabin so far from a road? Brad thought of the long bundle he had watched the people carry. For some reason, that was the hardest piece of all to make fit. What could those people have been carrying that was so important to make them stomp around in mud and darkness?

Brad sipped his coffee. *It looked like those people were carrying a damned body.*

Was it the nightmare that left him so unsettled? Whatever the reason, Brad knew he couldn't spend the day feeling so agitated. There had to be a way to settle his mind. He chose the same medicine as always, the thing that he always relied on as an antidote to whatever ailed him: a workout. Brad jumped into his truck and headed to the meadow.

A few early rising joggers and mountain bikers shared the trail as Brad worked his way through the valley and up the mountain that were the treasured centerpieces of his hometown. Morning's chill evaporated as the sun climbed in the sky. Before long he was drenched with sweat.

His tired legs reminded him of yesterday's steep hike. Before Elizabeth's illness, he had been able to run this trail like the wind. Brad resolved that he would do so again. After his run, followed by pushups and sit-ups in the grassy meadow, he drove home.

With a glass of orange juice, Brad felt like a new man. While running, it had become clear that something sure as hell wasn't right. His old friend and partner, Kurt Riddle, was the person to talk with. Kurt had a way of seeing through haze, and his instincts were seldom wrong.

But before he could call Kurt, there was something he had to do. Brad had avoided it all morning but could postpone her no longer. Brad walked through his house and stood before Elizabeth's photograph. It was just as he had feared. There was no sparkle in her eyes. They had not changed one bit since last night. Her eyes were somber, severe, almost begging. Once again, Brad knew he was missing something. What was it? He tried to read her eyes. He tried to listen. Shaking his head in resignation, he sighed. Elizabeth refused to back down. Her gaze was unrelenting.

Before making his call to Kurt, Brad headed to the shower.

———

KURT RIDDLE WAS AN OLD-FASHIONED COP. He wouldn't be caught dead in anything other than boots and jeans and beneath his easy-going country manner was a razor-sharp intellect. He was stronger than a mule, loved politically incorrect jokes, and could smell bullshit before it hit the ground. When he heard Brad Walker's voice on the telephone he drawled, "Well, if it ain't J. Edgar Hoover's shoeshine boy. How the hell are you anyway?"

"You buzzard, I was doing great until I thought about you. Now I'm not so sure."

Kurt was a deputy sheriff and worked the county where Elk Run Fly

Fishing Resort was located. Brad knew Kurt to be one of the finest investigators ever to grace law enforcement. The two men shared fond memories of investigations as well as love for each other's family. Riddle and his wife had been with Elizabeth and Brad during the toughest days before Elizabeth died. The two men respected each other deeply.

"Hey, listen, Kurt, I hate to bother you, but I need to talk. I suspect you're going to tell me that I need a vacation in a Prozac factory, but something is bugging me. And I'm not having any luck sorting it out."

"Fire away, my friend."

Brad related the events of the previous evening to Kurt. He deliberately omitted the part about his nightmare and certainly did not discuss the surreal experiences he felt with Elizabeth's photograph. He would prefer that his old friend not hang up on him.

After listening to Brad's story, Riddle spoke with no hint of sarcasm. "Well, I understand why you've got funny feelings about what you saw, and I sure don't have an explanation for what the hell was going on. I suppose there may be a reasonable explanation. I just can't think of one at the moment."

"I can tell you for sure, Kurt, I've been going over this since I walked away last night. The more I think about things, the more bizarre the whole deal seems. I'm starting to get a bad feeling that I screwed up by not doing something."

"I guess I understand how you feel, but I can't say that I would have done things any different."

"It's too late now, but the whole deal is bothering me so badly I decided to give you a call."

"I'm glad you did. Gives me an excuse to bust your chops a bit. You know, Brad, that resort is about as high end as it can be. Without really deep pockets, don't expect an invitation to their summer picnic. From time to time we get some calls from somebody out there. Pretty much what you might expect. You know, stuff like some drunken husband pinching the ass of a twenty-five-year-old waitress and his wife clobbers him. Or better yet, the wife takes a roll beneath the pines with a twenty-five-year-old fishing guide and all hell breaks loose. Ain't it amazing, Brad, rich people have genitals just like everybody else."

Both men laughed.

Riddle continued, "We don't have anything going at the ranch right now. At least not that I'm aware of. But I'll keep my ears to the ground and make some calls. The resort manager is a young kid who recently inherited the place, and he's not inclined to be cooperative with the police."

"Yeah, I've heard the same thing about the kid. I appreciate your help. Just give me a whistle if something crosses your screen, not that this old retired guy could do anything about it anyway."

"Listen, Brad," Kurt said earnestly, "you and I both know that one of the few things in this world that qualifies as a sin is for a cop to ignore his instincts. If you've got a feeling, pay attention. Don't ignore it. I agree that what you saw is mighty strange. I'll check around, see what I can learn, and I'll call you back."

"Gotcha. Thanks a million."

———

BLUE SKIES and sunshine were making Brad restless. He decided to take advantage of the beautiful morning and run a few errands. His car was filthy, he had no cash, and even the stale pizza was gone. While he was at it, a plate of enchiladas with smoking hot, green chili sauce sounded like the best thing this side of heaven. Maybe a tamale for dessert.

Brad drove about town running errands. He saw old friends and made small talk, always promising to get together soon. He loved this town in the mountains. It was a special place, and he could not imagine why anyone would choose to live anywhere but here. But then, he surely was glad that most people didn't live here.

As soon as he returned home, Brad listened to his telephone messages. "Hey daddio, check this out." Brad knew instantly that it was his youngest son, Michael. Only one year younger than Meghan, he was also in college and was thinking of someday going into law. Brad would never push him, but he sure did hope Michael would become a prosecutor. Not only would he be dynamite in a courtroom, it seemed a real tribute to Elizabeth.

Michael and Meghan had each spent the summer attending school before beginning their regular classes in September. Brad missed them terribly but knew that after losing their mom, staying busy and out of the house was the best thing. Brad smiled as he listened to his son's message about his university adventures and the antics of goofy professors he was forced to tolerate. Michael never stopped cracking jokes, and he had a way of making everyone happy. Physically, he was a mirror image of Brad, six-three and slender. The sound of Michael's voice was a reminder about how much he missed his children.

The next message was from Kurt. "Hey, Brad. Just wanted to let you know that I checked around just to be sure and our department doesn't have anything going at Elk Run. If something pops up, I'll call you in a heartbeat. However, I thought you might be interested in knowing that I just spoke with Sam Trathen over in Aspen. He's had a brand-new case drop in his lap. Too early to tell whether or not it's the real deal, but a super wealthy woman has either vanished or run away with her dream lover. Sam said they were just getting into it. He doesn't know too much yet, but it may turn out to be a biggie." Kurt paused. "Then, Brad, that crazy guy said something that I absolutely do not understand. He said he misses working with your sorry ass and would love to hear from you. He must be losing what's left of the tiny little brain he ever had. Why don't you give him a call? Later old man."

Brad listened to the message again. Aspen was three to four hours away from his home and about the same distance from Elk Run. There certainly was no reason to connect a woman reported missing from Aspen to what he had seen last night. But still, Kurt's message had caused a bell to ring. Brad shut his eyes, recalling the darkened image of something being pulled from the trunk of an automobile. He had seen something that was long and awkward to handle. Damn if it hadn't resembled a body rolled in a blanket. Brad shook his head and grinned, embarrassed with his own thoughts. *Am I going nuts? If I were still on the job, would I get this worked up over a couple of cars driving in the woods?* He asked himself the question sarcastically, but the answer really didn't seem so clear. Brad brought it all into his mind again. He saw lightning and rain and three people struggling with a bundle. Brad saw a man with a ponytail.

His earlier conversation with Kurt Riddle had been a pleasant reconnection with a friend. Brad contemplated how quickly friendships can grow stale. He knew that after Elizabeth's death he had become way too reclusive. Not a good thing. On an impulse, he dialed Sam Trathen. Sam's voice mail kicked in and Brad left a message requesting a return call. Sam Trathen was a police officer in Aspen and like Kurt Riddle, he was salt of the earth, rock solid.

Brad glanced around his house and realized there was no reason at all for him to hang around. It wasn't like important stuff was waiting. Why not drive to Aspen, see Sam, and go fishing? Decision made. Within minutes he had a bag packed and his fly rod and gear ready to go.

His telephone rang.

"How's life in the retirement home? Has anyone been by to change your diaper today?" It was the unmistakable growl of Sam Trathen.

Brad smiled at the voice of his old friend. Without losing a beat Brad fired back. "Kurt called me this morning. Said you were floundering as usual, like a catfish at a formal ball. He suggested I drive over there and give you a little guidance. How about coffee in the morning? I'll do all that's humanly possible to straighten you out. Then I plan to fish the Frying Pan River."

"Christ, you Feds never go away, do you?" Sam moaned. "OK, but I'm busy. Doing police work. Something you wouldn't understand. How about seven o'clock at our old regular?"

"Sounds great, Sam. See you in the morning. Consider it your lucky day."

"My ass." Sam hung up.

Brad walked through his house. It was an old habit he developed through years of raising kids. Before leaving on a trip, he had to be sure the lights were off, no toilets were running, and the trash was removed to the garage. After making his rounds, Brad stopped beside Elizabeth's photograph. Would she approve of him blasting off to Aspen? Should he look at her? Could he not look? Brad felt as foolish as a schoolboy hoping to glimpse the most beautiful girl in seventh grade, but desperately not wanting to be caught sneaking a peek. Brad peeked. Elizabeth sure as hell caught him. He was pretty sure he saw approval in her eyes, but he didn't look for too long as those eyes had half frightened him last night.

Brad climbed into his truck and was ready to travel.

He decided to go the long way, over Independence Pass. This would take him through one of his favorite areas of the state. Brad wanted to reach Independence Pass before nightfall so that he could enjoy its majesty and spend some time with a few memories that lived there. Heading west on Interstate 70, Brad passed Idaho Springs and George-town. The Eisenhower Tunnel took him through the spine of the Continental Divide, then ejected him like a torpedo at eleven thousand feet in the sky. In dazzling sunshine, Brad was eye to eye with the Ten Mile Range and the ski resorts of Summit County. Willie Nelson's "On the Road Again" was perfect company.

Things felt right. It was good to be moving. Something told him this was a step in the right direction toward figuring out what he had seen last night.

Traffic was light and Brad made good time. He headed south on Colorado Highway 24 toward Leadville. With Mt. Elbert, the highest peak in Colorado, in view, Brad made a turn onto Highway 82. It was time for the big climb.

Independence Pass, a contorted sinew of asphalt, backtracked on itself again and again. The climb snaked through alpine meadows and spruce forests. Each twist of the road delivered new breathtaking views. Brad delighted in the brilliance of high-altitude meadows but sadly bid farewell to the last remnants of summer's wildflowers. As the road clawed its way higher into the sky, the air became paper thin. Trees and vegetation gradually disappeared. Colossus boulders and walls of stone were the only survivors in this twelve-thousand-foot tundra.

Upon reaching the summit, Brad parked his truck.

A brisk hike led him to an overlook that always took his breath—sheer grandeur. This was the place where he had stood with Elizabeth on their honeymoon. This was the reason he had chosen to travel this road. Elizabeth had been raised in the Deep South and, to her people, anywhere else was viewed almost as a foreign land. As far as her family was concerned, one who wandered from the South did so with real risk of being transformed into a pillar of salt. Elizabeth thought she was in another world when she stood here for the first time. She had come to love the mountains of Colorado as much as he did.

Brad stood where they had stood—where he had held her. A gallery of wind-sculpted stones scattered across the landscape. Regal giants of grey, black, and brown granite stood in stoic silence at the threshold of heaven. Nothing but the wind. She was here. He could feel her. Brad stood, his heart aching, savoring her presence.

The walk back to his truck helped him settle down. Despite the pain, Brad was glad he had come. Standing beside his truck, he breathed deeply. He was going to make it.

To orchestrate his descent into Aspen, Brad selected Sarah Brightman's "Don't Cry for me Argentina" in Spanish: *"No llores por mi Argentina."*

Brad didn't stop in Aspen. Lodging in this glitzy town was out of his league. Another half hour took him to Glenwood Springs where he was to meet Sam the next morning. Traveling the familiar road caused Brad to realize how much he missed his old friend. It would be great to see the old codger again.

SATURDAY, SEPTEMBER 8

THE AROMA OF COFFEE, bacon, and cinnamon rolls greeted Brad when he walked through the door. The restaurant they referred to as their auxiliary office oozed with nostalgia. Wood-planked flooring, grey with age and warped from the residue of thousands of snow-covered boots, provided a sturdy platform for pine tables and chairs. A red brick wall held mounted game trophies and black-and-white photographs of the bearded miners who had settled the valley. In perpetual defiance of winter, a massive wood-burning stove dominated the dining area. One intuitively understood that creamy lattes would not be found on the menu.

Keeping with tradition, Sam was ahead of schedule and already seated at their favorite table beneath a mounted bull elk head. Although dressed sharp as a tack in a grey suit, white shirt, and tie, it was readily apparent to Brad that his friend was operating on minimal sleep. Despite his haggard look, Sam offered his infectious smile as he stood to greet Brad.

"By golly, I'm glad to see that you didn't get lost driving over here. Knowing the way your little brain can get confused, I was worried that you might end up in Arkansas."

"If I was in Arkansas, I wouldn't have to put up with the likes of you."

After more mandatory insults, they reminisced with stories of the old days and caught up on their respective families.

Elizabeth had loved Sam. She thought he hung the moon. For years Sam and Brad's oldest son, Cody, had played a game together. On their respective birthdays they exchanged the same pair of women's sized XXL pink panties. Every birthday the same jokes and derogatory remarks were bantered about over who was most deserving of the prodigious bloomers. It became a tradition as predictable as Christmas that continued until Cody joined the Navy.

Kurt, Sam, and Brad had been a team for years. Well known throughout the law enforcement world, they were generally referred to as the Three Horsemen because of their love of riding horses into remote wilderness areas to fly fish. Shared memories, humor, and family traditions held the men close.

Knowing that his friend had much to do, Brad curtailed small talk and spoke about the troublesome events that he had seen while sitting in the cave.

As the story unfolded, Sam played with his food and listened. "That's a mighty bizarre story for sure. If I were in your shoes, I'd be thinking just like you are; what the hell did I just see?"

"You gotta help me here, Sam. Maybe I'm just looking for an excuse to visit with a pleasant voice from the past but after the crazy stuff I saw at that cabin, then hearing about a missing woman over here in Aspen, something made me feel like I had to drive over and see you. I know there is absolutely nothing to connect the two events, but I don't know, Sam. Something just ain't right." Brad grinned. "Now, go ahead and tell me I'm crackers, but I sure would like to hear a little bit more about your case."

Sam threw his head back and laughed. "I knew you were crackers long before this morning. I only tolerate you because I feel sorry for you."

Brad rolled his eyes. "I'm sure as hell glad I drove hours just to listen to your wiseass comments."

Sam laughed. The weary police officer rubbed his tired eyes and thoughtfully replied, "No, Brad, I don't think you're crazy at all. In fact, I would have called you this morning anyway. I spent some time on the telephone yesterday with your old agency. I can't really say they were assholes, but they came darned close. The world ain't what it used to be, Brad."

"You are so right. What happened?"

Sam contemplated the breakfast that was growing cold. Both men were quiet before Sam spoke.

"Okay, Brad, how should I start?" Sam tapped his fork on the table, thinking before he spoke. "This darned thing started for us with a private charter pilot who was scheduled to fly a woman named Christine Reynolds from Aspen to Phoenix. The pilot sits around waiting for his passenger, but the lady never shows up. After a while, the pilot gets worried. He can't raise her on her telephone or anything, so he calls her husband. Now, the husband is a super-rich business guy named Brandon Reynolds. Mr. Reynolds doesn't like what he's hearing so he gets on the horn immediately. That's what starts the ball rolling for us here in Aspen. Initially, we have no idea if we're dealing with a nutcase or somebody legit. We begin to nose around and find her rental car at the airport. Turns out she has a regular driver who picked her up at the airport on the day she arrived. He drove her to her hotel and left her with her car. They had done this many times before. When she left Aspen, she would leave the car at the airport."

Before Brad could ask the question, Sam said, "Oh yeah, we talked to the driver at length. He's a very decent guy, and believe me, he is some kind of major upset. Hell, I think he's about half in love with the woman. He carried on about Mrs. Reynolds and how wonderful she treats him. He claims this is absolutely out of her character. No way would she just run off." Sam shook his head. "Brad, I'm convinced that the driver is legit and telling us everything he knows."

"Okay, that's a good start."

"Anyway, things heated up a bit once it becomes obvious that we have something serious on our hands. We decided pretty quickly that she really was missing. The big question, of course, is why, or how, she went missing."

Brad watched his friend closely. It was apparent Sam was stressed. He knew that the grey in Sam's neatly trimmed hair was from too many cases like this.

Sam sipped his coffee and continued. "It's taken some time to sort through it all, but the bottom line is that Christine Reynolds is a mega rich lady, even by Aspen standards. She flew out here to attend a party thrown by some other rich folks named Cotter. You know their place, Brad. It's at the end of Paradise Valley where we hiked with your boys up to Carbon Lake a couple of years ago. At the time, they had just started to build the house, and we stopped to look the place over. We talked about what an incredible setting they had for a home."

Brad shook his head. "Oh, yeah, I remember it well."

"According to her driver and her husband, Mrs. Reynolds had planned to spend an evening at the party, return to her hotel in Aspen, and fly back to Phoenix the next morning. We've been able to confirm that she attended the party, and everything was fine. She's not a drinker. She left the party stone-cold sober a little after ten o'clock. Whammo! She's gone. Her car is sitting at the airport right where it's supposed to be, but no Mrs. Reynolds. No sign, no word, no clue."

"Wow!"

Sam Trathen's eyes drifted about the restaurant, almost as if he expected to see Christine Reynolds seated across the room enjoying coffee before a flight to Arizona. Sam brought his eyes back to the table and continued. "According to the hotel, her room appeared to have been used and her bed slept in. Unfortunately, the cleaning people had already done their thing, and it was tidy as could be before we even realized that a problem existed. We did all the crime scene stuff anyway, including her car. No real surprises there, tons of prints, hairs, and the usual stuff. The lab work is still in process, but I'm not optimistic we're gonna get much of a break."

Brad visualized each step Sam Trathen described. He could hear the conversations and feel the anticipation, the building excitement of a new case. Nostalgia stirred uncomfortably. What was he doing on the outside looking in? What's wrong here? Brad looked down and simply swirled his coffee.

"A few strange things have popped up, though. A telephone call was made from her room after midnight to the Bellagio Casino and Hotel. Las Vegas of all places. We couldn't trace the call to a specific location inside the hotel, so we don't know where the call ended up. But there sure as hell was somebody in her room long after she left the party. The next morning, her credit card gets used in a coffee shop near the hotel and her cell phone records indicate another call was made to the Bellagio."

Elbows on the table and fingers intertwined beneath his chin, Sam became quiet and looked for a reaction from Brad.

"Las Vegas?" Brad asked slightly surprised. "Is her husband aware of those calls?"

Sam grinned. "Oh, yes, and is he ever going nuts! He has no explanation for the calls to Las Vegas, but he swears they have a great marriage and no way is she messing around with any jet-setting Las Vegas type. He's calling our department, he's calling the Denver FBI, and, apparently, he is even talking with the friggin' director of the FBI. Christ, the guy can get through to the damned president if he wants."

Brad grinned and shook his head. "And what did the old Bureau have to say about this?"

"Jesus, it was frustrating. They wouldn't even send an agent to talk with the husband in Arizona. We got Phoenix PD to help us with that. The Bureau says that there is no body, no indication of abduction, and no ransom demand. According to their infinite wisdom, that translates into the fact that they see no reason why they should stop pursuing terrorists and protecting the defenseless citizens of the Free World simply to go chasing after what is probably just a horny, rich broad looking for something to keep her excited for a few days."

Brad shook his head. He could easily imagine what Sam had endured, and a sinking feeling began to settle into his stomach. "What did Arizona have to say about things on their end?"

"I know the investigator in Phoenix. We went through a homicide school together, and we've worked some cases over the years. He's a good guy, and I trust his instincts. He says the Reynolds are absolutely a legit couple and this definitely is not a case of rich folks simply behaving like fools. The hubby is falling apart, genuinely terrified and heartbroken. Hell, the guy is demanding that he be given a polygraph just to validate what he's saying. The Reynolds family has an excellent reputation. Even though they are super-rich, they still have their feet on the ground. They donate millions to the community, and everybody loves them. Not exactly your typical celebrity assholes that are absolute trash but just happen to have money out the wazoo."

Brad held his coffee mug in both hands.

Both men gave time for thought.

Brad lifted his eyes to meet Sam's face. "What do you think, Sam?"

Sam was quiet, measuring his words. "I think it's a little too early to know. We're still interviewing and learning. We need to track down more people who were at the party she attended. More family and staff have to be interviewed. It doesn't look like the lab people will come up with anything that's going to blow this open. We have more work to do with credit cards and telephone records. All the regular stuff." Sam tossed a sarcastic smile across the table. "Now, wouldn't it just be fucking peaches if the good old Federal Bureau of Investigation would maybe offer a little help? You know, like making available a few guys around the country to get to the bottom of this in a timely manner. We're not looking for a new world order here, Brad. Maybe just some help with out-of-state leads to get to the bottom of this thing quickly." Sam paused and leaned over the table and continued, "Cause let me tell you, Brad, if it turns out she was grabbed, this is gonna be a big one. People with this kind of money and political connections don't just vanish into thin air quietly. Know what I mean? If something bad has happened, it's going to be a big case. It'll involve investigators from all over the country. The big bad Bureau is gonna get sucked in whether they like it or not. But it will be just a tad late!" Sam gave Brad a hard look.

What had begun as a mere sinking feeling was now twisting into a hard knot in Brad's stomach. "I'm sick about it, Sam. Who have you been talking to in the Denver office?"

"Guy named Barnes."

"Yeah, I know him. He's a good agent."

"I don't doubt that, and he seemed nice enough. I tried using your name, and it got me exactly nowhere," Sam grinned. "The poor guy really was catching it from all angles. His boss was yelling at him; my boss was yelling at him; the damned FBI director was calling from Washington. Brandon Reynolds was calling everyone on the planet, screaming and demanding immediate action. What a mess. But at the end of the day, it was your esteemed director who made it clear: no FBI involvement. He said this was a local criminal matter and refused to commit any resources."

"Sam, you have no idea how badly that pisses me off."

"Oh, I think I do," Sam chuckled. "Barnes seemed like a great guy. He would be here with us right now if he had his way. It's the brass at the top." Sam's voice singed with sarcasm. "You know those guys who see the really big picture, who have a global perspective far beyond the capabilities of a mere cop or FBI Agent who want to determine if an innocent woman has been murdered or kidnapped."

"Yeah," Brad said. "You know, Sam, the Bureau really started changing after September 11. All anyone could think about was terrorists, weapons of mass destruction, and all that stuff. Then, along came the bombings in Spain and England, and the mess in Iraq and Afghanistan. It was all like salt in a wound. Maybe it's the way things have to be, but to some extent, it seems like the Bureau has morphed into a bunch of people just chasing shadows on their laptops. I don't have an answer, but it sure as hell seems like there could be a better way to run a railroad."

"It's nobody's fault," Sam sighed. "Just the way the world is." He looked across the table at Brad and gave a weak grin. "All this talk and I guess I never did answer your question. You asked what do I think at this point?" Sam thought for a moment, staring at the table. He leaned forward and with intensity in his face he said, "I think there's a damned old snake in the woodpile, Brad! It's all too neat. Calls to Las Vegas making it look like some sort of romantic fling. Who the hell calls a secret squeeze in a hotel anymore? She would have called her lover on a cell. I have doubts about the whole Las Vegas thing, but we have to check it out anyway. We're trying to get the FAA to give us information on any flights that left Aspen that morning with a flight plan to Las Vegas. Now, Brad, don't take this as a compliment, but the FAA, TSA, ICE, and Homeland Security are a thousand times more fucked-up than the FBI. Maybe we'll get something, but I doubt it."

Brad couldn't keep a smile off his face.

Sam was on a roll. "Also, why would a rich woman like Christine Reynolds pay for a lousy cup of coffee with a credit card? And, the card hasn't been used anymore since the coffee shop. Hell's bells, Brad. That just doesn't make any sense. It all strikes me as a big charade. And another thing that strikes me as out of whack is that Christine Reynolds apparently left the hotel without saying squat to anybody. She didn't check out, sign any papers, nothing. She just left. Okay, maybe so, but the hotel has no record of anyone being called to help her with her bags." Sam shook his head. "This is the part I don't buy, Brad. From what we've learned, she's a very nice lady, but I sure as hell don't see a woman like Christine Reynolds carrying her own damned luggage from her room, through the hotel, and loading it into her car. Not in a million years. No way, not while an entire hotel staff stands around chewing gum and scratching their ass."

"I have to agree," Brad nodded.

"And, Brad, you know there is no electronic record that she used the hotel parking lot that night. I suppose it's possible that for some reason she may have chosen to park on the street after her party, but I don't think so. Why wouldn't she use valet service or pull right into a secure and covered garage?" Sam shoved his plate away. "We had no luck at all in determining when her room was last entered. The hotel had already cleared those records out of their computer before we even contacted them. They keep the garage records a lot longer."

Brad offered no response as he waited for his friend to continue.

Sam was quiet. Brad could tell he was visualizing every detail of the story. Then Sam spoke again. "Brad, I just don't see her being grabbed in the airport parking lot. At the time her flight was scheduled, it was broad-assed daylight and people are thick as flies around that place. I can't say it's impossible, but my gut says whatever happened, it wasn't at the airport."

Sam's face betrayed his discouragement.

Brad looked closely at his friend. "I'm with you all the way, Sam. I absolutely agree with every conclusion or doubt that you've mentioned. If someone grabbed her for straight-up robbery, rape, or murder, then the telephone calls from both her hotel room and cell phone don't add up. Why waste a stolen credit card on an insignificant purchase?" Brad placed his coffee mug on the table and leaned forward. "But for heaven's sake, Sam, if she was snatched for ransom, we are way the hell overdue for a demand. Give me a break. What kind of friggin' bad guy is going to just sit around and hold her for God knows how long before asking for money?"

Sam shook his head. "I couldn't agree more, Brad, and I have no answer for you. I am one puzzled guy."

Neither man spoke. Brad sat back in his chair and did what he had always done when he worked a case. He tried to imagine with how Brandon Reynolds must be feeling. Had their last moment together been a kiss or an angry word? If the moment could be recalled, what changes would be made? Was it a memory to cherish or a prayer for one more chance to get it right?

Brad spoke softly. "Sam, can you imagine what the husband is going through? Talk about emotional devastation. Something like this could tear a person apart."

"I've been thinking about that very thing ever since this deal began," Sam replied. "That's why these cases are so damned tough. We're talking real people here, real lives. When I think that a mistake on my part could cause another person harm or death. . . . Hell, Brad, I don't have to tell you what it's like. You've been there plenty."

Brad nodded.

Silence again fell over the table, each man lost in private thoughts of family, children, and wives. They remembered past cases similar to this. Not all of them had happy endings.

"Has the Reynolds' house been set up to receive a demand?" Brad asked.

"Yeah, we were sure hoping for some help from your guys in that regard. But since the Bureau said no go, Phoenix PD is handling it for us so far. But Holy Christ, we're talking a bunch of manpower here. If there is a crime at all, it's in Colorado. Phoenix is not too anxious to commit a ton of guys to a Colorado case that may turn out not to even be a case at all. In fact, Brad, I gotta tell you, if after the basic investigation is completed and we don't have something solid, or if there isn't a demand pretty soon, my boss is going to tell me to back off this thing. Wait and see if a body shows up or she comes riding back into town after her fling with Vegas lover boy, or whoever."

"I understand," Brad replied. "I don't think it will make any difference, but I'll talk to Barnes. I feel sure his hands are tied but it doesn't hurt to talk."

Both men sat in silence for a few moments just thinking about all the unanswered questions.

Brad broke the moment. "Look, Sam, it has been great to see you, and I appreciate your time. I know you have a million things to do, and I need to let you get going." Hesitating for a moment, Brad thought before continuing. "I can't say for sure why I felt such a need to talk with you, but, Sam, there's something about what I saw the other night. Those crazy people were out in the forest. It was dark as hell. They were up to their ankles in mud, dragging a long bundle out of their trunk and carrying it into an old cabin that looked like it could fall down in a strong wind. Christ, Sam, it's burning a hole in me. When I heard about your case here in Aspen, hell, I don't know, it just hit me. On one hand, I feel like an idiot. Then I think about things and damn if a little voice doesn't scream at me. Something like, open your eyes, moron!" Brad gave a shrug and a grin. "What's your diagnosis, Sam, too much Moosehead?"

Sam smiled. "Ain't no such thing as too much Moosehead," he said. "Surely you know that by now. That may be the most moronic thing I've ever heard you say, and you've said quite a bunch in the years I've known you."

"Okay, okay, I take it back. Maybe I'm not drinking enough Moosehead."

After a chuckle, Sam peered across the table, his face becoming deadly serious. "Listen to me, goofball. For the moment, I'm lost on this one, but I don't intend to stay lost. This will all come together and soon, I hope. You and I have put a whole lot of people in jail over the years, and half the time all we started with was a hunch. Some damned little voice talking to us. The day you stop listening to those little voices, my friend, that will sure as hell be the day I stop listening to you."

Brad smiled and gave a knowing nod.

"I don't know what the hell you saw out there in the woods," Sam continued. "But for heaven's sake, folks carrying things around in the middle of a stormy night, things that look like a body, what the hell is anybody supposed to think? Hell, I don't know what it means." Looking squarely into Brad's face, Sam pointed for emphasis. "Don't ever ignore it when those little voices talk to you. Listen to the bastards. They usually have something important to say." Sam leaned back. He had nothing more to say.

With a short laugh Brad acknowledged his friend. "You got it, Sam. I suppose that's the sermon I needed, the reason I drove over here. I appreciate it." Brad paused and then said, "I'll call Barnes when I get home. Tell him you're a pain in the ass."

Sam laughed as he stood to depart. "Anything you can do is appreciated. Stay in touch."

Shaking hands, the two friends parted company.

OUTSIDE THE RESTAURANT, Brad climbed into his truck and just sat. He needed some time to think things through. His original intention had been to go to the Frying Pan River and fish for a few hours, but after talking with Sam, he was rolling inside. He didn't think he could settle himself adequately to concentrate on fishing. Everything seemed upside down: a party filled with rich people that had somehow turned into a woman vanishing and an investigation that held more questions than answers and his old FBI too busy to lend a hand in a matter that held a person's life in the balance.

Brad recalled the hike he, Sam, Cody, and Michael made to Carbon Lake. It was a beautiful trail that wound up out of Paradise Valley to a trout-filled gem of a lake. How could they have imagined on that day, as they looked at a house barely under construction, the significance that the scene would someday hold? Brad closed his eyes in thought. *Who had known Christine would be there that night? Was there any connection with the party and her disappearance?*

Brad understood the math involved here. Big money equals big houses equals big parties equals lots of people involved to arrange a gala affair. It was anybody's guess how many people may have known about the party and that Christine Reynolds would be in attendance.

With the turn of a key, Brad started his engine. "What the hell," he muttered as he pulled away from the restaurant. He turned in the opposite direction of the Frying Pan River and headed to Paradise Valley.

A half hour later, Brad slowed as he approached the end of the valley and the drive leading to the Cotter estate. He eased his truck to a halt and gazed at the sprawling manor where Christine Reynolds had spent her last hours before vanishing. Even though he had seen it under construction, he was flabbergasted with the opulence of the residence and its surroundings. What a dramatic change from the piles of newly excavated dirt he had seen such a long time ago. Brad pulled to the side of the road and stepped out of his truck. Looking at the driveway to the house, it reminded him more of a runway than a driveway. "Could land a 747 here," Brad mumbled. He took a few minutes to study the layout. In the past when he had been involved in cases like this, he had always made it a point to visit the scene where the abduction had taken place. It was a way to get close to the victim, to develop a feel for what had transpired. Taking a breath, Brad realized that this was as close to Christine Reynolds as he could get.

A virtual palace stood at the end of the drive. Brad could only imagine the opulence of a party in such a place. Had the event served as an opportune ruse for an evil-minded scheme or was it merely a coincidence? Brad stood still, absorbing the sight as he contemplated what had happened. Christine Reynolds would have had to travel this driveway and turn onto this very road. *What happened after she departed?*

Staring at the empty drive, Brad thought of missing person cases from his past. There was no sweeter joy than reuniting someone with his or her family and nothing more heart-wrenching than discovering the body of a victim. Maybe the very worst were those that had no end, no resolution, only questions and infinite grief.

Once back in his vehicle, Brad eased away, driving slowly. He was in no rush to distance himself from this place. In only a few hundred yards he was surprised when he reached the trailhead to Carbon Lake. He had not remembered how close the trail was to the Cotter estate. Brad pulled into the parking area and stopped. Only two vehicles occupied the space, which meant very few people would be on the trail or at Carbon Lake. Brad looked at the blue sky and knew the day would be warm. Still, he left his truck and started up the trail.

It wasn't clear in his mind if he would hike the entire distance to Carbon Lake or simply walk for a while and enjoy a beautiful day. After talking with Sam, any kind of a walk struck Brad as the perfect way to do some thinking.

The initial portion of the hike was steep and rocky, so Brad had no choice but to keep his eyes focused on the trail. But his thoughts were not so easily focused. Like replaying scenes from a movie in his mind, he imagined images of an elegant house, a plush party, and a woman vanished. Without conscious effort, the mental images transformed into a dilapidated cabin, rain, mud, and the mysteries of that dark night. Brad thought about himself too. He had sat alone in a dark cave not understanding what he saw. He had stood before the cabin, debating what to do. Now, doubt gnawed at him, questions demanded answers. *Did I do the right thing?* Brad realized that what he had done was not the source of his angst. It was what he had not done that now haunted him.

After a short distance, the trail leveled, allowing Brad's mind to wonder. He thought about the wildflowers that he remembered from his hike with Sam. Now few flowers remained, but the alpine beauty was still all about him. He loved it here.

Brad enjoyed hiking slowly so that he could really pay attention to details such as moss-covered stones, brown grass, and bushes turning crimson in preparation for autumn. That's how he saw nature. As he looked for broken blades of grass or vegetation recently disturbed, something grabbed his attention. Brad halted and squinted his eyes. He discerned a scarcely perceptible path leading away from the main trail. It was not something caused by hoofs or paws of an animal. The broken grass blades had been crushed by a human foot. His eyes traced the course of the diminutive track until it disappeared into a stand of ponderosa pines. Brad studied the disturbed thread of land, trying to imagine why anyone would leave the trail at this point when only a few more minutes of walking rewarded hikers with the treasure of Carbon Lake. Brad engaged his mental map to determine the perspective of where he stood in relation to the valley below. Even though trees and rolling topography obscured the view, he quickly visualized the unseen landscape. It had to be! This nearly imperceptible path would lead to a point very near the Cotter estate.

It took less than a minute for Brad to cover the distance of the faint path until it ended in a semi-circular configuration of boulders. Looking back, he realized that the stand of ponderosa pines offered total seclusion from the main trail. Taking a few more steps, he reached the brim of a precipitous ledge. Brad held his breath. Standing as if transfixed in the sky, he now hovered directly over the Cotter estate. He had a perfect vantage of all that lay below. Brad felt chills prickle his skin. He knew this sensation from his old life. It happened when some small detail unfolded that turned out to have great value in solving a case.

Examining the ground about him he saw nothing, but yet the presence of another human filled this space. Brad stood motionless trying to decipher his feelings. Within the shadowy confines of these towering boulders, someone or something felt trapped. The trees seemed to have acted as diligent sentinels, precluded the escape of something that had transpired here.

Lowering his body to the ground, Brad breathed deeply, holding his breath and asking what occurred in this place? After a few moments, he realized that what he felt was exactly what he had experienced while standing in darkness outside the old cabin. Something was unseen. Something was speaking. But just as when he had been at the cabin, try as he might, Brad could not quite identify or focus on what beckoned.

After several minutes, Brad reluctantly admitted that despite his efforts, it just wasn't coming together. He could not grasp the intricacies of what had happened here. He lifted his body from the ground, knowing he had to return to Aspen and talk with Sam. But what would he say? That he had found a possible lookout over the Cotter place that gave him strange vibes? Brad laughed at the thought. He was confident that something was here. He just could not articulate exactly what the hell it might be.

Before leaving, he took a few moments to poke around in the dense brush that rimmed the clearing about the boulders. Nothing. Brad felt the same reluctance to leave as he had experienced when he walked away from the cabin. He tried to think of a reason to stay, but no logical purpose struck him. It was time to go.

After retracing his steps and returning into Aspen, Brad called Sam and told him of his discovery. Sam was quiet for a moment. "We've had talks in the office about an observation point somewhere up there. We just haven't had time to send anyone to check it out yet. It's a big ass mountain and nobody has had the time to poke around up there for a logical survey. The fact you found a trail that looks to be recently used sure as hell may turn out to be relevant. It's one more thing to think about."

"Who knows, Sam," Brad said, "someone could have gone there for any number of reasons. I can only tell you that it seems more than coincidental to me that there is a recently forged path that leads to such a perfectly strategic spot. The view of the entire estate is incredible. Maybe you should talk to the Cotters and see if they have an explanation."

"I agree. We'll ask them today. I suppose it's possible that they could have hiked up there just to take photographs of their place. Hell, anything's possible. I just don't know yet where this thing is going. We can't examine every inch of that entire mountain and the whole damned valley when we don't even know what we're dealing with."

"No, of course not, Sam. You've got a ton of things to do to get things untangled and headed in the right direction. But I'm just telling you, Sam, when I saw that place, I had a feeling. That's all I can say. Here I go again, my friend, feelings and those damned little voices."

"Well, we sure as heck don't have anything concrete, so your feelings are as good as anything else we have right now. I think all doors have to be left open."

"Okay, Sam, thanks for listening to me today."

"Hell's bells, I'm glad you came over. I needed to have a good sounding board."

"I may swing by the Frying Pan for a while and then I'll probably scoot back to Denver. I'm dying to know how this shakes out, so stay in touch."

"We'll talk soon, Brad. It was good to see you again."

———

EVEN THOUGH HE wanted to fish, Brad had now reconciled that today was not the day. There were too many things to think about. Just the same, he wanted to go to the river for a while. Being close to water was always a good thing. He didn't know what to make of his talk with Sam, and the experience of finding a clearing that so perfectly overlooked the Cotter estate clouded his mind even more. There was no logical connection with the case here in Aspen and with what he had seen at Elk Run. Brad pressed the accelerator. "It's those voices. Those damned little voices." Brad's whispered voice was drowned by the sound of his truck making its way to the Frying Pan River.

The territory was familiar, and Brad knew where to park. He did not carry his rod or put on his gear. He just wanted to make it to a certain place to look at something. Brad walked upstream, rounded a bend, and saw the familiar boulder that held a deep, quiet pool. This was what he was looking for. This portion of the river held fond memories of fishing with his brother, Matthew. Brad grinned to himself. Matthew was the quintessential fly-fishing snob. He viewed any type of angling, other than that accomplished with a lightweight rod and a delicate fly, to be crude and prehistoric. Fly rods were like the Holy Grail to his brother. Brad recalled the day that Matthew had been fishing near this particular boulder when a man passed by on the river's bank. The man had stopped to observe Matthew's efforts. After a few minutes, the stranger chose to comment on the obscenely expensive, handmade rod that Matthew held.

"Nice pole there, bud." The man drew his words out in a slow drawl.

For someone to call a fly rod a "pole" was sheer blasphemy to Brad's brother. Matthew and Brad had decided to name this place in memory of the man who made the offending comment. The Neanderthal Hole became the name of this special place that always held a trout. Brad smiled with the great memory. He longed to fish with Matthew again. But for now, a memory would have to do.

Finding a cushion of thick grass that provided a comfortable perspective of the river, Brad lowered himself and sat in silent contemplation. Brad loved rivers. He loved them for reasons far beyond a momentary pleasure of casting a fly rod. Brad thought of rivers as storytellers, among other things. Just like the crinkled old men from the heart of the Smoky Mountains who could spin a yarn that would ignite one's imagination, rivers could do the same. Spirits of ancestors live again in the magic of a storyteller and in the flow of rivers.

Rivers tell stories, Brad had told his children. One only has to listen. Voices are there, winged sirens in the canyons, singing their stories to those who will listen. Stories of the land. Stories of the deer that stepped into the river an hour ago. Stories of the wooly mammoth that crossed eons ago. Stories of native women at water's edge preparing hides. Stories of last week's picnic. Rhythms of seasons, years and centuries, they all drift in rivers.

Brad needed to listen to the river to hear its whisperings. What stories would it tell? If he listened closely, would it murmur secrets? The secret of the cabin, a bundle carried through rain by a man with a ponytail. Did the river know the secret of Christine Reynolds? Would it tell?

Was anyone listening?

Brad sat by the Frying Pan River. He closed his eyes and listened.

———

AN HOUR LATER, Brad and his truck were heading home. This time, the drive was all interstate. There was no time for Independence Pass and reminiscing. He did not listen to Willie or Sarah. Michael Crawford held no appeal. He drove with purpose. Brad knew what he had to do. It was time to undo his mistake, handle what he had failed to do.

———

IN UTTER AMAZEMENT, Felix Gomez gripped his cell phone tightly as he listened to the words of Mark Whitman. He remained silent as a mental image developed. The arrogant man was surely in his Washington office. He imagined him relaxed, feet propped on his desk, rocking his chair slightly, and a sneer on his face. With this picture clearly in his mind, Felix absorbed Whitman's incredibly detailed account of what life had been like in the Reynolds' house since the time of the abduction. The lawyer laughed frequently, taking obvious pleasure in telling how Brandon Reynolds was frustrated beyond words with the pace of the police investigation and the FBI's refusal to get involved. Whitman was able to actually quote some of the questions the police had asked of Reynolds. The police were suspicious of Mrs.

Reynolds. They thought she may have been involved in a romantic adventure or that her disappearance was a result of marital discord. Whitman took particular delight in this aspect of the story. Felix was astute enough to grasp that Whitman thoroughly enjoyed having inside knowledge. The man relished that he alone held power to withhold or disseminate information to his underlings.

But there was more to it. Felix was certain that the reason for Whitman's delight was more complex than merely being privy to inside information. He had recently begun to see a sadistic side of Whitman. Felix now thought it was likely that the man derived a certain pleasure simply from Brandon Reynolds' torment. Could it be that Whitman actually enjoyed tormenting Christine Reynolds?

Felix didn't really care what motivated Whitman. He didn't know or care what made the man tick. That was irrelevant. What was relevant at this moment was that Whitman was somehow able to obtain such accurate and detailed information about Brandon Reynolds. It was amazing that he miraculously knew what was happening inside the Reynolds home and even the progress of the police investigation. In the early days of their planning, Whitman had told Felix that he had an inside source, but he was careful to never divulge the identity of the source. Felix knew better than to ask Whitman the person's identity. He could live with that. All that really mattered was that someone was damned sure inside the Reynolds house and talking freely to Whitman. Felix held the phone and silently breathed his thoughts, "Just let that someone keep on talking."

"Is she secure?" Whitman asked.

"Yes, she's in the cabin. But we're going to move quickly, or I'll have to relocate her. The only bad luck we've had so far was with the weather. As we were moving her to the cabin, there was a hell of a storm and now it's one huge muddy mess. We were lucky that we got in and back out again. It's going to take some time for things to dry out. The conditions make it hard to feed her, get her to a bathroom, and all that. How long? What are you thinking?"

"Another few days I'm sure," Whitman replied. "The way the FBI and local yokels are handling this, in no time at all there won't be any fucking cops involved period. Plus, Felix, why not let old man Reynolds sweat a bit, soften him up for the demand. Hell, he's going to love us more than he loves the police before this is over. He may even want to pay us a few extra million." Whitman laughed as though he were witness to something outrageously funny.

Another few days! Gomez almost choked. He felt his heart sink. What the hell was Whitman thinking?

He held his voice steady, cautious not to betray his frustration. "Okay then, if we're looking at that much time, I'll move her tonight. But I vote to get going soon. The longer we delay, the more chance for something to go wrong."

Gomez heard Whitman inhale sharply and knew instantly that he had misspoken. He anticipated Whitman's tirade a split second before it erupted. Gomez prepared to hold his breath for its duration. He knew too well that once Whitman started, nothing could stop him.

As Whitman spoke, his voice rose, becoming increasingly shrill with each word. "I think I have made it perfectly clear. You don't have a fucking vote. Let me repeat, you do not have a fucking vote. You are about to make millions by ensuring that nothing goes goddamn wrong. So don't give me any soured shit about your vote! You just keep that twinkling little bitch out of sight, and we'll be rich men in a few days!"

Felix clenched his jaw to maintain his composure. He swallowed Whitman's insolence, struggling not to gag. "Yes sir, I understand. No problem." He listened to Whitman's breathing, visualizing the man's face as he waited for the lawyer to relax. This was part of the process after such outbursts. Whitman's composure would return quickly enough. Felix prayed that he could maintain his own.

After Whitman calmed down, he spoke, "Good! That's handled. Now, listen, is everything in place for the other job, the special job?" Whitman now sounded as if nothing unusual had occurred.

Felix camouflaged the anger that boiled in his gut and said in a slow, deliberate voice, "Absolutely! All I have to do is make a telephone call."

"Okay, that's good because when the time comes, it's got to happen fast, really fast. No second chances. First time is the only time. This part of the deal is just as critical as what you're doing in Colorado. Be ready to act in a heartbeat."

"It's a piece of cake. I've done it before, and everything is set. I have good people on it."

"Okay, I'll be in touch and keep you posted on rich boy and his troubles."

"I'll wait to hear."

"Now, tell me Felix, don't you agree that this beats the hell out of any goddamned episode of *Desperate Housewives*?

Whitman was howling as he hung up.

Felix did not know what to think. Jesus, he didn't want to go back to that cabin tonight and move the woman. Bouncing around in mud, moving from place to place, that was risky shit. But maybe more important than anything else, Felix needed some time to think about Whitman. Why in God's name did he want to drag this out? Did he not understand the need to finish this?

Felix sat quietly, recalling his relationship with Whitman and how it had evolved over the years. Questions rolled within his mind. What's changing here? What makes that man do what he does? Felix then contemplated something that had been bothering him for some time. Felix was becoming more and more convinced that Whitman had turned into a madman.

———

AFTER SPENDING hours in his truck returning from Aspen, Brad was happy to have some time to stretch his legs. With another drive ahead of him in a few hours, he needed to move around a bit. After unloading the fly rod and fishing gear that had not been used, he thought about how best to pass the time until night arrived. Brad felt absolutely comfortable with the decision he had made while sitting beside the Frying Pan River, but he had some time to kill before doing what had to be done. A workout sounded like the perfect thing and his gym bag was always ready. He glanced at the afternoon sky, calculating time left until nightfall. Things should work out perfectly. He would grab a workout, call his old FBI friend, Rick Barnes, and then it would be time. All he needed was darkness.

Brad was focused and, just like the old days, he ran hard. Then after some time on the weights, he called it quits. He felt great, ready for whatever the night held in store.

Back in his study, Brad called Rick Barnes. He knew Barnes to be a hard-working and very competent agent. He also knew that the poor guy had been placed in a tough spot yesterday. In addition to Sam Trathen asking for help, Barnes had also dealt with the boss of the Denver office and the director of the FBI telling him what to do. Then throw in a super-rich guy like Brandon Reynolds, and he had all kinds of people yelling at him and demanding something different. What a no-win situation! Brad chuckled quietly as he thought about Rick Barnes stuck right in the middle.

Sarcasm greeted Brad when Barnes' voice came on the telephone.

"What took you so long?"

Brad laughed. "I felt sorry for you. I couldn't kick you while you were down. Retirement has made me a kinder and gentler person."

"Man, I wish you would kick me. Kick me in the head and put me out of my misery. After I talked with Sam Trathen yesterday, I've been expecting your call. I can only imagine that you're wondering what the heck is going on."

Brad laughed again. "Yeah, that's a fair assessment. What's with my old outfit? I leave and everything goes to hell."

Barnes moaned before continuing, "What a friggin' goat rope. But I have to tell you, I think we would have done the right thing and jumped right into that case yesterday if Mr. Reynolds had just not called the director."

"Really?"

"Oh, yeah. The director has been making a big deal in Washington about how the FBI should be fighting white-collar crime, political corruption, and international terrorism. He says that the police are the ones equipped to handle regular criminal stuff and he's really taking a stand on this. Plus, the director is a stiff-lipped guy who is supersensitive to politicians or big business types attempting to interfere with the FBI. Now, whether you like him or not, you can't hold that against him."

"No, Rick, I absolutely agree."

"Anyway, two of the director's primary criteria for managing the Bureau were on the line: investigative priorities and political influence. He dug in, and I mean he wouldn't budge. The director made it clear to everyone that unless there is a ransom demand with a clear interstate nexus, this is a local case and we are not to get involved."

"My aching ass! So if Mr. Reynolds had just stayed out of the loop, you would be working this case with Sam Trathen right now?"

"That's exactly the way I see it. Not exactly your father's FBI is it?"

"Well, this is pretty much what I expected to hear, but I needed to hear it straight from you. Nothing like the old horse's mouth. I had breakfast with Trathen this morning. He's not real sure what's going on, but he thinks something bad may be brewing in this thing. He has nothing concrete to take him in any direction and that's pretty frustrating."

"Oh, I know, Brad. He has a tough one on his hands."

"Well, Rick, you've done your best. Thanks much. One thing is for sure, though. My old friend, Sam, is feeling pressure, and he sure would like a little company as the canoe floats down the river cause there sure as hell might be a waterfall up ahead."

"I understand and believe me," Barnes replied in exasperation, "I'm ready to rock and roll. But right now, my hands have been tied by the old federal bureaucracy, and I don't really have a choice."

"I understand. I know what you're up against. I haven't been gone so long that I've forgotten how the game is played. Thanks a million and let me know if anything changes. Sam and I go back a long way. I'd like to help him."

After the call, Brad allowed his thoughts to settle. He had made the effort with Barnes because he had promised Sam. No surprises were gleaned, but he had promised. Brad sighed. Empty promises were not going to help either Sam or Christine Reynolds. He looked out the window. Darkness would be here soon. It was almost time to leave.

Brad ran his hands over the oak rolltop desk where he sat. His father had worked for the railroad for forty-three years and found the old desk discarded in a trash heap, dumped on railroad property. His dad didn't have two nickels to rub together, but he had heart and imagination. With only a few tools and determination, he had rebuilt the desk piece by piece and turned it into a magnificent work of art. He had been so proud. Dad had passed two years before mom. For Brad, having the desk in his house was like having a part of his dad. What a solid memory.

Brad showered, giving the sun a bit more time to disappear. He wanted total darkness. After a sandwich, he packed the gear he'd need for the evening. This time a fly rod and waders were not part of the inventory. As he walked out of his house, Brad made a point to pass Elizabeth's photograph. Her face and eyes were just as he had expected, not a hint of a smile. She was relentless. Brad spoke, both to himself and to Elizabeth, "For heaven's sake, give me a break. I'm going, I'm going."

Brad pointed his truck southwest and began the drive into the gathering dusk. With a clear sky, Brad knew that the evening star would soon appear. His chest tightened. He had lived another day without Elizabeth.

———

No other cars or hikers were at the trailhead. Brad checked the sky and breathed in the air. The night was clear and calm with no hint of an approaching storm. "I sure as hell don't need any weather surprises tonight," Brad mumbled softly as he secured his pack about his waist. With a miner's lamp positioned on his head to illuminate the trail, he sucked a determined breath and began to hike.

The air was pleasant, and his boots made little noise as he traversed the path. Brad marched with purpose. Only two nights ago he had walked this same trail. That evening had begun as a stroll, a simple walk to fish and enjoy solitude. Shaking his head as he hiked, he considered the mystery of that experience. Was it only two nights ago? It seemed more like a year.

Brad lowered his head and picked up his pace.

Well in advance of the private road and gate into Elk Run Fly Fishing Resort, Brad lifted the lamp from about his head and held the focus low to the ground. Once he broke out of the trees and stepped into the clearing across from the gate, he killed his lamp and remained still. Despite the cool evening, Brad realized he was sweating, and it was not a result of physical exertion. It was nervous anticipation of what he was about to do.

Holy shit! Brad couldn't believe his eyes. Coming directly at him, out of the darkness, were headlights. Brad dropped to his stomach, whispering in exasperation, "What the hell is it? When I show up here it always turns into a regular traffic jam." He pressed his body onto the cold soil, wishing himself to be invisible and thankful that he had extinguished his light.

The vehicle was inside the ranch. It was coming from the old cabins and heading straight toward the gate, straight toward Brad. It was a damned repeat of the other night! Unconsciously clawing his fingers into the ground, his mind raced. What are the odds of this? Brad lay without breathing as he watched the gate swing open. The vehicle passed through, turned onto the private road and drove away. Still, Brad didn't move, watching as the red glow of taillights faded into the night. Lying on the cold ground, Brad almost cracked a smile as he thought of the old Yogi Berra line, "de ja vu all over again."

After several seconds, Brad raised his body from the ground and took a few deep breaths before he dared move his feet. Once again, he was struck by how dark and silent it was. He needed his headlamp, but no way was he going to use it at this point. He inched forward without light, not much faster than a crawl. He had to concentrate to visualize where he was on the trail. Finding the exact spot that would place him in front of the cabin would be a challenge. After what seemed an eternity, he knew he had to be getting close.

God, it was dark.

Straining to see, trying to calculate his position in the night, his eyes actually hurt. Despite their effort, nothing appeared familiar.

Brad looked up, only stars and black. He moved a few feet further, his senses on high alert. He felt it before he saw it, something in the air, a weight pressing down. Just as in his dream, the structure seemed to simply materialize before his eyes. There was the cabin. A shiver moved through his body as he recalled the vision of his mother in the window, beckoning.

What is it about this place? The question repeated within Brad's mind.

Brad crept to the fence, dropped to the ground, and slithered beneath the wire strands. He didn't think that any other vehicles would be parked around the cabin, but it was possible. A car could be parked a distance away, hidden by the night. He had no way to know.

Heart pounding, Brad inched toward the door of the cabin. What would he do if the lock was no longer on the door? What in hell had someone been doing here?

Scarcely moving, he shifted his feet as silently as possible. He had to see if the lock was on the door. A few more steps, and he would be able to see. Thank God! It was still there. Brad breathed a bit easier. If someone was inside, then they were locked in. Was that good or bad?

As he covered the final distance to the door, Brad's mind was spinning. *Had someone been left behind? Why would anyone be left? What was inside this cabin that called for people to come here regularly? Was there something inside that required someone to stand guard? Who or what was he about to encounter?* He had to calm down, focus on what had to be done. Whenever Brad was stressed or frightened, he would talk to himself, sometimes in whispers and sometimes in his mind. Brad now whispered, "Okay, you got yourself into this, now get on with it." Reaching into an outside pocket of his pack, he retrieved a tiny flashlight and his lock tools. Holding the light in his teeth, he had the lock open in a matter of seconds. Gently lifting the lock from the door and placing it on the ground, Brad exhaled gently. There was no way to release the latch and open the door without making noise. Another breath. Brad wrenched the rusting knob, threw his shoulder into the door's center and heaved. Almost weightless from decades of exposure, the door flew open. Brad did not budge. He waited, listening.

Silence.

In the distance an owl hooted.

Holding the flashlight in his left hand and extended away from his body, Brad stepped inside, shinning his light as he moved. The walls were dusty, spiders' webs glistened like liquid silver. Rapidly he crossed the floor, and in only seconds he knew he was alone. Returning to the entrance, he closed the door and secured the rusty old latch to lock himself inside.

For a few moments Brad stood still, settling himself before beginning a more thorough and methodical examination. There wasn't much to survey. The place was empty except for an old table and a crumbling cabinet on the floor. Deteriorating wood, dust, and rodent droppings were all Brad found. "Why the big old shiny lock on the door?" His softly uttered question sounded hollow in the emptiness.

Once again, Brad stood quietly, listening, feeling, certain he was missing something. He walked through the cabin a second time. Had the dust on the floor been disturbed? He couldn't be sure. A shiver rippled Brad's spine. The beam of his light seemed inconsequential, totally inadequate in the pressing darkness. The light scarcely left his flashlight before inky blackness sucked it away, like a wind gust that snuffs light from a candle. Stale air clung to Brad's face. He felt as though he moved through sticky spider webs.

Once again placing the miner's lamp on his head, Brad could see his surroundings in more detail. It was basically a single room structure and could be examined simply by standing in the center of the living area. A recessed alcove along one wall had probably been a kitchen, and a small bathroom appeared to have been on the opposite side. In the back of the cabin was another recessed area that was almost large enough to be another room. Brad calculated that this had probably been the community closet for the entire dwelling. No doors hung over the opening, but from where he stood, he was unable to see into the deepest recesses of the closet. Brad stepped closer, casting light into the hidden corners of the closet.

Oh God! Brad's heart raced, and he held his breath, sealing putrid air within his chest. His mind recoiled in horror. *Please, God, don't let it be what I think it is.* Hot, salty sweat burned his eyes. Brad blinked, trying to clear his vision as he focused his light on the floor: dirt, splintering wood, remnants of some sort of nest, mouse droppings, and two brand-new stainless-steel eye bolts. About eight inches long, each had been screwed securely into the floor at an angle, gripping the solid joist underneath the flooring planks. The glistening hooks were located at each end of the closet and it took but a second for the heinous message to register: one for the hands, the other for feet. Strands of snow-white rope were attached to each bolt, obviously new and freshly cut. *A human being had been imprisoned here!* Realization of what he saw seared his very consciousness.

Only with deliberate effort could Brad make himself breathe. A matter of minutes had separated him from unspeakable evil in this closet. There was no doubt in Brad's mind that the vehicle he had seen departing the resort was a part of that evil. He could feel it. Their body heat remained. He could smell their breath.

Nausea gripped Brad's stomach. He didn't know if it was because of fear or anger, but he had to trap his hands beneath his armpits for a few seconds. "Jesus Christ! A matter of minutes!" He no longer whispered. Thoughts of what might have been registered in his mind. What if he had arrived ten minutes earlier? Brad refused to let the thoughts take hold. Now was not the time for such speculation. Whoever in hell these people were, they were gone, and he had arrived too late.

Brad realized that he had to sort out a plan. He was looking at a crime scene but realized he was breaking the law just by being here. Brad stepped back from the horror and scanned his light about the cabin. He saw nothing else but suddenly felt an urgent need to escape, step outside where he could breathe and figure out what to do. He moved toward the door, his mind gyrating from the implications of what he had discovered.

In less than a blink it happened. The beam of his light reflected back into his eyes. Something shiny was among the dusty fractures of the wood floor. He swung his light again. Nothing. Again. There it was, from underneath the floor, between the cracks of the planks, a flicker of light. Brad adjusted the beam, altering its angle as he shifted his body. When everything aligned perfectly, it was easy to see. Something was concealed beneath the floor.

Tracing the planks of the floor with his light, he followed their splintered surfaces to where they met the wall. Once he really looked, it was easy to discern. Three parallel planks were not secured to the joist or the wall. He traced the planks in the opposite direction. Same story, no nails or screws existed to secure the planks.

Using only his fingers, Brad easily lifted the three planks from the floor. Blackness of the newly exposed crevice leapt up as if attacking his face. Sweat now soaked his shirt. Lowering his head, the beam of his headlamp stabbed the darkness like an ice pick. Brad's eyes adjusted. Clumps of dried mud and rock-infested soil stared back, a long-forgotten, ghostly white from decades of entombment in a sunless crypt seemed to stir. Brad shuddered. He felt he had disturbed a slumbering creature, but he forced himself to peer into the crevasse. His eyes followed the beam of light to where it focused on the object that had captured his attention. Brad stared, gradually comprehending the implications of what he saw. He had no choice. He sure as hell did not want to do what he knew had to be done. With some deep breaths, he summoned courage. "Damn raider of the lost ark," he mumbled. "Why in hell can't I stop shaking?"

Lying on his stomach with his face on the brink of the black pit, Brad felt as though he were entering a grave. He held his breath and extended his arm into the exposed abyss, half expecting serpents or a monstrous spider to spring from hiding. His hand touched cool metal. He lifted a rectangular box from the pit and placed it on the floor. It was a relatively cheap metal container, about eight inches by eighteen inches. A small nail inserted through a hasp was all that secured its lid. Brad realized that whoever had placed trust in this metal chest was relying on its concealment beneath the cabin for security.

Dragging a shirt sleeve across his face, Brad considered how he had discovered the box. It would have been impossible to observe the buried object in daylight hours. Only a perfectly focused and directed shaft of light between the floor planks, contrasting against darkness and ricocheting off of the metal, had allowed Brad to see the buried object. It was the happenstance of being in the cabin at night that had allowed the discovery.

Contemplating his situation, Brad once again needed to hear a voice. "Screw it," he spoke softly. "I've crossed the line. It's too late to worry about tainted evidence and technical legal crap now."

Brad opened the lock and lifted the lid.

Even if his headlamp had not cast a harsh glare into the box, even if sweat had not clouded his vision, it would have taken seconds for Brad's brain to comprehend the putrid waste that his eyes did not want to see: horrific images of abused children, graphic sexual depravity that sickens bowels and shatters hearts.

Brad had seen plenty of this stuff over the years. A few cases of this ilk had crossed his path in the Bureau, and Elizabeth had been a sex crimes prosecutor. There was nothing here that was new, but that sure as hell made no difference; callousness provides no shield from the toxins that ooze from such evil.

Anger mixed with bile in Brad's throat as he sorted through the photographs. There was no rhyme, reason, or pattern to the pictorial depictions of children engaged in sexual acts with adults. The children were of both sexes and appeared to range in age from about nine to fourteen years old. Some of the photos were crystal clear while others were grainy and clouded. It was Brad's guess that some of the photos had been taken surreptitiously, but he couldn't be sure. As he worked his way through the images, he realized that while many different children were involved, only half dozen or so adults were depicted.

Revulsion brought cold sweat that trickled down his torso. As he neared the bottom of the box, Brad saw something obviously out of place among the photographs. Unsure of what to expect, he lifted a spiral type notebook, five by seven, with a cheap cardboard cover. Across the outside was a computer-generated label: KING SOLOMON.

Holding the notebook under the beam of his light, Brad flipped through dozens of pages that held handwritten inscriptions, scribbled in a careless style. He tried to make sense of it. Was this a diary? Most of the entries were scrawled haphazardly but some were printed in block letters. Brad flipped through the pages to the inside of the back cover. Here was the telephone directory.

Brad paused for a moment, thinking about what he had instinctively done. Why had he so quickly turned to the back cover for telephone numbers? He had done so without thinking, automatic pilot, simple reflex. *Jesus!* It dawned on Brad like a bell sounding in his ear. This was a prison diary. He had seen hundreds of them. They all looked and smelled exactly alike. He flipped back to the inside of the front cover to verify what his instinct told him. In a clearly printed line, a date had been etched, followed by the words, "Virginia State Prison."

Brad returned to the telephone directory. The numbers were written in a neat column, consuming almost the entire inside cover. The names meant nothing to Brad, but he realized that most of what he saw were just nicknames anyway. As he studied the names and numbers it was apparent that many of the area codes were from Washington, DC, or Virginia. Brad appreciated that in all probability a treasure of information existed within these pages, outlining some type of criminal activity. But on the surface, it made little sense.

Using his cell phone, Brad photographed the names and numbers and everything that he had found within the box, as well as the interior of the cabin. He gave his eyes a few minutes to recover from the harsh flash and then replaced the photographs and notebook into the container, as close as he could recall to their original order. After closing the box, Brad shined his light underneath the floor for a last check; nothing. He lowered the box to its original resting place and secured the floor planks as they had been.

One final look. Brad cast his light about the cabin: old wood, ancient dust, and the glaring steel of eye bolts, crucified into the floor. Unseen demons remained in this forgotten cabin under the Colorado night sky.

Brad needed some time to allow his eyes to adjust to total darkness before he left the cabin and returned to the outside. Turning off his light, the cabin plunged into utter darkness.

Allowing time to pass, Brad stood perfectly still, the sound of his heart pounding within his head. He thought about why he had felt so ill at ease all evening, on the verge of fear in what he had done. He had been frightened many times in his career, but tonight had been different. He had not exactly felt fear but something close to it, even worse in ways. As he analyzed the evening, he understood why. When he was on the job, he had usually worked with a partner. At least someone had always known where he was, or he had radio or telephone contact with another person. Tonight, he had spoken to no one about where he was going or what he intended to do. The eerie apprehension that had persisted throughout the evening was a feeling of absolute isolation, being totally alone.

Thoughts of the cramped, filthy closet filled his mind. The eye bolts, the blackness, the silence. Who had been confined there?

Brad could not conceive of being abandoned in this darkness. Unimaginable loneliness.

Without turning on his light, Brad cautiously crossed the dusty floor, stepped outside, and breathed deeply, hoping that fresh air might purge what he had just seen. Replacing the lock on the cabin door, Brad walked away. He had a long hike ahead.

SUNDAY, SEPTEMBER 9

MIDNIGHT'S quiet rode as a passenger and the silent companion was perfect company. Brad welcomed the hypnotic rhythm of his truck gliding over painted stripes of the deserted highway. He needed to sort things in his mind and think how to proceed. Too many times he had seen the counterproductive effect of an illogical or disjointed initial response to a crime scene. Tons of people pouring onto the ranch or into the cabin could easily backfire and cause more harm than good. Whatever had happened in the cabin had happened. It was history to be examined, not a future calamity to be prevented. "I just need a little time." Brad spoke softly into the night as he allowed his mind to drift, taking him back through recent hours.

Dampness of the cave seemed to fill his truck as Brad relived the inexplicable events he had witnessed. He could hear his conversation with Sam Trathen clearly, and the image of his friend's troubled face materialized. Brad felt himself hovering above the Cotter estate, foreboding feelings wrapping about him like a cocoon. Most vividly, Brad recalled what he had just experienced. The horror of the cabin was sickening.

God, it had been dark inside that cabin!

The town slept as Brad reached his home. The long night was

finally coming to an end. After scrubbing his hands with soap and water as hot as could be tolerated, Brad then drenched his face in icy cold water. He watched the water swirl down the drain hopefully taking the evening's repugnance with it. It was definitely Moosehead time. In long gulps, he downed one and then opened another.

Elizabeth's photograph waited. Brad had felt her the moment he stepped into his house. Was he ready for this? Carrying his Moosehead, Brad walked across the room to be near her. A part of him desperately wanted to see her, yet he felt a dread at what her look might say to him. He had been through enough for one night. He had to do it. Cautiously, Brad's eyes found her photograph. Elizabeth did not hesitate. She looked directly at him, her gaze slicing straight through him. Her eyes didn't sparkle but they were different. Had they softened? Brad stepped closer and looked again. Something was there. He concentrated, trying to see, to listen. *Was it a twinkle? Yes, her eyes twinkled!* But it was not her usual loving twinkle, not at all. Elizabeth was taunting him. Yes, that's what he saw. Elizabeth's eyes delivered her message loud and clear: *See, I told you so!*

Brad lifted Elizabeth's photograph and carried it along with his Moosehead to his bedroom. He placed Elizabeth on his nightstand, emptied the Moosehead and collapsed on the bed. The ghastly images would not leave. Brad felt them burrowing into his brain as ants devour their way into a rotting melon.

There was no warning. Windows strained as the wind struck. It blew harder, increasing in intensity, whistling around the walls and over the roof of his house. Then, in a horrible roar, a full-blown attack came from the peaks of the Continental Divide. A west wind charged from the mountains like an army of howling savages. Brad sat up, dismayed at what he heard. These storms were commonplace in the winter, but it was only September. This was an ill wind. It was too early in the season, out of rhythm with nature. "Everything is upside down," Brad spoke softly as he lay down again, feeling his house sway on its foundation.

Memories and wind were all that Brad could feel; memories of how he and Elizabeth had spent so many nights together in these raging storms, pressing their bodies together, combining their strength, waiting for sunrise, and hoping for calm. Reaching for Elizabeth's photograph, Brad pulled her to his chest. Closing his eyes, he ached for her touch, yearned for her voice, and prayed for sleep.

Time passed, whether it was minutes or hours Brad had no idea. Stiffness invaded every joint of his body as he rose from his bed, and in darkness, he stumbled through his house. He turned on a lamp and settled in at his dad's old desk. The wind continued to rage, and in the loneliness of the predawn hours, Brad sorted out in his mind how best to proceed. He began by writing notes and compiled a chronological diary of all that had happened, beginning with the night he sat in the cave. He included his conversations with Kurt Riddle and Sam Trathen, as well as his hike to the Cotter estate. When he wrote out everything he had seen in the cabin, his heart again hammered against his chest. Next, Brad dug out some old telephone numbers that he intended to call as soon as a decent hour approached. He glanced out his window. It was still pitch black. The sun was nowhere near the eastern horizon. The storm raged on. Sorrowful wails shredded the night.

Pollution from the cabin had permeated his skin. Brad recognized a need to cleanse both his body and his mind. A shower and a mug of coffee later, he greeted the first hint of light to seep through his windows. He checked his watch and grunted, "Good, a few minutes after six. That makes it after eight on the East Coast. Close enough." He reached for his telephone.

"Virginia State Penitentiary. How may I help you?"

"Officer George Randall, please."

"One moment."

Silence followed. Brad thought about the music that was usually forced upon a helpless public while waiting for phone calls to transfer. He could think of no melody that would be appropriate for a prison. Silence was definitely the best option.

"Officer Randall here." The voice brought back memories. Brad could recall the man as clearly as if it were yesterday. Short with strong, muscular features and skin black as midnight, Randall was one of Brad's favorite people ever. His shaved head was his lustrous trademark, always polished to a shine. Whenever Randall spoke, his voice projected an ever-present sense of humor, always looking for an opportunity to deliver a wisecrack, no matter the topic being discussed.

"Hound Dog, you senile SOB, this is the most handsome white guy you ever had the pleasure of knowing. How the heck are you?"

"As I live and breathe, my old friend Brad Walker. What a surprise! You still trying to get accepted into the Boy Scouts? They don't usually take cheese dicks like you."

"Screw you, Hound Dog. I didn't call across half the continent to listen to your crap. How about a little respect?"

"That will sure as hell be the day. How are you, old friend?"

George Randall had been with the Virginia State Prison System for years. He and Brad had met during the course of an investigation in which a prison inmate had attempted to arrange for the murder of a key witness in a federal arson trial. The case had developed into a terrific undercover operation in which an FBI agent played the role of a hit man. Brad and Randall had taken an instant liking to each other and had maintained contact long after Brad's transfer to another assignment.

One of Randall's treasured accomplishments in life was his nickname. He was called Hound Dog because of his tenacious personality. On his first day on the job, Randall realized the inmates referred to each other by nicknames. Through the years, George "Hound Dog" Randall maintained meticulous records of inmates' nicknames, matching them with their true identity, their associates, and various other bits of pertinent information. He kept everything in log, which he kept up to date and which he and Brad referred to as "The Holy Scriptures According to Hound Dog Randall." The scriptures had been of invaluable assistance too many times to count.

"Hey, boss man, I need some help on something," Brad said. "It's a long shot but worth a try if you have a few minutes."

"Of course, I always have time for you. But what's going on here? I thought you was a retired Fed. Somebody file a paternity suit against you?"

"I should be so lucky," Brad laughed. "No, this is nothing as fun as that I'm afraid, but I sure hope you can help me out, Hound Dog. Could you check the scriptures, your holy book? I'm looking for something on a guy and all I have is probably just a nickname. King Solomon is all I have. Could you take a peek, let me know if he's in your book?"

"King Solomon!" Randall snorted. "Kiss my beautiful black ass. I don't need no book on that one. He left here about a year ago. Asshole of all assholes. I hope he's into something that will put him back inside the joint, just not inside my joint. I hate that buzzard fucker."

"Damn, Hound Dog, stop beating around the bush. How do you really feel?"

"There aren't enough hours in the day for me to tell you how I feel. Even in this place, he stood out as one of the worst. You just tell me, Brad, what do you need to know?"

"I guess give me anything you have on the guy. What was he in for? Who put him there? What's he look like? All the regular stuff."

There was no hesitation. "This is an easy one, my friend. His real name is Antonio Padilla. He's a half-breed, half black and half Hispanic, about thirty or so. Kind of a small to medium-sized guy who thinks he's Muhammad Ali. Struts his ass around, long straight hair down to his shoulders, real pretty boy. Goes fuckin' crazy if someone calls him by anything other than King Solomon. Not King, not Solomon. It's King Fucking Solomon. I used to drive him nuts 'cause I called him Little Sol Baby. God, he hated that. He would kill me in a heartbeat if he ever had the chance."

"Make sure he never gets the chance then, Hound Dog."

"Don't you worry your pretty little head, Mr. FBI. I get up way too early for that inbred creep."

"Is he just a regular street punk? What was he in for?"

"I sure as hell don't consider him a regular street punk. No, Brad, he's beyond that. He got popped outside of Washington. I think it was kidnap and false imprisonment on the paperwork. But the real story on Sol Baby is that he's a traveling pimp, specializing in kids. Takes little girls, barely in their teens. Takes them all over the country so sick bastards can get their jollies."

Brad dropped his head in a silent prayer of thanks. He had the right guy.

"I think he worked a plea deal and got away with five years. Should have been five hundred."

"Oh, my gosh, Hound Dog. You have no idea how much I appreciate this. I think I've stumbled onto something that old Sol Baby is probably involved with. If I'm right, he is still up to his same "old tricks.""

"Brad, I can promise you he's still up to his same old stuff. King Solomon is one asshole who will never change."

Brad paused a moment before speaking. This was unbelievable. "Okay, I appreciate your help, but the last thing I ever want to do is jam you up for giving me information, you know all that super-secret stuff that only the newspapers and afternoon talk shows get. I'm supposed to be retired and no longer an official member of the brotherhood."

Brad was forced to hold the phone away from his ear as Hound Dog's voice shouted. "Fuck the fuckin' rules. I've only got a year to go myself and anybody don't like what I do can kiss my sweet ass all the way around this here country club for assholes."

Brad could hardly contain himself. Clear as day, he could visualize Randall's powerful black face on the other end of the call. How many times had he seen Hound Dog just like this? He would flash his brilliant, mischievous smile as he proclaimed disdain for rules and those who made them. Then, his eyes darting, he would wait for a reaction from his audience.

Brad laughed into the telephone. "Okay, okay, Hound Dog, don't get yourself all worked up into a frenzy. You're too old. Don't stress that heart of yours, no telling what may happen. How about friends, or his visiting list, anything there?"

"No friends at all inside. In fact, we had to watch him pretty close cause most of the population hated his prissy ass. The whole time he was here, I kept expecting to find him dead with a blade between his shoulders. And let me add, my friend, I was very disappointed that it didn't happen. If you have a minute, I'll pull his file, check his approved visitor list and all that happy horseshit."

"If you've got time!? I promise you; I've got time."

"Alright, hold on."

Walker sat in silence while he was on hold, half dazed at the bombshell that seemed to be exploding in his face.

In minutes, Randall came back on the line. "Okay, Junior, here you go. He's got three visitors on his list: His mom, a lady named Anna Padilla, a friend named Maria Sanchez, and a friend named Felix Gomez."

"God love you, Hound Dog. I take back most of the bad things I've ever said about you."

"You're too easy."

"That's what the ladies have always said. Now, how about giving me phone numbers and addresses for those fine citizens. Also, where was Sol Baby supposed to go after release? He's got to have a parole officer responsible for keeping an eye on him."

"Hold on, Brad, let me read through this stuff."

Brad listened to the sounds of shuffling papers.

"It's your lucky day on The Price is Right," Randall boomed. "He was paroled out of state to be near his dear mother. Now, hang on, cowboy, listen to this. King Solomon left Virginia to take his beautiful little ass to, of all places, Denver, Colorado!"

Walker felt his knees go weak. "I can't believe it. This is exactly what I need."

"Great, I hope to hell it helps put this shitbird away forever."

"This may be the ticket my friend. I'll take whatever you have in that file."

"I'm looking, I'm looking. Okay, here we go. Got your crayons and tablet ready, FBI man?"

"Lay it on me."

"A condition for being granted out-of-state parole was to show that he had a job. Says here he would be assigned to a parole officer named Phil Taylor and that he would be working for an uncle, guy named Lawrence Acosta. He's supposed to be working as a groundskeeper at some place called Elk Run Fly Fishing Resort." Randall paused. "Elk Run Fly Fishing Resort! Now, isn't that just fucking hoity-toity. You suppose I might find me some black brothers vacationing at a place with a name like that?" Randall cackled. "Yes sir, absolutely. Wouldn't be a few blue-eyed, white faces lounging around on that home on the range now would there?" Randall was having fun. "I can see it now. White wine and portfolios. Yep, I can see it all." Randall's howling laughter almost burst Brad's ear.

Brad wanted to laugh with Randall, but he was too busy trying to keep from having heart failure. He copied identifying data on Padilla, telephone numbers and address information. Brad already knew how to contact Padilla's parole officer. Thank God for working years in the same city and knowing almost everyone in law enforcement. Phil Taylor and Brad had worked together on multiple occasions. Phil was now one more name to add to his list of people to call.

"Hound Dog, I have never owed so much to anyone in my life. I'll be sending you a box of cigars."

"Sounds great, you asshole. But do it right. Make them real cigars. Cuban. I don't want dog turds. Cuban, man, Cuban."

"You'll get them if I have to swim there myself, Hound Dog."

"You owe me absolutely nothing, my friend. Talking to you brings back memories of the old days. I'm out of here myself in just over a year. But this book of mine, the one I've been writing for twenty-five years, The Holy Scriptures According to Hound Dog Randall, she goes with me. Call me anytime."

"I'll let you know how this turns out."

"Be safe."

Brad sat in stunned silence. What an incredible telephone call! He quickly compared the telephone numbers that Randall had given him against those he had copied from King Solomon's diary. Nothing matched up, but he wasn't surprised. The exhaustion Brad had felt only minutes earlier had amazingly vanished. Driving purpose and excitement now charged his body.

With a sense of urgency, Brad punched the keys of his telephone so hard his finger hurt. He had to speak with Kurt Riddle. The information from Hound Dog threw an entire new twist into whatever was going on. Kurt's answering message kicked on and Brad spoke into the recorder. "Good morning, Grumpy. After you've finished doing your nails, call me ASAP. It's very important."

Within the stack of old business cards that Brad had retrieved was one for the National Center for Missing and Exploited Children in Alexandria, Virginia. His old friend, Bob Callahan, was the next person he needed to speak with. After Callahan retired from the Bureau, he took a job with NCMEC and was still working as hard as ever. Brad knew from their FBI days that Callahan almost always used the quiet of Sunday mornings to catch up on paperwork. He doubted anything had changed.

A friendly voice answered the telephone at NCMEC and informed Brad that Callahan was on his way into the office and should be arriving shortly. Brad left a message requesting a return telephone call as soon as possible.

With another mug of coffee in his hands, Brad leaned back in his chair, savoring the warmth between his hands. As he sipped, he realized that his house was no longer shaking. Brad walked across the room and stood at the window. Outside, the trees stood perfectly still; there was not a breath of wind. Dawn's pink had given way to the soft gold of early morning sun.

He had made it. The horrible night was over. Brad set his coffee down, locked his fingers behind his head, and stretched and twisted his lanky frame from side to side. The night had seemed endless. Now, a warming sun streamed into his window bringing with it promise of a fresh beginning, clean air, and a better day.

———

RAYS OF DAWN edged around the seams of closed shades. A new day arrived for Felix Gomez. Awake but groggy after another sleepless night, Felix lay on a couch wishing for time to pass more quickly. How could he sleep when Whitman made life so miserable with his mindless nonsense? It had taken hours to get the broad out of the cabin last night and now she was right here in the house. She was just down the hall, for Christ's sake. After finally arriving home, Felix had spent the remainder of the night angry and frustrated. He was helpless to make things happen and with every minute that Whitman screwed around, the chances increased that something could go wrong. Felix tried to think of something to lighten his spirit. Maybe today would be the day.

A ringing cell phone shattered the quiet of early morning. Gomez sat up as if he had been shocked. "Must be Whitman," he mumbled as he reached for the device, hoping that this would be the call he wanted.

"Felix, we have fucking problems! *Come verga*! We have fucking problems!" The voice was shrill, filled with panic. Like ice water in his face, Gomez was instantly alert. It was not the crass voice of Whitman. Instead, it was a familiar, heavily accented, and completely hysterical voice that jolted Felix into his new day.

"What's wrong, Victor? Calm down. What the hell is wrong?" Victor was his associate in Oklahoma who helped to transport kids around the country and sometimes helped in arranging their sexual encounters with clients.

Victor continued, his voice tight, "Things are bad. We've got fucking problems. Remember that TV preacher that I've been taking care of, the one that lives in Oklahoma?"

"Sure, I remember him, he likes teenage girls."

"That's right. And that's our problem. That's your problem, Felix, your fucking problem. How could you do this to me?" Victor shouted a torrent of obscenities, half in Spanish and half in English.

"Victor! Slow down, talk to me." Felix wanted to scream right back at Victor but knew that would be a mistake. He managed to speak with a deliberate cadence, exuding a calmness that he certainly didn't feel.

Felix sensed impending doom.

With a deep breath, Victor resumed speaking. Felix could at least now understand what the hell he was saying. "I brought him to Colorado a few times so you and Maria could set him up with girls you had there."

"I remember."

"I should have known better. You fucked me!" Victor again screamed a torrent of incomprehensible obscenities.

Felix felt his temper beginning to burn. He fantasized crawling through the telephone and using his bare hands to choke Victor into silence. Somehow, he managed self-control as he again spoke with forced restraint, "Victor, you have to slow down. Talk to me, Victor. What's wrong?"

"The minister got his ass caught in Oklahoma City. I don't know exactly how it happened, but the cops caught him in a motel with a thirteen-year-old girl. Caught him in the act."

Intending to respond with an obscenity of his own, Felix's voice failed. A slow moan was the only sound escaping his lips.

"All hell is breaking lose." Victor was shouting again, alternating between English and Spanish. "Every news show and TV station in the state is carrying the story. The preacher had a bunch of people besides us who were supplying him, and he has told the police everything. Cops are everywhere. They're pulling girls out of massage parlors, strip clubs, everything. Politicians and police are screaming that this is only the beginning. They say that there are underage girls outside of Oklahoma that are in danger, and they intend to rescue them. This is one fucking mess, Felix!"

Now standing, pacing back and forth, Felix tried to maintain his cool. He had to think. "Has there been any talk about Colorado?"

Victor seemed to calm a bit. "I can't tell you that because I'm fucking out of here. I'm going back to Chicago. I have to get far away from that preacher and everything in Oklahoma. I have no choice but to lay low until this blows over."

"I understand, Victor, I just wish to hell I knew what the cops are doing that might come down on me here in Colorado."

Again speaking in Spanish, Victor continued. "Like I said, I don't know for sure what's the latest. But I sure as hell know that last time I took the preacher to Denver, you had me take him straight to your house. I couldn't understand why we didn't use a motel like we always do, but you were yelling that you didn't have time to screw around and to bring him to the house. You fucked me, *pendejo!* You fucked us both!"

Felix squeezed the phone; his knuckles turned white. He had no response to Victor's accusations. He realized he had made a really big, really stupid mistake. Felix clearly recalled the incident that Victor was talking about. After travelling to Denver with the preacher, Victor called, saying they were ready for a young girl. Felix and Maria had been busy setting up another deal and King Solomon was not around. So, instead of doing things right and taking a girl to a motel, they had been careless and told Victor to bring the preacher to the house. The whole thing with the young girl had been over in thirty minutes. At the time, it had seemed routine. Now, it was back to haunt him.

Memories of his arrest in Phoenix years ago flashed in his mind. He had made a stupid mistake then and had vowed never to do so again. Now, here he was on the verge of the biggest opportunity of his life, and he had fucked up terribly. This couldn't be happening!

Felix closed his eyes. He had to be smart, no more mistakes. He spoke quietly, shifting to Spanish. "Victor, it was afternoon when you brought him here, well before dark. Do you think the preacher could find this house again? Could he show it to the cops?"

"How do I know? But from what I heard on the news before I left Oklahoma City, he will sure as hell be telling the cops about every trip he has ever taken." Victor moaned as if in agony. "I don't know if the cops can put it together or not. Preacher doesn't know my real name. All he has is my cell phone number, which is billed to a guy in Miami. I'm pretty sure it's going to take some time for the cops to figure stuff out. But how long, who the hell knows."

"Christ!" Gomez felt his body wilt.

Victor sounded like he was on the verge of crying. "One thing I do know, Felix. I'm out of business."

Gomez spoke, returning to English. "Alright, Victor, I understand. You get to Chicago and stay out of sight. I have to figure out what to do out here. Let me know if you learn anything."

Victor took a breath. "Yeah, sure. I'll call you from Chicago."

Felix rubbed his eyes, his stomach was in knots, and his body was sagging in disbelief as the ramifications of Victor's call continued to sink in. *The damned Oklahoma preacher had been inside this very house! He had used the very room where the woman is now.* Felix sank onto the couch and buried his face in his hands. How could he have been so careless?

At any other time Felix would have taken such news simply as a matter of routine business—unpleasant but routine. Maria and he would load the kids into a van and have someone move them. Clear the house and be gone. The police had no knowledge of Felix or Maria. Victor used a variety of names and had already left for Chicago where he would lay low until the storm passed. Friends of King Solomon had rented this house. It would take days for the police to figure out who was doing what. There was no reason why they would not be able to stay ahead of the cops indefinitely or just go to Mexico if things got too hot.

Groaning softly, Felix knew that this could not be handled as a routine business problem. Not with the broad, Whitman, and the deal of a lifetime to think about.

Clammy sweat gathered in his hands and under his arms. What timing! They had just moved the damned woman into the house last night because Whitman couldn't get off his ass and conclude this operation. Now, here he was stuck with a house full of kids and the woman. How could things get so fucked up so fast?

Again pacing, Felix stood and started pacing as he thought about the situation. He had planned to hold the broad here in the house where it was easier to watch her. He had to keep her alive and well until the demand was made and the money delivered. After that, King Solomon was supposed to take care of her. As Felix continued to consider what had happened, the seriousness of his problems sank in. There was no way in hell he had time to be screwing around taking care of the broad and moving kids all over the place while Whitman played games. Felix knew that he had to focus on one thing: the big job with the woman. That was all that mattered, and to make it happen Maria and King Solomon needed to stay close by every minute to help him handle things when Whitman called. He sure as hell didn't have time for a bunch of kids.

All he had to do was make this one last deal come together. Then, he would have no more worries. No more dealing with crazy Whitman, crazy Victor, or crazy preachers.

Felix cursed himself for being careless, but it was too late for that now. What if the minister could identify the house? It was not a chance he could risk.

What he had to do was obvious and Felix intended to do it quickly.

———

CHRISTINE REYNOLDS LISTENED. Her hands and feet were tied, securing her to a bed in a small room. A shower and access to a bathroom had seemed like heaven and she had been given a meal and water. This was so much better than being strapped to a filthy floor. But Christine knew she was in deep trouble. After being abducted, she had been blind-folded. It seemed obvious to her that as long as her captors kept her eyes covered, they may have plans to release her. If they intended to kill her, why should they care if she saw them or not? After moving her, they clearly did not care if Christine saw their faces.

Christine wished for the blindfold.

Since being brought to the bedroom, Christine heard many types of sounds. It was a welcomed relief from the torture of silence she had endured in the dark cabin. She could hear occasional traffic noises from outside and noises from other areas of the house. They were like music. How long had it been since she had listened to a bird? But it was human sounds that Christine most longed for, any human sound, even if the sounds came from her captors. There had been a few times since being moved that Christine thought she had heard the voices of young children, but she wasn't sure.

However, there was no doubt about what she was now hearing: angry voices, screaming just outside her room. It was the three people who had taken her, two men and a woman. They were in the midst of a heated argument and clearly did not care if she overheard.

Christine listened to the woman's voice. "We have to move now, damn it. The police could show up anytime. Are we just going to sit around and wait for them?"

One of the men said, "I don't give a shit about the girls. I know nigger pimps all over the place where I can get a dozen girls. Girls are easy, but the boy is valuable. To get a boy I have to deal with the assholes that smuggle people across the border. It's risky and expensive. We can't just walk away from what we have here."

"What the fuck is wrong with you?" said another voice. Christine recognized it as the man with a ponytail and the person who Christine had determined was the leader. "Here we are, setting on the verge of millions and you worry about losing a few thousand on that little bastard! I don't want to hear this shit anymore. King Solomon, listen to me and listen good. You get those damned kids handled and do it now! Maria and I will get the broad out of here. I don't like doing this shit any more than you, but we have no choice so let's get it done."

———

CHRISTINE KNEW things weren't good. She felt a great weight pressing her body onto the bed. A seam of light appeared as a corona around the blackened shade that sealed her single window. She missed the sun. Since being confined on the dirty, wood floor, her desire for sunshine had become an obsession. She remembered times in Arizona when she had grown tired of the sun, even tried to get away from it. Christine now longed for its brilliance, if only for a minute.

Jumbled thoughts and blurry images were like a mist inside Christine's brain. She could scarcely even recall what her house looked like. How could that happen? She thought of Brandon. What must he be going through? Was the hell that he or her children suffered any less than hers? Was it possible to concentrate hard enough or to pray fervently enough that he would be able to feel her, or she him? Should she wish him into her hell? Right or wrong, she did wish for him. How many times had she prayed since this began? She prayed again. Please God, if I have to be in hell, let Brandon be with me.

The quarrel that was taking place outside Christine's door had grown louder and now sounded out of control. Shouting and cursing came from all areas of the house. Something crashed to the floor, shattering glass and more screaming. For certain, she now heard children's voices. Adult voices shrieked commands and made obscene threats that were followed by hysterical young voices. Children's cries were pleading. More cursing. A door slammed shut.

Silence.

Christine was terrified when the shouting first began. But after a few minutes, the unsettling effects went away, and her heart no longer pounded so rapidly. With the slamming of the door, she was in a silent world once again. She was now resigned to her fate and was becoming too tired to be frightened. Slowly, her mind succumbed and her body surrendered, as though anesthetic trickled into her veins. She tried to pray but her words never reached heaven. Christine Reynolds drifted, her mind suspended between some level of artificial sleep and ghastly reality.

———

MERE FEET away from where Christine lay bound, Felix sat in his own silent world. He had another problem, one that he had not mentioned to the others. If Whitman somehow learned about the mess with the minister, there was no telling what he may do. The opportunity of a lifetime may very well go up in smoke. How could this have happened?

Things had been going so perfectly.

———

WHEN KURT RIDDLE returned Brad's telephone call from earlier in the morning, he tried to make a joke, but Brad cut off small talk and began spitting words like an auctioneer. He related the story of what he had done and seen at the cabin on the previous evening.

"Good Lord, Brad, that's a hell of a story."

"And you ain't heard it all, my friend." Brad then explained what he had learned from the Virginia State Penitentiary.

"This is incredible, Brad. I'm not sure what to think."

"I'm not sure either, but you have to help me think through everything. Of course, first there is the part that I had no right to be in the cabin in the first place."

Riddle chuckled. "Too late to worry about that now. That's water under the old bridge, toothpaste out of the tube, all that stuff."

"I'm afraid you're right, Kurt."

"Don't lose any sleep over it. Not the crime of the century." Kurt, as always, evoked an aura of calm.

"Yeah, I know. But also, I remember that before Clayton Price retired from the Department of Wildlife, he told me Elk Run was owned by a guy named Owens, big oil money from Texas."

"That's correct," Riddle confirmed.

"Well, Clayton also told me the old man is a great guy and would help anybody. But the kicker is that he turned the ranch over to his son. Apparently, his son grew up a spoiled, rich little shit. So, his dad is having him manage the ranch to try to teach him responsibility."

"Right again."

"Fat chance on that social experiment," Brad droned sarcastically.

Riddle chuckled.

"According to Clayton, the kid is a wild ass, coke-snorting, knucklehead who hates any type of authority, especially the police. Clayton warned me to never go to him with anything."

"That's exactly right," Kurt replied. "The guy is a major pain in the ass. We've had a few cases where we needed a little help, and we learned the hard way that he is not at all bashful about telling us to screw off. I wouldn't trust that guy with anything."

"Alright, Kurt, the way I see it is this: a crime scene exists in that cabin and all the rest of those old cabins out there need to be searched as well. But the problem is if an army of cops show up everyone is going to know about it, including the spoiled rich kid. If this Antonio Padilla guy, King Solomon, still works there and is involved in something, he's also going to know. It may sure as hell blow any chance to quietly figure out what's going on. We have no idea if even the Owens kid himself is involved. You agree?"

"Yeah, I'm hearing you."

"Kurt, I'm just wondering, do you think it would be smart to hold off for a while, do some homework first? Phil Taylor is his parole officer. He and I go way back. If you don't mind, I would love to talk to Phil about what he can tell us about King Solomon. I've also got a call in to a guy I know at the National Center for Missing and Exploited Children. I'll give him the names and numbers from the prison diary and see what shakes out. Who the heck knows who may ultimately turn out to be involved in this mess?"

"You are exactly right, Brad."

"It seems risky to me to go tipping our hand to the ranch before we have a better picture of who is doing what to whom."

Kurt was silent for several seconds. "I'm trying to think of everything that I haven't thought of. Not easy for an old guy like me, but I'm thinking that you may be right for once in your life. We could sure as hell do more damage than good if we aren't careful."

"I feel better knowing you agree. I think we're looking at some serious stuff here, and I would hate to make a big mistake right out of the box."

"You got it. Go ahead, call Phil Taylor and talk with NCMEC. I'll run the names and numbers and start to do some digging in my office."

"That strikes me as the best plan, at least for right now."

"I agree. Give Phil my regards."

"Okay, I'll call him right away. When you do decide to go into the cabin for a search, my guess is that you and the lab crew will find prints on the box and maybe the photographs. I don't know about the room with the bolts in the floor. Strands of hair or something. Could be anything I suppose. But whatever is found will be for naught anyway if the wrong people find out too soon that somebody's snooping."

"Yeah, you're right, Brad. We're on the same sheet of music. Let me chew on this for a while. I sure as hell would like to get inside the cabin with a search warrant. But that damn Owens kid may be in the middle of this himself. We gotta be careful."

Brad was quiet for a moment. "Something tells me that just a few hours of checking things out before exposing this to the whole world could make a big difference. I can't get Sam Trathen's case of the missing lady out of my mind. Those bolts in the floor—Kurt, I'm telling you somebody was tied up there."

Kurt's voice softened. "I've thought a lot about Sam and what he's dealing with. I don't really see any certain connection yet, but I think it would be a big mistake to eliminate any possibility."

"Yeah, I think so too."

"Okay, let's do what we can and see what we learn."

"I'll start making calls as quick as I can."

Kurt spoke again. "You know, there is another thing we should probably do. What would you think of putting a lookout on the cabin? I think we need to seal the place off and keep an eye on the area until we get things sorted out? I know it's remote up there, but I sure would like to know if anyone else comes or goes while we are getting started."

"Oh, heck yes, I agree completely." Brad recalled the small cave he had used for a shelter a few nights earlier. "Concealment for a couple of your guys won't be an issue at all. There are plenty of places to hide. Whoever you send in should go right back to the place in the rocks where I saw this whole deal begin. It won't be that comfortable, but at least it's protected and dry. The way it's situated, someone could hide out for a long time without being spotted. Just be sure to carry in plenty of food and water." Brad paused. "A flat screen TV and sound system would also be nice. I know you sissies don't take hardship too readily."

"Okay, wise ass. I can get a guy in there right away. Can you sketch me a map showing the exact cabin and the location of your cozy little cave? Maybe fax or e-mail it to me?"

"Absolutely. I'll diagram the whole thing for you and include the names and telephone numbers I have for you to start your checks."

"I'll look for your info."

"Also, Kurt, I've got the photographs I took inside the cabin. Maybe they would help the evidence folks figure what they want to do. I'll shoot them to you right away."

"Okay. I'll talk to the lab crew and let you know."

"If you don't mind, I'd like to call Sam Trathen. We had breakfast yesterday, and I want to hear what he has to say. See what's happened in the last few hours."

"Sure, no problem."

"Thanks, Kurt. I'll tell Sam to give you a call and then you guys can figure out the best way to proceed."

"Sounds good, Brad. Catch you later."

Brad stood to stretch. He touched his toes and did a few knee bends before placing his call to Sam. Even a little exercise always seemed to help when there was no time for a workout. Once he felt blood flowing in his body again, Brad made the call. Sam picked up on the second ring and Brad wasted no time in bringing him up to speed on all that had happened.

"Holy smokes, Brad, something's going on there, and it ain't good." Sam's voice sounded weary but excited. "There's nothing to connect what you saw to my case here in Aspen, but then there sure as hell is nothing to say it's not. I'm not blowing it off. I'd love to get with Kurt and take a look inside that place."

"He's expecting your call to work that out. It's driving me nuts, but I'm not really in this anymore. The real police have to do this."

"Don't be so hard on yourself. Sounds to me like you're doing pretty damned fine police work as a regular old civilian."

"Thanks, Sam. Boy, the last couple of days have really been something. I wasn't prepared to jump back in the middle of something like this."

Sam gave a slight laugh. "No, I don't suppose you had this penciled in on your calendar." He paused to think and then laughed out loud. "Forgive me, Brad, I forgot that you're way past pencils and calendars. You're a high tech guy, probably have one of those goofy telephone things that you stick in your ear all day, walk around looking like an alien that just stepped out of a UFO." Sam Trathen laughed. Brad loved Sam's deep, full-bodied laugh.

"Yeah, Sam, I'm a real techie sort of guy. My goal is to be as futuristic as you. Any chance I could borrow your typewriter and some carbon paper when we write up the reports on this thing?" They both laughed.

"It's a funny thing, Sam, most days since I left the Bureau, I've been happy to be out. Haven't missed anything too much. I guess maybe this stuff right now is my first big test. But man, since all this started, it's hit me with a vengeance. Feelings that I thought were in the past have come roaring back, and I sure am missing the old days." Brad paused. "Actually, it's the old guys I'm missing more than the old days."

Sam chuckled. "I understand completely," he said with sympathy in his voice. "But don't let it get you down. This will soon pass, and life will get back to normal. You'll be fine; I'm sure. Old and forgetful but fine."

"Screw you! What's happening with your missing lady? Any changes?"

"Well, we've been conducting interviews and record checks till we're blue in the face. We've talked to everybody we can think of on this end. Brandon Reynolds is about to explode, and he's driving everyone crazy. But who can blame him? He wanted to come out here to Aspen, but Phoenix PD talked him into staying in Arizona in case someone tries to make contact with him. If a ransom demand does happen, I think we need him out there."

"I would agree with you on that one." Brad thought for a second. "Sam, I haven't even watched the news since who knows when. What's the media doing with your case?"

"Oh, wow! They're on it big time! The whole story and photographs of Mrs. Reynolds are everywhere. But so far, nothing new has developed. No unidentified bodies have been discovered, no ransom demand, no nothing. I don't know, Brad. Something ain't right in River

City, but I haven't figured out exactly what's wrong. Phoenix PD has interviewed the logical people. Everyone says she's the greatest lady in the world, ideal marriage and all that stuff. Zippo, my friend. We got zippo."

"Strange, ain't it?"

"Indeed, it is, but I'm nowhere near ready to give up. Something's going to break. We just need a little more time."

"I hope you're right. I sure hope you're right."

"An old coyote like me ain't throwing in the towel yet."

"Look, Sam, I may be getting ahead of myself and complicating things, but, with the new twist of child porn in the cabin, maybe you or Kurt should make another run at the Bureau? They could help in figuring out the names and phone numbers that were in that notebook and in locating this King Solomon guy. There are leads all over the country that need to be tracked down. Seems to me even the director would have a tough time defending a decision not to get involved once he knows about those photos."

"You're probably right. Child porn raises everybody's antennae."

"Hell, I think you can go straight to Barnes and get help. Screw all the damned bureaucrats and leave their pencil-pushing asses out of the loop entirely."

"I'll call in a heartbeat, Brad. Just let me talk to Kurt first."

"Hell, Sam, I may be in more trouble than anyone for breaking into the cabin in the first place. But, give me a break. I can't just walk away and pretend I didn't see what I saw."

Sam Trathen's deep voice rumbled: "I'm happy as hell you looked inside the damned old cabin, and when this is all over, I'll buy you a steak dinner for your help. You know, Brad, at first thought it seems like the cabin thing is its own separate deal. But when you look at the entire picture of what you saw from the cave coupled with the eye bolts and rope, it's not that much of a stretch to connect it with our case. It's darned sure as good as anything else we have going. At least that's the way I see it."

"Sam, you are so right. I can't get those thoughts out of my mind."

"Okay, then, tell me this, Mr. FBI. If she was grabbed for her money, why no ransom demand? That part makes no sense to me. On the other hand, if we're dealing with some sex sicko, why all the bullshit about phone calls to Las Vegas and credit cards in a coffee shop? Things don't add up."

"I can't give you any answers. All I've got are feelings."

"I know you do, Brad. This will all come together, but it sure as hell is puzzling right now."

"You and Kurt work out what you can. I know you have to keep your chief there in Aspen happy, and Kurt has to keep the big county sheriff down here happy. Not always easy things to do. Let me know if I can help."

"Will do. I'll talk with you later."

Trying to keep things straight in his head, Brad sat quietly. Had it only been a few hours since his vile discovery in the darkness of the cabin? It seemed a lifetime ago. He walked to Elizabeth's photograph. Her smile was there but what were her eyes saying? They looked at each other. Brad touched the photograph, brushing her smile with his fingertips as he whispered, "I wish I could talk to you. I could use a little help right now." Elizabeth looked back. Her eyes drilled into him.

Back at his desk, Brad sketched out a diagram for Kurt and fired off the promised packet of information. He had a second to think. There was another person Brad desperately wanted to talk with. It was his older brother, Patrick. They had led parallel lives in many ways. Patrick had retired from the FBI two years before Brad, and they pretty much saw the world through the same lens. For years, Brad had relied on his brother's advice on just about everything. Patrick would know what to do. Patrick always knew what to do. However, now that he really needed him, could use a little counsel, Patrick was nowhere to be found. He was camping in Alaska for two weeks and completely out of touch. Brad recalled the last words he had spoken to Patrick, telling him that since no self-respecting grizzly would eat his sorry ass, freezing to death was the only real danger he faced. Brad smiled. Patrick and he had enjoyed some pretty cool camping trips together. Those were the good memories. It was time to create more. He silently vowed that he would put a trip together with Patrick before winter.

Brad looked around his house, his eyes coming to rest on the family piano. It had remained untouched now for over a year. He had loved it beyond words when Elizabeth played, happy sounds filling their house. Her music book was still opened on the rack. Brad had not summoned courage to even approach the piano in all these months. He sure wasn't going there now. He had never imagined it possible to miss a person so desperately. Touching the piano would be too much.

———

WAITING for a call from Bob Callahan at the National Center for Missing and Exploited Children was the next orders of business. Brad admired the dedication and professionalism of the folks at NCMEC. He knew all too well how every day they had to peer into the sewer, dig through the bottom of the muck, soiling their hands with what most people cannot even imagine. In Brad's mind, NCMEC was a genuine hero to America's most vulnerable and his friend was typical of the outstanding people who worked there.

Brad was starving and his truck's gas tank was bone dry. Since he was simply waiting for a return call, a quick trip for fuel and a burrito for breakfast seemed like a good thing to do. Before he could think about it further, his cell phone rang, startling him so badly he jumped. It was Bob Callahan.

Within seconds, the two men were laughing as they recalled stories of their past days together and caught up on their respective families. Brad then provided the details of all that had happened in Aspen, his own experiences in the cabin, and the information from the Virginia State Penitentiary.

Callahan took it all in. "Damn, you're a busy little bee. You were supposed to get this stuff out of your system before you retired. You're not being too smart here, Brad. Why don't you get a job selling something in a shopping mall? You would be a natural in handbags and shoes."

"You're right, Bob, I'm not very smart. Cause if I was smart, I sure as hell wouldn't be wasting my time with a donkey like you. Now, can we talk business?"

"Don't have a stroke now. What can I do for you?"

"Would you mind taking the names and numbers that I took out of the cabin and the ones from Virginia State Penitentiary and give them to the departments in your area? Give them to whoever you think is appropriate. See if you can come up with anything? Most of the numbers are from your area of the country."

"Sure, that's not a problem at all."

"First, let me give you the telephone number to reach Kurt Riddle. He's the county investigator working this and a super guy. I've worked with him for years. You can call Kurt at his home or at the sheriff's office with the results. I know I'm not official anymore, but I just wanted to say hello and see if you can help jump-start this thing. Since it's a weekend, if you can get the wheels turning without a lot of official baloney, it may save a bunch of hours. I don't know where this deal is going, but I'm thinking the time factor may turn out to be pretty important before this is all over."

Bob Callahan replied with the spirited enthusiasm that Brad remembered. "Sure thing, I'll get on this right now. I'll start with Fairfax County since they will be plugged into all the Virginia state records. I know those folks well and they'll jump right on their computers At least the preliminary stuff should be pretty fast. Tracking down specific investigators working individual cases will take a little longer."

"I understand that perfectly, no problem. I'll take whatever I can get, Bob. Thanks so much. This is really bothering me big time. Sam Trathen and Kurt Riddle are the best guys ever, and they have incredible instincts. I can tell you they smell a rat here."

"Of course, Brad, I'm happy to help. I'll call your friend, Kurt Riddle, with the gory details. You're too old. You'll just get things all screwed up and forget half what you hear. The case will never get solved. I prefer to deal with responsible adults, if you know what I mean."

"Go sit on a chili pepper."

Laughter ended their telephone call.

Brad's stomach was screaming for some food, but he decided to go ahead and finish his telephone calls before leaving. He dug through the rubble that cluttered his desk looking for a business card for Phil Taylor, his old friend from Colorado State Department of Parole and Probation. After a few minutes of scouring through piles of old papers and multiple episodes of swearing, Brad found the card he needed. Phil's personal cell number was scrawled on the back.

On the second ring, Phil answered. It sounded like he was in a restaurant, so Brad kept small talk to a minimum. When Phil heard Brad mention the name King Solomon, his reaction was immediate. "Listen, that guy is bad news. If you're onto something involving him, you better take it seriously."

"That's what I need to know. What can you tell me about this guy?"

"Look, Brad, I'm having breakfast with some friends. Let's do this right and not screw around on the telephone. Give me a couple of hours and meet me at my office. I'll go over his file with you. I've got photos and everything. I've been expecting someone to call me about this guy. I just didn't think it would be a retired guy who should be out fishing."

"You're right on that one. I didn't think I'd be making a call like this either. But something smells very rotten here, and I'm sure as hell glad to have you to talk to. I can't tell you how much I appreciate this."

"Don't give it a second thought. The office is locked up on Sundays. I'll tell the security people at the main door to expect you. Just knock on the office door or ring my phone. I'll be waiting for you."

"Gotcha. I'll see you soon."

With a glance at his watch, Brad calculated his schedule. He had just enough time. He found his old briefcase, threw it in his truck and headed out. A gas station was his first stop, then to his favorite roadside stand for a burrito.

Wanting to feel outside air for a while, Brad decided to enjoy his food at one of his favorite places, Three Sisters Park, so named because of three mountains encircling a large meadow. He parked at an overlook that offered a panorama of the popular recreation area. "Great spot for a quick picnic," he mumbled to himself. He and Elizabeth had walked for miles through the hiking trails that webbed the meadow. He felt a welcomed sense of calm as he saw mountain bikers, walkers, and runners everywhere. It was a glorious day and a glorious location. "This is what life is supposed to be," he spoke to the meadow. "No abused kids and missing women."

Brad savored a bit of serenity in his truck, listening to Willie Nelson's "Blue Eyes Crying in the Rain." He needed this respite for a few minutes. It seemed as though his insides had been tight for days.

After his meal, Brad made his way to the interstate and began the descending drive from the mountains to Phil Taylor's office in Denver. Traffic was light and Brad took advantage of a carefree drive to anticipate what the next hours would likely disclose. Whatever information Phil and Callahan were going to provide, there was a good chance it would have a major impact on how this case would get off the ground and how quickly it might unfold. He knew that the beginning stages of an investigation could be tricky. It was critical not to jump to premature conclusions. Once such a mistake was made, it was easy to try and make subsequent developments fit the conclusions rather than allow hard evidence lead the way. Brad sensed that a wealth of information was about to flow. He just had to be careful how to handle it.

Soon after his exit from the interstate, Callahan called. Brad pulled to the curb and parked as he listened. "Hey man, I don't have a lot but certainly enough for someone to do some poking around. I just got off the phone with Kurt and he has the entire story. He told me he would pass it on to your guy in Aspen."

"Thanks for your help, Bob. What's the word?"

"In a nutshell, Brad, here's the story. It looks like your friend, Antonio Padilla, the King Solomon guy, is involved in a human trafficking case that's being investigated in a joint effort by several agencies across the country. No one has made a solid case yet, but it appears that he is probably involved in some serious child prostitution stuff as well.

Kurt has the details, and he said he's going to run with it and start calling all the involved investigators. I came up with nothing on the other names you gave me. But based on what you found in the cabin and from the prison records, it sounds like there's a lot more to the story and there has to be other connections."

"Okay, Bob, I'll stay in touch with Kurt. Human trafficking is not something I've dealt with much, so I'm certainly no expert."

"There are very few experts." Callahan's laugh was more of a snort. "Just a lot of phonies parading before a camera or microphone claiming to be experts."

"Isn't that the damned truth!"

"Turn on the television, and there they are, telling us all we need to know about how to conduct our lives."

"I hear you. I know enough to recognize that these matters are a serious problem."

"They are for sure," Callahan replied. "Helpless people are getting smuggled into our country like crazy. Mostly it's for cheap labor and poor people simply looking to make a better life. But sex and abuse are certainly a part of it. There's no shortage of people like this King Solomon guy who are absolute predators."

"It just shouldn't be that way, Bob."

"Is that ever the truth! What a sad state of affairs. But I have to tell you, every once in a while, I see progress being made. There have been some dynamite prosecutions around the country, and let me tell you, my friend, they have been incredible eye-openers. When this stuff gets laid out in a courtroom with real people telling their stories in plain words, that's when the staggering tragedy of these crimes is shoved right in your face. Believe me, it will make you go home and count your blessings. You know, hug your kids and all that stuff."

"I can only imagine what you and the folks there at the Center must deal with every day."

"It's frustrating as hell, but like it or not, it's life, the way things are. Look, Brad, we could talk forever but I've got to run. Stay in touch with the police and let's hope this thing has a happy ending."

"Bob, you have no idea how much I appreciate you getting this off the ground this morning. The time you saved may turn out to be critical."

"Absolutely. No problem at all. I miss our old days, running around like there was no tomorrow. We had a lot of fun before we had to grow up."

"Growing up was a big mistake, my friend."

"You nailed it there," Callahan replied with a laugh. "I hope the folks out there can put this together. There may be a hell of a case in the works. I think they should talk with the Bureau since these cases are usually national in scope. I hope you'll encourage them to do so."

Brad gave a short chuckle. "Don't worry about that. Kurt Riddle and Sam Trathen will both beat the drum loud and clear. They ain't exactly the quiet and shy types. Thanks, Bob. Thanks a million. I'll be in touch to let you know how this all turns out."

Brad pulled back onto the street and made his way to Phil Taylor's office. The streets were practically empty. On the way, Brad reflected on what Callahan had said about human trafficking. Images of bolts, rope and the sickening photographs were never far from Brad's mind.

Parking was easy on a Sunday morning. A security guard directed Brad to the proper office. A sterile corridor of fluorescent light and rows of closed doors stood like a column of silent soldiers, guarding the state's bureaucracy until Monday morning. At the end of the corridor, Brad faced a wooden door with a simple, stenciled sign: Colorado Department of Probation and Parole. Brad knocked. A moment later the door opened, and Phil stood there with an extended hand. "Hey, Brad. Good to see you. Come on in."

"Good to see you, too," Brad spoke as he grasped Phil's hand. "I'm really sorry to bother you on a Sunday, Phil. Thanks so much. I owe you for this one."

"No worries, no worries at all. What you told me on the phone makes me think this may be something that shouldn't wait until regular banker's hours. Come on back to my office. Can I get you something to drink?"

"No, thanks. I drank enough coffee this morning to float a ship."

"If I had gotten into what you got into last night, I think I might be drinking something more than coffee."

"I've been thinking about that very thing. Why don't we try to figure this stuff out and then plan on a little fishing and some cold Moosehead?"

"You won't have to ask me twice. The crap that happens around this office on a daily basis could drive anyone to drink."

"I couldn't do your job, Phil. I'd have to kill someone with my bare hands at least once a week."

The men laughed as they took seats and then Brad said, "Now, look, I don't want to get you jammed up in any way here. I'm no longer with the Bureau, anything you tell me today I'm just going to give it to Kurt Riddle. I'm simply trying to save everybody some time and get this thing launched."

Taylor grunted and twisted his face. "My aching ass. Don't sweat the small stuff. We're so damned politically correct around here it makes me ill. This is serious shit, so let's get with it." He opened a file that lay on his desk. "You know, Brad, I've been doing this a long time. It's always a balancing act to keep things in perspective. Most of the people I work with are just plain young and dumb, never had a chance from the day their useless parents brought them into the world. If I didn't feel sympathy for their lot in life, I wouldn't be human. Then, there are a few who I have trouble figuring out. They're half evil, half stupid, half smart, and completely screwed up. But sometimes I think that maybe, just maybe, with a little help, they could possibly turn their lives around." Phil Taylor shook his head in contempt. "But every once in a while someone like this King Solomon character comes along. Someone who just makes my blood run cold. No redeeming qualities. I mean none at all, Brad, none at all. This guy is a bad actor and ain't nobody—you, me, the Easter Bunny, or even the Pope—will ever change him. He is what he is."

"That's pretty much what my friend at the joint in Virginia had to say."

"For the life of me, I really don't understand why Virginia agreed to let him transfer out here, but they did. So now, for better or worse, I got the bastard."

"You're just a very lucky guy." The sarcasm in Brad's voice brought a smile to Taylor's face.

"All right, Brad, let me start at the beginning and give you what I have. Like your friend told you, King Solomon took his hit in Virginia on a plea deal that really watered down what he was actually doing. The guy is a lot worse than a regular pimp. This asshole pimps mostly little girls and little boys, like eleven to fourteen-year-old kids. He kept a few girls that were older, some were even over eighteen, but mostly he handled young ones. He seems to have a network throughout several cities that trades kids around like baseball cards."

"If he's into this crap, why in hell did Virginia let him plea to such an easy deal?" Brad gave a questioning shrug. "There's a story here, I'm sure."

"You're asking the same question I asked when I talked with the police and the prosecutor out in Virginia. And, yes, there is a story here. Partly, it boiled down to girls too young and too afraid to testify. But it's more complicated than that. They had King Solomon identified as part of a group that smuggled kids from Mexico. When King Solomon needed kids of a certain gender or age, he would contact his people in Mexico and virtually place an order. Then he would go to a designated city, usually in California or Texas, sometimes Arizona, and pick up what he had specified. Just like you or I would drive to a market to buy fresh fruit."

"God, Phil, I was just talking with a friend of mine at NCMEC about this very thing."

"I'm sure NCMEC gets this on a regular basis." Disgust filled Taylor's voice. "It's more than I could handle. Anyway, the cops in Virginia worked this case for months. They had him under surveillance and had an informant who was giving them the inside scoop. As time went by, they developed a pretty good picture of what King Solomon was doing for a living. They also knew that he kept written logs that detailed the really important stuff, you know, his contacts on the border, his customers, lists of kids traded, and all kinds of critical information. He kept these records in his house and car. Of course, records like that would be a gold mine so the police tried to get a search warrant for King Solomon's car and house. But they couldn't get a judge to sign off since uncorroborated confidential information was the only basis for the warrant."

Brad nodded. He understood the issue.

"If the search warrant route wasn't going to work, they had to come up with another plan. Since they knew King Solomon always carried a gun, they did the next best thing: they nailed his ass in a traffic stop. The officer who pulled him over easily spotted what appeared to be a gun in his pants and, of course, carrying an illegal and concealed weapon opened the door for a search of his car. When it was all over, they found some, but not all, of the records they were hoping for. There was plenty of evidence pointing to a teen prostitution operation, but not the stuff needed on the human trafficking across the border." Taylor looked across his desk at Brad. "So, they took a gamble, and when it was over, they were stuck with what they got. No way to change history."

"My guess is that what they really needed to make a solid case against him was inside his house."

"Yeah, I imagine that's the case." Taylor shook his head in agreement. "But they had other issues also. The problem was that the car King Solomon drove was actually registered to another person. So, King Solomon feigned ignorance. He claimed the records were not his at all, said he had never even seen them."

He knew what was coming next. Brad shook his head and gave a sad laugh.

Taylor's voice swelled in sarcasm. "Now, King Solomon made this claim even though police surveillance had him driving the car every day for weeks. And if that wasn't enough, King Solomon's fingerprints were all over the records!"

"I don't wanna hear the rest of this." Brad threw his head back and looked to the ceiling.

Taylor grinned. "Okay, Einstein, you've already figured out the next chapter. Since most of the evidence came from records found in the car, the search itself became the focal point of the case. King Solomon lawyered up with a high-priced firm. His attorney screamed illegal stop, and racial profiling became the central issue. The lawyers went nose to nose for a while, and it looked like the entire case could be in jeopardy. Thus, my friend, they hammer out a plea deal and King Solomon got off on the relatively minor charge of false imprisonment. The case they ultimately nailed him with involved a girl who happened to be over eighteen. Since she wasn't a minor, King Solomon avoids hard time. So, Goldilocks, this brings us to the end of this little happy-ever-after fairy tale."

"Wow!" Brad understood the frustration of weeks of work only to be lost in a torrent of legal wrangling.

Taylor leaned back in his chair and rubbed his eyes. "What happened to the rest of the case and the other people involved, I don't know. I'm sure that could all be tracked down with some work in Virginia and other places. All I know is that I'm stuck here in Denver with the King himself. Good old King Solomon and yours truly. We're a team."

"Don't forget to count your blessings." Brad's eyes twinkled.

"Every day, Brad, every day."

"What do you know about what he's doing now? How does he spend his time, make money? Who in the heck is he running with?"

Taylor gave a grunt. "Well, somehow he convinced Virginia that he would be better off here in Colorado because he had a job opportunity. He's living with his uncle, a guy named Lawrence Acosta, just off Federal Boulevard, about half mile south of Sixth Avenue. The two of them work at Elk Run Fly Fishing Resort. You and I both know what an exclusive place that is."

Brad nodded. "Top of the line."

"His uncle is apparently a decent sort of guy and has been employed there for a bunch of years. I guess he managed to talk the resort into hiring his nephew. So, King Solomon works at the resort on a part-time basis, general cleaning and maintenance duties. Stuff like that."

"How much is part-time, any idea?"

Shaking his head in disgust, Taylor replied, "It's a mighty sweet deal. He only works a few hours a week, but that gives him access to employee housing and full access to the resort. When I have my talks with him, it's either at his uncle's house or he comes here to my office. I really don't know how he spends his time when he isn't working, but I promise you he isn't doing volunteer work for his local parish. The uncle works full time and, since it's a pretty good drive to the ranch, my guess is that he spends most of his time out at the resort in employee housing. But I don't know about King Solomon. He could be bouncing back and forth between Elk Run and the city, anywhere he chooses."

Brad jotted some notes before speaking again. "My friend in Virginia told me his mother lives out here. You know anything about her?"

"Yes, I've spoken with her, but only when King Solomon first got to Colorado. She seemed like a very decent lady, actually. Based on what she said to me, she sure as hell doesn't fit the normal mold. You know how mothers almost always defend their little darlings, no matter what they've done?"

"Oh, yeah." Brad smiled.

"Everything is the fault of someone else. The world ganged up against their child."

"I hear you, Phil, but thank God for mothers. Otherwise you and I might not have any friends at all." Both men laughed.

"Well, I'll tell you, Brad, she wasn't that way at all when I spoke with her. She was mad as hell with her son, ready to disown him. It's her brother that got King Solomon hired at Elk Run, and she says that was the last chance anyone in her family will ever give the guy. She didn't want him around her house, and she sure as heck didn't plan to give him money."

"Wow! That is a different twist to the usual story."

"Good for her is the way I see it, Brad. She works her ass off cleaning hotel rooms in downtown Denver and has no patience for his nonsense. I honestly think she would be the first to call the cops if she knew he was up to something."

"A few more mothers like her and you might not have such good job security, Mr. Taylor." Brad grinned.

"Job security is not one of my worries. You can bet your ass on that."

Taylor paused. "I'll get you her address and everything I have, but I feel pretty confident that old King Solomon is too wise to run to Mama if he gets his ass in a jam."

Brad thought for a few seconds, digesting what he was hearing. "What's this guy like when you talk to him, Phil? Can you read him in any way?"

"Oh, yes, I can read him. I can read him like a large-print book. This is the part that's creepy and plain scary to me, Brad. He is absolutely friendly when we speak. It's not like he's got the shitty attitude that street punks usually have. He is intelligent as hell, very well-spoken, and presents himself like a pro. He can bullshit with the best, I promise you. But to me, more than anything, it's his eyes. They look right through you, like damned ice picks. But those eyes are laughing. That son of a bitch is talking to me with his eyes. I can hear them. It's like they're saying, 'You're not even capable of understanding how evil I am, and there is nothing you can do to stop me.' He is an ice-cold fucker, Brad, ice cold. And I warn you or anyone else who has to deal with him, watch your ass my friend. Watch your ass."

A grave silence fell. Brad nodded his head as he contemplated this.

"Now, in all fairness, I admit that my perceptions are probably tainted because I've read his psychological reports from Virginia."

"I was going to ask you what the shrinks say about him."

Taylor leaned forward to emphasize his words. "Well, you know how those goofs write their reports, Brad. They use a bunch of eleven-syllable words and doublespeak bullshit. But the bottom line at the end of the report on King Solomon is that he is a mean-ass bastard who has absolutely no conscience. Remorse is an emotion he has never known, except when he's caught by the police, of course. He is deceitful in all aspects of relating with people and he has an irrepressible need to exercise control over others. That's probably why he deals with kids. The report basically says he is a ticking bomb waiting to explode. It's a matter of when, not if."

"Jesus, that's pretty unusual language for an institutional report." Brad rolled his eyes. "Those things usually read pretty much the same, the standard hocus-pocus about why the poor guy has troubles: his mother didn't breastfeed him long enough or he didn't have a father figure. They never see anything that a little counseling and rehabilitation from a twenty-two-year-old social worker can't cure. Paid for by taxpayers, of course."

"Ain't that the sad truth!" Taylor laughed out loud. "Most times those reports read like Mother Teresa wrote them. That's why this one jumped out at me."

"Hell, yes, it jumps out."

Taylor looked hard at Brad before continuing. "I just know in my bones, Brad, there is something wrong here, big time wrong. He calls when he is supposed to call, never misses an appointment, and his piss tests are clean as a whistle. But I'm telling you, he's dirty. I don't know exactly how, but he's dirty. I've told the Denver Sex Crimes Unit about him, and they say he hasn't popped up on their radar screen. I tell them it's because he's a stealthy son of a bitch."

"I don't think I've ever seen you this concerned about anyone before and that scares me."

Phil Taylor thought for a moment. "You may be right on that. I've been doing this a long time and King Solomon definitely makes the all-star team for straight up evil dudes."

"How about a photo, his uncle's address, and any other known associates you have on him?"

"You can have anything you want. Here, look at this while I make you a folder of everything I have." Taylor lifted a photograph of King Solomon from his papers and handed it to Brad.

As Taylor walked down the hall, Brad looked at the photograph. There was no surprise. Based on just the words that Hound Dog and Taylor had used to describe King Solomon, Brad would have made the identification in a second: a sculpted face with high cheekbones, milk chocolate skin, and thin lips. Straight, dark hair hung to his shoulders. His hair looked as though it was lovingly groomed for hours each day. In a feminine sort of way, he was handsome. But Phil was right. It was the eyes. Even when looking into a camera for a mug shot they mocked: 'You just *think* you've caught me.'

Returning to his desk, Taylor handed Brad a folder filled with papers. "Here you go. Let me know if I can do anything more."

"Thanks, Phil. I appreciate it. By the way, Kurt Riddle sends his best."

"Lord have mercy on us all, it's frightening as hell for the two of you to be back together again; just when everyone thought it was safe to go back into the water!"

"Yeah, well, if you go back into the water, please don't wear a Speedo. Talk about something frightening!" They both laughed as Brad continued. "Listen, Phil, we've got almost two months of good weather ahead of us if you're interested in a day on the river."

"You just call me, Brad. I'll blow out of here in a heartbeat. Also, tell Kurt if he needs anything, I'll get it to him as fast as my little legs can run."

The men shook hands as Brad left.

In his truck, Brad leafed through the sheaf of documents Taylor had provided. He stopped when he came across the photograph of King Solomon. Holding it in both hands, Brad stared for several long seconds, memorizing the image. *Christ, the guy is creepy!* Just looking at him caused Brad to chill.

The same chill he had felt in the cabin.

———

BRAD HAD INITIALLY PLANNED to return home after seeing Phil Taylor. It couldn't happen. He couldn't just drive away. Not after all that he had learned. He had to follow his gut. Brad turned his truck toward Federal Boulevard and spoke to himself, "Let's go take a look at where Mr. King Solomon lives."

Driving west, Brad left the downtown area, and then went south on Federal Boulevard. After a few blocks, Brad smelled the fragrance that was the very essence of autumn in the southwest: the aroma of green chilies being roasted over an open flame. The smell seduced Brad, taking him back to his boyhood in New Mexico. He stopped to purchase a full bushel, vowing to himself that he would soon invite friends for one of his famous enchilada dinners.

From Federal Boulevard, Brad turned west onto a side street that took him past the house of Lawrence Acosta, King Solomon's uncle. It was like every other house on the block: wood-framed with a small front yard and a chain-link fence enclosing the rear yard. A detached, one-car garage sat next to the house and Brad could tell by looking that it had the old-fashioned type of door, the kind where someone had to get out of the car to open it. There was nothing fancy to be found here. Children played in the street, and it seemed to Brad that the entire neighborhood was vibrant and happy. Windows and doors were opened wide and people gathered on porches or in front yards, enjoying a pleasant Sunday. Brad circled the block to drive past the house again. It was the only house in the area with its doors closed tightly and its curtains drawn, no sign of life whatsoever. It seemed out of step with the neighborhood.

King Solomon could be anywhere. He could be at Elk Run. Where else could he be?

Further up the street, Brad spotted a small park. Swings and a merry-go-round were alive with children as adults sat, sipping from cans and talking. He parked and got out. King Solomon's house was in easy view. Even though the neighborhood was racially mixed Brad stuck out like a sore thumb. Anyone could tell that he didn't belong here. But no one seemed to be paying him much attention. Why not keep an eye on the house for a while? Brad took a seat on a bench and savored the beautiful morning.

People moved about and the day grew warmer. Nothing changed at King Solomon's house. Brad walked back to his truck and again drove through the neighborhood. He found another place to park, this time just over a block from the house. He wasn't sure why he did this. Even if he saw Lawrence Acosta or King Solomon, what would he do? Maybe he should talk to Kurt, see what he thought about Callahan's information and tell him about his visit with Phil Taylor. Brad reached for his phone.

As he was pressing the numbers, it happened. There was no way in hell Brad could explain how he knew, but he was as certain as he had ever been of anything: the dull, red pick-up truck coming straight at him, and still two blocks away, was the one he had seen from the cave. He knew it. All he had seen that night was a silhouette, not much more than a shadow, but it was enough to discern that it was a pick-up truck. Now he saw it in broad daylight. This was it. Brad watched the vehicle speeding toward him. He knew it was going to turn into King Solomon's drive well before it actually reached the house. The driver slammed the brakes, barely making the turn. The tires skidded across the gravel drive before coming to a halt. When the pick-up truck was stopped, it squarely faced the garage. Brad was mesmerized as he watched the events unfold. The truck sat there and looked just like it had at the old cabin. Brad felt a chill in his spine, and his truck suddenly smelled like the cave.

The door of the pick-up truck flew open. The driver leaped from the vehicle, and for a fraction of a second, the man glanced down the street, looking straight in the direction of Brad.

For the first time, Brad Walker saw the live face of King Solomon, and his preened shoulder-length hair.

In a sprint, King Solomon ran to the front door of the house and was gone, out of sight. It had all happened unexpectedly and quickly. Brad couldn't tell whether or not King Solomon was afraid or angry or in a panic, but he was clearly distressed about something. Brad placed his cell phone back onto the seat. This was not the moment to call Kurt.

He had no time to think. Within seconds Brad saw King Solomon sprint back out again, jump into his pick-up truck, and pull out of the drive, spinning the tires as he drove away. Brad sat half stunned. What had he just seen? This had been a man on a mission.

Instinctively, Brad started his engine and followed. King Solomon had almost a two-block head start, so Brad pushed his speed as much as he dared to close the distance. He saw the pick-up truck turn east toward Federal Boulevard. Brad turned a block behind him and paralleled what he anticipated would be King Solomon's route. When he reached Federal Boulevard, King Solomon had already turned north and was driving toward Sixth Avenue. Brad had no choice but to push his old truck harder than he liked just to keep King Solomon in view. Once they reached Sixth Avenue and headed west, things got easier. Brad managed to pull to within a few cars behind the red pick-up and then held his position.

At Sheridan, King Solomon exited north. After driving close to a mile, he turned west and then made a series of turns, winding his way through a quiet, middle-class residential neighborhood.

Now, it was just the two of them. There were no other cars for cover, and Brad grew increasingly nervous. Whatever King Solomon was up to, the last thing Brad wanted was for him to notice he was being followed. Things quickly got worse. King Solomon turned his vehicle onto a short street that ended in a cul-de-sac.

There was nowhere to go. Brad drove past, not making the turn. He drove on for a short distance before turning around and again driving past the cul-de-sac. The pick-up sat empty in the driveway of the last house on the circle. He caught only a glimpse of King Solomon's body and long hair as he ran into the house without knocking.

Brad continued driving through the area. Damn if his heart wasn't pounding again! He cruised slowly, observing that the houses were modest, fairly well maintained with small yards. Some had privacy fences enclosing the rear yards. This neighborhood was different than the one where he had sat while watching King Solomon's house. Children played in backyards, not on the street. Houses with privacy fences shielded their yards from the eyes of passers-by. He drove past the cul-de-sac again. He saw no cars or signs of life at the house, only King Solomon's empty pick-up truck.

Uncertain about what he should do, Brad continued to cruise. He parked his truck and walked back to the cul-de-sac where he had last seen King Solomon. The pick-up truck was gone. Whatever King Solomon's business had been at the house, it had been short.

The driveway of the house was empty and the house that King Solomon had entered showed no signs of life. Brad studied the setting. The same old feelings chilled his skin. The house beckoned him; an invisible hand pulled. The hair of Brad's neck stood up. He walked casually, making his way down the cul-de-sac. Within seconds he reached the house. A curving walkway led from the driveway to the front door. The door looked to be made of heavy wood and across the top was a circular stained-glass window that gave the effect of a church door. It seemed terribly out of place.

This house was clearly not as well maintained as the other houses in the neighborhood. The yard was ragged and brown. A privacy fence in the back was in need of paint, and one section was leaning to the ground, on the brink of collapse. Brad moved slowly past the house, trying to memorize its image. As he came to within mere feet of the walls and front door, a sense of dread again enveloped his body. It was just as on the night when he had stood outside the cabin. He shuddered. *What is it about this place?*

Brad walked through a few more blocks of the neighborhood before returning to his truck. He contemplated his options. What he wanted to do was watch the house and see who showed up. It sure would be nice to get a better feel for the house and the entire cul-de-sac. But his gut told him that it wouldn't work. In this neighborhood, people would be wary of strangers. Brad knew sure as hell that if he hung around for very long, sitting in his car or walking, someone would call the police. He couldn't risk anything that might attract the attention of King Solomon or whoever lived in the house. With the same reluctance he had the night he had walked away from the cabin, Brad started the engine of his truck and drove away.

Darkness was approaching, and it had been way too long since his breakfast burrito in Three Sisters Park. Brad pulled into a restaurant for a hamburger and a chance to call Kurt. He found a table in an empty corner. After ordering, he dialed his friend. Visions of King Solomon's troubled face and the house on the cul-de-sac lingered in Brad's mind. Something didn't feel right. Maybe a talk with Kurt would help.

The sound of his friend's voice was reassuring. Brad told Kurt of his visit with King Solomon's parole officer and the unexpected afternoon adventure of following King Solomon. He gave Kurt the addresses of both houses and the license number of the pick-up truck.

Kurt spoke as he flipped through stacks of notes. "Well, I didn't put a bunch of miles on my car like you did. I've spent the day on the tele-phone, sitting right here on my wrinkled old ass. After I got the infor-mation from your pal at NCMEC, I went to work trying to get through to individual investigators from different agencies. I was hoping to determine what kind of investigations, if any, are still pending. The stuff you got from Phil Taylor at parole matches up with what I learned about King Solomon's last arrest. But I have a little bit more to add to the mix."

"Good, there has to be a lot more to what this guy is up to."

"Well, I think you're right. I'm still waiting for some calls to come back to me, so I don't have the entire story. I honestly don't think there is a clear picture anywhere out there. The people I've talked with today are all pretty frustrated with how difficult their investigations have been."

Brad was dying to know something. "Is there more to this than the Virginia case? Phil Taylor only had details of the teenaged prostitution matter, but he was sure it went beyond that. He mentioned a human trafficking investigation."

Kurt grunted. "Oh, hell, it's way larger than just one state. There's a task force in Virginia that's working with several agencies all up and down the East Coast and some western states as well. The crux of the case has been along the Mexican border. That's where it all starts. People are smuggled across the line in all kinds of ways: cars, buses, boats, freight containers, you name it. Some are simply walked across the border. Once they're inside the United States, they are placed into vans, trucks, trailers, or, hell, most any type of vehicle and then their real journey begins. There are highly organized networks that distribute these poor people all over. Sometimes the victims get transferred to different vehicles with different drivers and multiple transfers before they reach a final destination."

"This is the same old shit, Kurt, but it just keeps on happening."

"I know, it's awful, Brad. But at least for regular laborers, they get to a city or town and go to work. With the kids, there is no final destina-tion. The animals that smuggle kids are smart. They never stop shuf-fling them around. They keep them moving every few weeks without ever letting the kids really learn where they are or even who they're with. It's a very cruel psychological trick that leaves the kids with absolutely nowhere to go. Makes me sick."

Brad interjected. "And nobody knows anybody so when something goes wrong, like the police snooping around, there's no way to really trace what the hell has happened."

"You got it. However, in this particular case, Virginia came up with a couple of good sources who identified your friend King Solomon as being a middle man in this stuff. He dealt at a high enough level that he actually knew who worked for who and who was paying who. I suppose Phil told you the sad story on how they didn't make a solid case on him."

"Yeah, he told me all about it."

"I talked with a Virginia investigator just an hour ago, and he told me that after King Solomon got popped and worked his plea deal, the case pretty much stalled. They didn't have a good hammer over his head to force him to bargain, so Solomon refused to cooperate and took his minimal jail time. Because of the way the case was finally resolved, a bunch of loose ends were left dangling. The investigator said that, unfortunately, they just rolled on to other cases, and the extent of King Solomon's noble enterprise was never fully determined. They moved on to a new crop of names and faces."

"What a sad story."

"Yeah, it's very much like working drug cases. Endless supply and endless demand."

Brad spoke with a harsh tone. "That's true, but there's a hell of a difference. I've worked a bunch of drug cases over the years, and they don't tear your insides out like this shit does."

"Absolutely, absolutely! Anyway, from what I learned today, King Solomon had pretty much faded into history until some damned old retired FBI guy stirred the pot and got everybody all excited again."

Brad laughed. "Gotta do something besides fish."

Kurt continued. "They say that the big players, the real controllers, don't change all that much, and King Solomon is probably still very much in the thick of things. Virginia would love another crack at him. Lord, Brad, they hate him with a passion."

"Kurt, have you noticed that he seems to evoke that emotion from everyone?"

"Yep, that sure seems to be the case."

Brad paused and then asked, "By the way, have you heard from Sam today?"

"He left me a message. Said nothing was breaking for him. He's pretty discouraged."

"He has to be. That's a tough one. But I keep getting these feelings that maybe, just maybe, there is some sort of connection with King Solomon, the cabin, and Sam's case."

Kurt sighed and then continued, "I know, Brad, I agree with you. But we need something more than your goofball feelings. You know, those pesky little things called facts or evidence. Ever hear those words in the FBI?"

"Give me a break. When did you ever let facts get in the way of any of your genius conclusions?"

Laughing, Kurt said, "Look, I have no more time for you. Let's talk tomorrow if your busy schedule will allow. I'll let you know what I learn about these addresses and license numbers your super-sleuthing turned up."

"Sounds good."

Speaking as an afterthought, Kurt asked, "Hey goofball, I forgot to ask, have you listened to any news today?"

"No, can't say that I have."

"Well, there's a pretty big story coming out of Oklahoma. Some big-name television preacher type got caught playing hide the weenie with a little girl. All hell is breaking lose in Oklahoma and the good preacher is telling all, brother, telling it all. The cops in Oklahoma City and all over the state have been doing a major house cleaning the last couple of days. They're getting really good stuff for the church bulletins."

Brad listened intently.

"This part isn't on the news yet, but I just talked to Denver PD and, sure as hell, the preacher claims that one of the people who fixed him up with little girls has brought him to Denver a few times for a roll in the hay with an underaged maiden."

Brad felt his nerve endings fire. "No shit!"

"Yeah, he usually went to a motel where a girl was brought to him. However, one time the preacher got taken to a house, and the girl was already there. Preacher boy thinks there were other kids in the house also."

Brad squeezed the telephone as his palms grew sweaty. "Does the preacher know where this house is located?"

Kurt was sarcastic in his answer. "God bless the holy man. He said he would be able to find the house again, and Oklahoma brought him out here to point it out. But ain't no miracles happened yet. They're somewhere in Denver with him right now. I talked to them just a little bit ago. Those poor guys are pulling their hair out. Several Denver cops, Oklahoma City cops, and an FBI guy from your Oklahoma City office have spent the entire afternoon with this idiot. But so far, he hasn't been able to find the house of pleasures. When I talked to them, they were giving serious consideration to just shooting him on the spot, put him out of his misery, and save everyone a bunch of trouble."

"What about the guy who made arrangements for him, actually lined up the girls and brought him to Denver? What does preacher say about him?"

"Usual routine. It was some guy who lived there in Oklahoma City. But, of course, preacher only knew him by a street name and a cell phone number. Oklahoma City PD is hot on it, and the FBI is working some leads they have out in Chicago to find the asshole."

"Kurt, this is too much. How much coincidence can happen in a day? What part of town are they searching? Did the preacher at least give them a general area?"

"Somewhere on the west side is all I know."

"Damn, Kurt, here I go again with my hunches, but isn't it possible they could be looking for the house of King Solomon's uncle or, who knows, maybe the place where I just followed King Solomon?"

The phone was quiet for a moment before Kurt replied. "Hell, Brad,

I guess it's possible. I don't know if it's trying to cram too many things in a single pot here, but yes, it sure as hell is possible. All I know is they are on the west side of town; I don't know exactly where. Why don't you call Skip Watkins? He's the Denver guy I spoke to a little while ago. He's the man to answer your questions."

"Heck, I know Skip. A few years ago, we worked together on a robbery case that was wild as the dickens. Do you have his number handy?"

"Yeah, hang on."

Brad fumbled for a pen as he listened to Kurt shuffling papers. He was reluctant to tell Kurt what he was actually feeling. The second Kurt had told him how the preacher had traveled to Denver to have sex with a young girl, Brad had felt a sense of urgency, like he couldn't move fast enough. The afternoon flashed through his mind. Why had King Solomon been so rushed at his uncle's house? Brad visualized the anxious expression he had seen on King Solomon's face as he ran from his vehicle to the house. Brad again saw the way King Solomon had sped away with purpose. He thought of the ominous feeling he had as he walked near the house on the cul-de-sac. Brad felt close to something that he could not quite define. It was all around him, but he couldn't get his hands around it. He just couldn't grab it. Visions of repugnant photographs flashed in his mind.

Kurt interrupted his thoughts. "Here's your number, Brad."

As Brad scribbled the number, he again felt like he was in the cave. He could smell the cabin and the mustiness of the address book.

"Thanks, Kurt. I'll call Skip right now."

"Sounds good, catch you later."

Brad held the telephone in a death grip. He already knew what he was going to hear. He pressed the numbers.

"Watkins," the voice on the other line barked.

"Skip, Brad Walker here, a blast from your past."

"Heaven and earth! Brad Walker. How are you?"

Brad forced himself to engage in small talk for a minute then cut to the point.

"Skip, I just spoke with Kurt Riddle. He told me you've been in an old-fashioned revival meeting all afternoon, spending quality time with a real hellfire-and-brimstone type from Oklahoma."

"Oh, God, don't make my balls hurt more than they do already. Did Kurt tell you what's going on?"

"Yeah, I know the basic story."

"Jesus, Brad, does this guy ever smoke my hairy ass. Between Sunday school and passing the offering plate, this shithead comes to my town to violate little girls. He's crying the blues now, but that's only 'cause he's been caught."

"Seems like that's always the case, isn't it?"

"I'm afraid so. He's helping us look, but so far, he hasn't been able to find the exact house. We've been like a squirrel in a wheel all day, and we got nothing to show for it. I felt pretty optimistic when we first started, thought we would have ourselves a search warrant before night. Now, I don't know, Brad. After a day with this toad, I'm thinking I may have been dreaming."

"What's his state of mind, Skip? Is his heart really in this?"

Watkins contemplated his response before speaking. "I honestly do think he's trying, but he only went to the house a single time. All the other times he was in a motel. He just can't remember how to find it again. I think he's given us his best, but I don't think we're anywhere close. And we sure as hell ain't playing horseshoes, my friend."

"Look, Skip, I'll explain later why I'm asking, but for now, can you just tell me where you're looking and what type of house he is looking for?"

"Yeah, sure, Brad. We're on the west side. We've been up between Sheridan and Wadsworth going north from Sixth Avenue all the way to Eighty-Fourth. We've been in dozens of neighborhoods but there are about a hundred to go, and our preacher is getting more confused by the hour. It's dark now, and we're all exhausted. I think we may knock off for the night and give the guy some rest. I don't know what we'll do tomorrow. We can't totally give up, but we sure do need to focus in a single area."

"Holy Mary, Skip. This is so incredible I don't know where to even begin. Please, don't tell me I'm crazy until you hear the entire story, but I think I know the house your reverend friend visited."

"Jesus, Brad, talk to me!"

Brad was trembling. How much more could happen to him in seventy-two hours? "Look, Skip, let's try this. Write down this address and go take a look at it. Just by yourself. Don't let the good shepherd even know what you're doing. If you look at the house, and it fits the description of what you've been looking for, then take the preacher to look at it for a positive identification. I'm telling you, Skip, you're going to get a hit."

"You're on. Give me the address."

"Here you go." Brad relayed the address and then asked, "Where can I meet up with you?"

"That same gas station where we arrested the spray-paint bandit a couple of years ago, remember? I'm leaving to find this address of yours, but my partner is here with a Bureau guy from Oklahoma. Preacher boy is here also. Oklahoma City PD is sitting tight with him."

Brad had to laugh. "How could I forget that gas station? I'm on my way, Skip. I'll be dying to hear from you after you see the house."

"Fast as I can, Brad, fast as I can."

A waitress set a hamburger in front of Brad. He left money on the table and his food untouched.

———

As Brad arrived at the gas station, the smile on his face grew wider by the moment. A few years ago, Denver Police and FBI Agents had worked a surveillance on a guy who they suspected of having robbed several banks. He was obviously a nut job, but he used a gun, and everyone was afraid the idiot might hurt someone. This particular gas station was located across the street from the bank where it had all ended. They had watched as the crazy guy spray-painted his body until he was totally silver before walking across the street to rob the bank. Everyone was laughing so hard they could hardly pull off the arrest.

Pulling his truck to the back side of the gas station, Brad saw a marked police cruiser and an unmarked unit. It was completely dark in the alley where the officers were parked. He pulled his truck beside the unmarked unit, knowing the preacher was probably being held in the back seat of the patrol car. As Brad approached the driver's door, he did not recognize the Denver officer sitting behind the wheel. The passenger side door flung open as a short, powerful body emerged. A half-smoked, half-eaten cigar protruded from the man's square face. Permanent smile lines etched his tanned skin like a wrinkled shirt. Brad heard the words, "Hello, marshmallow dick."

"Yogi!" Brad raced to the man. The friends of more than twenty years shook hands and then embraced. Yogi had stood as the best man when Brad and Elizabeth married. He had delivered Elizabeth's eulogy.

Brad stepped back to speak. "I had no idea it was you on this deal. I didn't think you were allowed outside the state of Oklahoma."

"Well, hell, I'm not telling any of these guys that I know you. I have my reputation to protect."

The Denver police officer had walked around the car and now stood next to Yogi. Extending his hand to Brad, he introduced himself as Grant. Brad spoke with a grave tone. "My sympathy goes out to you for having to spend a day with this guy. I promise you, not all of the Bureau is as screwed up as this short-armed idiot. He played way too many football games with no helmet and spent too many years in the Marine Corps. He'll never recover."

"That's okay," Grant replied with a smile. "Everybody's gotta have a few guys like him. Cultural diversity they call it."

"Just don't let him drive," Brad warned. "His arms are too short to reach the wheel. It's a terrifying experience. Let me tell you a story, Grant, and, may God strike me dead if it's not true."

"I think I need to hear this," Grant said, eager for some humor.

Placing a hand on Grant's shoulder, Brad became deadly serious. "One day Yogi was driving me. He had a cigar in one hand and a cherry Slurpee in the other. It never occurred to him that maybe, just maybe, he should at least touch the steering wheel once every thirty seconds or so. Well, we're flying down the road doing about sixty, with no hands on the wheel. This moron here," Brad nodded to Yogi, "is puffing and slurping away. All of a sudden, ashes fall from his cigar and land right in his crotch. I mean to tell you, Grant, it was like the Hindenburg. Yogi's balls burst into flames, and we had ourselves a regular bonfire. Yogi's suit was smoking like a bunch of burning tires. Of course, he forgets he has a Slurpee in his hand and starts pounding on his balls to put out the fire. The car is filling with smoke, Slurpee is splashing everywhere, Yogi is screaming, and nobody's driving. I see my life about to end, so I grabbed the steering wheel and pull us over to the side of the road. Yogi just sits there; his nuts are like peanut butter; he has a hole in his suit, and cherry Slurpee covers everything. Now, does this idiot care about his manhood? Does he give a rip about his four-hundred-dollar suit? Hell no! All I hear is a grown man crying because he spilled his cherry Slurpee!"

Grant howled while the sheepish grin on Yogi's face betrayed the absolute truth of the tale. Shaking his head, Yogi meekly said, "That was supposed to be our secret, Brad. Thanks a million."

"Anytime, Yogi, anytime."

After they stopped laughing, the men settled in the unmarked police car. Brad sat in the back seat. He asked if they had heard from Skip Watkins.

"No word yet," replied Grant.

Brad gave the men a short synopsis of the events that led up to how he happened to call Skip with information about the house.

"Man alive! What a story." Yogi rubbed his chin as he spoke. "The Bureau has some leads on the guy who arranged little girls for preacher boy. We think he's in the Chicago area and the people out there are working like crazy to locate him and, hopefully, arrest his ass."

"Well, Yogi, you sit tight cause I'm telling you, when Skip calls, it is going to be the right house. Don't ask me how I know, but I damned well know."

"I hope to hell you're right," Grant said with a twinge of doubt in his voice.

"I hope like hell I'm right." Brad looked to Yogi. "If they can grab the guy in Chicago, who knows what all may happen."

Yogi's voice was thick with disgust as he pointed a finger to the profile of the preacher slumped in the rear seat of the police cruiser. "I hope you're right too, Brad. Spending the day with this sicko sitting over here has been like having teeth pulled."

"Yeah, I'm sure it's been a real delight."

Yogi moaned, "And that's only half the story, Brad. We ain't had no supper tonight, not a bite. You know how grumpy I get when I don't get my three squares."

Extracting crackers from his shirt pocket, Grant handed Yogi the morsels. "Here, I don't want you to cry like you did over your Slurpee."

Yogi took the crackers and examined them. "Is this it? One lousy pack of crackers."

Brad looked toward the preacher. "There's a holy man right there. Why don't you give him the crackers, let him bless them, feed the multitudes, and then deliver us a message of inspiration? Our own Sermon on the Mount, right here in Colorado."

Yogi rolled his eyes. "You can bet your sweet ass I wouldn't eat anything that pervert blessed. I'm not anywhere near that hungry."

Grant's phone rang. Skip's voice came through so loudly everyone in the car could hear clearly. "It's it, by God, it's it. The exact house our boy described. Stained glass window in the door, fence falling down, curved walkway, everything. Get his ass over here for an identification and statement. We're going to have our search warrant pronto!"

Brad tapped Grant on the shoulder, "Ask him if there's a red pick-up truck parked there."

Skip Watkins heard Brad ask the question and he shouted back into the telephone. "No, I don't see any vehicles at all. The place is dark and looks empty."

Brad leaned forward and said, "Okay, guys, you've got the information on what I learned from parole, everything Kurt Riddle told me and from what I saw today. Throw it in your affidavit for the search warrant."

Brad got out of the car. Grant and Yogi followed him to the front of the vehicle. For a few seconds the men simply stood silently facing each other. To break the awkwardness, Brad extended his hand to Grant and then to Yogi. "Okay, boys, I guess this is where the retired guy has to leave the performance, exit stage right as they say." Both men looked at Brad, uneasy in how suddenly the air had transformed from laughter and old memories to the harsh realities of the present.

"Go get 'em guys," Brad said feeling a little choked up. "Somebody call me and let me know how it all turns out." Grant turned away. Yogi and Brad faced each other in one final uneasy second of silence. Their embrace was short but solid.

Brad stepped into his truck, started the engine, and pulled away.

———

THE DRIVE HOME WAS A BLUR. It was near midnight, and Brad thought of his treasured memories of Yogi and Elizabeth and memories of investigations. He thought about how Yogi, Skip, Grant, and Watkins would be preparing their paperwork to get the search warrant. That would be followed by getting some poor judge out of bed and rounding up investigators and lab people. It would take a while, but before dawn they would be in the house, tearing the place apart. Then, decisions would be made about how to proceed with the case and King Solomon. Lord Almighty, he was missing it tonight.

The night was so still. His town slept. Sarah Brightman's voice came from his CD player, the song "Memories," from the musical *Cats*. Listening to the words, Brad Walker could not remember a time when he had felt so alone.

Straight to the refrigerator. Moosehead, bread, and cheese. Brad sat next to Elizabeth. He thought he saw a smile in her eyes, but he wasn't certain. He was too tired to think about it. It was so quiet. Brad looked at his watch, straight-up midnight.

It was a new day. What in the world would this one bring?

MONDAY, SEPTEMBER 10

Coffee machines brewed and computers spun to life for another day. For Senator Bertram Russert, the day felt anything but new as he sat behind the closed door of Mark Whitman's office. The lawyer's smile never changed as he glared across his desk, gently rocking in his chair. For the third time, Russert silently read the letter that had been prepared for Brandon Reynolds.

Whitman knew the document by heart. He had composed and typed it himself and was quite proud of it. The letter's terse words explained that to save the life of Christine Reynolds, Brandon must transfer fifty million dollars to an overseas account. The account had been established years ago by Russert and his wife as a tax shelter but now would conveniently serve as a depository for the ransom of a human life.

Savoring the silence and the moment, Whitman loved having a man with such prestige and immense wealth sitting before him, totally at his mercy. How could a person ask for more? Whitman's demented smile grew as Russert looked up from the letter in astonished disbelief. Whitman refused to speak. He wanted to let the weasel absorb what was happening, feel every agonizing detail as his privileged life melted like wax. Whitman had so looked forward to this moment, and he now intended to take his time to enjoy it.

He noted a flaring in Russert's nostrils, the only observable indication of life in his otherwise rigid body. Even his eyes did not blink.

How long had he planned for this day? Whitman could hardly believe his good fortune. He was a few keystrokes away from millions of dollars being transferred into his personal account. Whitman would then push a button and Felix would be paid. It was all like fucking magic.

Silence hung in the air. Whitman scrutinized Russert's face, delighting in the obvious agony that the man endured. Whitman loved it.

Finally, Whitman broke the silence with a sarcastic grunting laugh, more like a yelp. He tossed a small jewelry box across the desk. It landed perfectly in Russert's lap. Russert's eyes dropped for less than a second, all the time he needed to comprehend: a diamond ring, God only knew how many carats. Russert didn't have to be told that it had been removed from the hand of Christine Reynolds.

Whitman now spoke. "Come on, Bertram. Don't be so difficult The little lady is fine. Mister R can have her back, good as new. Nobody's even had any fun with her, which by the way, is probably the biggest flaw in this entire plan." Whitman laughed and his eyes grew expectant, as if he anticipated the senator to have an epiphany and realize the genius and comedy of the scheme contained in the letter.

Russert's entire body withered. Forcing his lips to shape words, he spoke in a choked staccato: "Have . . . you . . . lost . . . your mind?"

Here it came, weasel man's response. What fucking fun! Whitman smiled so wide, his white teeth and pink gums glistened in the light.

Russert gathered his words. He wanted to stand and shout, but he had no strength. Instead, he meekly said, "You are a recognized attorney and have practiced law in this city for years. You are a wealthy man. You have everything a person could wish for. Yet, you have kidnapped a woman. You threaten to kill her, and you expect me, a United States senator, to be a part of your scheme. You expect me to be complicit in this barbarous act of insanity? In the name of God, what is wrong with you?"

Guttural laughter bubbled from Whitman's mouth. His lips curled into a sneer as he remained silent, allowing the effect of his mirth to penetrate Russert's mind. Dreadful seconds passed before he spat a reply. "This is so fucking delicious I can't goddamned believe it! A senator of the United States is offended. He is offended because I have chosen to simply take a piece of the life that people like the Reynolds have enjoyed for years. The senator is shocked because he finds himself —what word did you use—*complicit*? Ah, yes, complicit. That is very senatorial, Bertram. I like that. Complicit indeed."

Leaning back in his chair, Whitman folded his hands beneath his chin, as in reflective thought, and looked to the ceiling. When he next spoke, he used a mocking sing-song tone. "*Complicit, complicit*, what a civilized word. I can just see it now. You are standing in the hallowed halls of the Senate, an adoring audience in rapture before your distinguished presence. Yes, yes, Bertram, I see at all so clearly. Your trim physique, silver hair, and you brimming with soulful sincerity. Oh, my God, I see it all. Yes! Yes! Your hands gesture to the sky. You raise your magnificent baritone voice to the heavens and cry out, 'I. Shall. Not. Be. Complicit.'"

Whitman halted his mocking soliloquy. His face burned red; his eyes jeered and beads of sweat erupted on his forehead. A visible tremor swelled. Whitman flung his body over his desk until his face was inches from Russert's. "Fuck me!" Whitman screeched. The enraged lawyer shot out of his chair as though he intended to tear Russert's flesh with his teeth. His veins swelled in purple rage, and his skin stretched taut across his face, as though he were on the brink of exploding.

"Complicit, my ass, you goddamned perverted baby-fucker. The United States senator who sticks his dick in young girls is offended? The United States senator who takes little girls right out of Brownies and fucks them, rams his cock down their tiny throats till they gag. He is offended!? The senator who bends innocent little girls over a table and rips their delicate bodies like a sheet of toilet paper he would use to wipe his esteemed, senatorial ass. You are offended!? Excuse me! The senator is offended! You baby fucking pervert. On what grounds are you offended?"

Whitman spewed condemnation as if he were ridding himself of rotting meat. His words hurled through the air, found their target, and splattered like hot fecal matter.

Remaining coiled over the desk, Whitman gasped for air as though he had just crossed the finish line of a marathon. The moment held. Gradually, he eased his body back into his chair. His breath slowed, but his eyes continued to rage in maniacal fury.

Motionless, Russert gaped. His face ashen and eyes dazed, he did not speak.

Whitman assessed the pathetic, ensnared figure before him. This is exactly what he had expected. No surprises. Precisely how he had thought Russert would react.

Never taking his eyes from Russert, Whitman withdrew a loosely bound bundle from his desk and flung it, striking Russert in the chest. The rubber band snapped, and photographs fluttered like confetti onto Russert's lap and the floor. Horrific images, unspeakable shame begging to be covered, were scattered everywhere. "If you need a little nudge to remember, baby-fucker, try these."

Russert barely moved his eyes. He could not summon the strength to confront the strewn photographs and their screaming pronounce-ment of his impending doom.

Whitman's lips again parted, curling upward over his teeth. Then, a hideous laugh stabbed Russert like a skewer through his brain.

No words, no movement from Russert.

Whitman eased his body more comfortably into his chair to speak again. He now used a gentle, condescending tone, as if speaking to a small child. "Now, Bertram, consider this. I know a very special and secret place. It is somewhere in the mountains of Colorado. Bertram, can you believe that this special place is where dozens of these wonderful photographs are kept? And, Bertram the baby-fucker, would you believe that I have copies and discs for reproductions right here in my desk? Isn't this exciting news?"

The twisted smile distended Whitman's face.

"Oh, yes, Bertram. I've paid baskets of money to photograph you and several other sickos for months. I've kept this marvelous collection, not knowing who the lucky winner would ultimately be. I had amazing choices: Senators, judges, ministers, businessmen, all kinds of sterling citizens competed hard for first place. But you, Bertram, blessed are you among baby-fuckers. Destiny has chosen you to be the key that will open my door. Baseball, apple pie, and baby-fuckers. Don't you just love it, Bertram?"

The laugh again was screeching.

Whitman analyzed Russert. He could literally see his nerves twitching, like hair sizzling over a flame. Whitman thought it was like watching a mutilated but living body dangling before a howling mob that screamed for more torture. He couldn't remember when he had enjoyed something so much.

Russert did not speak. His body was immobilized, his face grey. Dazed silence was his only reaction.

Calculating every motion, Whitman tilted his head. Casting his eyes upward, he searched for the perfect words. "Now, let's think about this, Bertram. Who would be interested in these photos? Come on now. You realize we're talking real Norman Rockwell stuff here, American fucking masterpieces. It would be a crime to the art lovers of the world not to allow these photographs to be shared. Don't you agree?"

Whitman sneered at Russert.

No response.

"How about this, Bertram. Why not put them in *Better Homes and Gardens*? I'm thinking maybe right between the sections featuring scrumptious deserts and fun ideas for a summer vacation. How absolutely lovely! They may possibly release a special issue just in your honor. Now, wouldn't that be a family treasure? Generation to generation, kids, grandchildren, everybody could read about good old Uncle Bertram."

The laugh.

Whitman rubbed his chin in contemplation. "Come on, Bertram. You're not helping me with this. Let's see, you don't seem too excited about my *Better Homes and Gardens* idea." He paused. "How about the *Washington Post* or *New York Times*? Are those better ideas, Mr. United States Senator?"

Another pause.

Delight illuminating his face, Whitman threw his hands into the air. "I've got it, Bertram! Why in the world did it take me so long to think of this? Why not send the photos to the *Denver Post*? Some of the best action shots were taken right there in their backyard. Rocky Mountain High and all that shit." Whitman grinned. "Sort of a new twist on becoming a member of the Mile High Club, isn't it, Bertram?"

Whitman howled at his own joke.

Russert remained immobile.

In an instant, all traces of humor vanished from Whitman's face. He leaned forward in his chair, bringing his body closer to Russert, Whitman shot a glare square into Russert's face. Silence pressed down like a second atmosphere. Whitman waited. He offered Russert time to respond.

Russert's eyes reached out across the desk in a pitiful plea for mercy. He opened his mouth to speak. His lips stirred but his tongue refused to move. He could not breathe. Russert appeared as a fish tossed onto a hot beach, grotesquely gasping before the mercy of death. Words did not come.

"Now, Bertram, this isn't so bad," Whitman said in a patronizing tone. "There is no reason why your family should ever see these photographs. No one at all need ever know. You will simply fly to Phoenix. Arrange an appointment with Brandon Reynolds. Show him the letter and the ring. He can call the number listed in the letter and ask any questions he wishes to ask, something that only she could answer. You understand, Bertram. Brandon Reynolds can do this for his own reassurance, so he will know for certain that his wife is fine. He can even hear her voice if he wishes. She will be able to speak to him. The rules are simple. All spelled out in the letter."

Russert did not move. He was no more than a statute.

Whitman continued. "This is it, Bertram, nothing complicated. Funds get transferred, old man Reynolds gets sweetie pie back into his little nest, and I go somewhere far away. I shall live the good life in another land. I have made my arrangements, Bertram. I've taken care of the details to begin a new life outside of this country."

Russert eyes glazed. He made no sound.

"Bertram, I know for a fact that Brandon Reynolds will pay the money and never make a stink. He just wants her back; that's all he cares about. You see I know what's going on inside his house. Hell, Bertram, I even know what's going on inside his head. The local cops are out of ideas, and the short-haired, white-shirted junior G-Men of the F-fucking-B-I won't touch this thing."

Unmitigated glee radiated from Whitman's face. "I'm not playing games with Brandon Reynolds. This is not some bullshit movie, not a bunch of *Mission Impossible* stuff, nothing that fancy. No secret letters hidden in a trash can in a park. No complicated procedures about how to transfer money so it can't be traced. None of that crap is involved here. This will be conducted in a businesslike manner between the two of you. Brandon Reynolds will simply electronically transfer the money into one of your family accounts. Now, Bertram, that's routine stuff for a man like Reynolds and business people such as your wife and you."

Whitman allowed a lull, creating time for reality to settle.

Like oil on water, the gravity of the situation was taking a while to sink in. Russert was incapable of speaking.

Whitman looked directly into Russert's eyes and commanded, "You will transfer the money to me. It's your business empire and you can make the transfer. You have full authority, and I expect you to do it."

Russert stared.

"It's easy, Bertram, easy. We'll all be winners. Queen for a fucking day!"

No response.

Whitman smiled again. "It's not like Reynolds and you are strangers. The two of you have previously met in your high-flying circles, and he knows exactly who and what he is dealing with. You tell him whatever you wish to tell him about me or why you are doing this. You do what you have to do. I don't care. Just get me my money, and I will uphold my end of the bargain and leave everyone alone."

Silence. Oil on water expanding.

"Bertram, you make damned sure you understand what I'm saying. If everything does not go exactly as I specify, my friends will take care of Mrs. Reynolds and you and you alone will be responsible for her death." Whitman paused. "And of course, your love for little girl pussy will be exposed to the world."

Silence. Russert was shaken; oil and water emulsified.

Whitman relentlessly stared into Russert's face as he continued. "I'm leaving this country, never coming back. My marriage ended long ago, and I have set myself up to live a new life in a whole new world. I have established a new identity. Mark Whitman will no longer exist, and I shall begin my new life whether you help me or not. My plans are set regardless of how this turns out." Whitman hesitated as he smiled. "I just prefer to leave with a few million extra in my account. Of course, I will like it better if I am never identified. But if I am, so be it. I am going forward regardless, and I will never be found."

Bertram Russert offered no response.

Silence.

"It's your call, Bertram. You cast the deciding vote. End of story, happily ever after, and all that good shit."

Silence.

Whitman felt detached. He wanted to let Russert decide the life or death of another person. Force him to decide how far he would go to save his own precious hide. Whitman held no doubt what the outcome would be, but it was an enjoyable torture to administer.

"I have very good information that Brandon Reynolds will do absolutely nothing after he gets his wife back," Whitman said matter-of-factly. "He wants this nightmare to be over and done with. No cops, no trial, no testimony, no reliving the whole thing. I know, Bertram. Trust me. I have someone on the inside. I know what Brandon Reynolds says every day. He wants this ordeal over with."

Russert still did not speak. His breathing was shallow, coming in scarcely audible gasps.

"What do you say, Bertram? Do the photos go back into my desk, or do I find a friendly post office? I want you on an airplane tomorrow.

Brandon Reynolds is home. I know he is. Schedule your meeting with him and this nightmare will be over for you in no time. Presto, you have your life back."

Hesitation hung in the air. The two men sat, evaluating, calculating.

"In fact, Bertram," Whitman continued. "It is absolutely accurate to say that you and only you can save your reputation and, of course, the life of Christine Reynolds. You are her executioner, or you are her savior." Whitman looked across the desk. He paused and then made his last pronouncement:

"The choice is yours, my good senator."

Russert managed to swallow hard.

The two men stared, neither blinking nor moving. Whitman glared, not backing down. Russert sought escape. None existed.

Russert moved for the first time since seeing the photographs. He brought his head down slightly and in a cracked whisper said, "I will do as you say."

"Splendid! Splendid!" Whitman's smile radiated as he clapped his hands together. "I knew you would do the right thing, Bertram. I have given you everything you need to resolve this quickly. Stay in touch as instructed and life will be grand for both of us."

Whitman's face beamed as if the past minutes had simply been a routine business meeting successfully negotiated with pleasant conversation. "Have a safe flight, Bertram. Enjoy some Arizona sunshine."

Russert nodded and tried to stand, but his legs quivered and refused to support his weight. He collapsed back into his chair, unable to move. He squeezed his eyes shut. Tears gathered in the cracks of his skin. As the droplets trickled down his cheeks, he opened his eyes to look at Whitman in one last plea for a shred of mercy.

Whitman smiled.

Summoning all his strength, Russert rose, holding to the arm of his chair for balance. Finally, he shuffled his feet across the floor, opened the door, and walked from Whitman's office.

———

IT WAS OVER. Breathing deeply, Whitman stood and walked to the door that Russert had left ajar. He quietly closed it and returned to his desk. Seated and with hands over his face, he processed what had just transpired. He went through the entire scenario again, visualizing every expression, every word. It had been perfect, and now his new life was within grasp. A smile appeared as he recalled the look on Russert's face. Whitman could not recall ever having enjoyed something so much.

There was no doubt that Russert would do exactly as he had been instructed. The man simply didn't have the balls to do anything else. Protecting his own ass was an instinct that was woven into the very fabric of Bertram Russert's life. He was as predictable as the sunrise.

After some time to enjoy the moment, Whitman called Felix Gomez. "Tomorrow we begin. Be ready."

"Good, we are prepared." Felix's voice betrayed both relief and anticipation.

"And Felix, the other job, is everything in place?"

"Absolutely."

"Tonight. I want it done tonight."

"Tonight it is. I'll call you when it's finished."

"Felix, you know how important this is. It must happen quickly and without problems. A lot is riding on this."

"I understand. I promise everything will go exactly as planned."

"Alright, I'll look forward to your call no matter the time. I have to know immediately."

"It will happen."

"And by the way, have you noticed that I wired half your payment to your account?"

"Yes, I'm aware of that. Thank you. This is almost over."

"Yes, my wealthy friend. It's only a matter of hours now. Stay in touch."

Rising from his chair, Whitman walked about his office, reflecting on the mementos that had taken years to accumulate: diplomas and awards, symbols of a life's work and accomplishment. He stood before photographs, recalling each event and celebrity with whom he posed. His eyes swept over the books that filled his shelves. Whitman returned to his chair, sat down, and traced his fingertips over the top of his desk. He felt its texture and thought of the countless hours he had toiled in this very spot. Muffled sounds of traffic came from the streets below and a murmur of cool air blew through vents in the ceiling. "I won't miss a damned thing," he spoke softly into the silence of his office.

Even if Russert should go to the FBI or police, let the simple-minded fuckers try to find me, he thought. *All arrangements are in place.*

Whitman glanced at his watch. A massage sounded great. He had made arrangements to fuck the black woman later that evening. He welcomed erotic visions into his mind, enjoying the warm pressure that surged between his legs. He wondered if all women from Jamaica, or wherever the hell she was from, had tits as beautiful as hers.

Whitman gathered the photographs that had been left strewn about the floor and placed them, along with a few other items, into his briefcase. He stood for a moment behind his desk. With a deep breath, he stood perfectly straight. With exaggerated and deliberate motions, he adjusted his tie, picked up his briefcase, and in measured strides, crossed the floor. Stepping through the door and without speaking to another person, Mark Whitman left his office for the last time. He walked away from his life. Forever.

———

BRAD MOVED AIMLESSLY through his house. Coffee mug in hand, he was unable to think of anything except what may have happened during the night after he left Yogi and Grant. He knew he would hear from someone as soon as they caught a break and had a chance to call. But waiting was a killer.

It was time to visit Elizabeth, see what her eyes had to say this morning. He poured fresh coffee and stood in front of her photograph.

His eyes traced the lines of her face, as beautiful as the night of their first date. After a few seconds, he spoke out loud, "Well, my dear, yesterday was quite a day. Do you care to tell me what sort of adventures today holds?" Her smile was there, illuminating and beautiful, but her eyes held the penetrating look of the past few days. No sparkle. Elizabeth was not backing down.

Brad walked through his house, sipping coffee and killing time. His eyes fell on a photograph of his two sons, fly rods in their hands and standing on the bank of Stone Creek. What a day that had been. He had meandered with his sons, admiring their ability to delicately place a tiny fly in just the perfect spot and then masterfully bring a fighting trout into their net. After each catch, just as he had taught them, there was always a moment of respect before the reverent release back into the river. For Brad and his sons, releasing a wild trout back into the water was not all that different from a religious ritual.

He and his sons had spent that magical day fishing and talking, sharing bits of their lives. As always happened when Brad embraced memories of fishing with his sons, his mind ultimately took him to Elizabeth and the life they had made together. He missed her more with every passing day.

Meghan's photograph sat next to his sons. She lived for music and Brad would never forget the brightness and pleasure his daughter had always brought into their home. He had watched her talent develop, and before she left for college, he would seek her out and say, "Come give your poor old dad a concert." Meghan's face would roll in contrived exasperation and say, "Again." But her blue eyes smiled. Her voice never failing to enchant him as she sang the songs he most loved: "Candle on the Water," "All I Ask of You," "Don't Cry for Me Argentina."

With thoughts of his children and Elizabeth churning within his mind, Brad took his coffee to the flower garden and sat beneath the aspen tree. A lot had happened yesterday, and he didn't even know all that may have happened in the night. This whole thing was feeling so strange. He had to come to grips with the fact that even though he was involved in a really good case, he was still on the outside, not working hard with the guys. Brad thought back to the cabin. Had his actions contaminated a crime scene?

He felt what was becoming too familiar: a knot in his stomach. His thoughts persisted. On the other hand, if it weren't for what he had done, no one would even know about the crime scene. If it weren't for his actions, the preacher would never have been able to find the house last night, and there would be no link between King Solomon, the house, and the preacher.

But what really gnawed at Brad went beyond King Solomon. It was a nagging feeling, something telling him that a piece of the puzzle was missing. Those damned little voices refused to go away. What about Christine Reynolds? How did her disappearance relate to any of this? There was no evidence to establish a logical connection at all to the cabin or to the bizarre activities of the preacher in Denver.

But those damned voices.

Brad knew that at some point in time, and probably pretty darned soon, the cabin would have to be searched. They could not postpone that much longer. Something had to happen to force this thing.

Just then his cell phone rang. Brad knew in an instant that his friend was on fire. "Are you sitting down?" Kurt asked with energy.

"It's about time. I've been dying to hear from you!"

Kurt grunted an insult before speaking. "Here's what I can tell you, Brad. About three this morning, Denver PD and your Bureau friend from Oklahoma hit the house that you spotted yesterday. By the way, Dick Tracy, nice going on that one. I guess even a blind pig finds an occasional acorn."

"Cut the crap and tell me what happened in the search."

Kurt Riddle gave a quiet chuckle. "Well, they tell me the place had been cleaned out. Obviously, someone left in a major hurry. But not in such a hurry that they didn't wipe the place down and leave everything polished pretty clean. Some clothes were lying around, stuff for both adults and kids. Mostly they found just trash and junk. Lab guys are still in there doing their thing, but they're not finding much."

"Oh man, I was hoping for something good."

"Don't give up so easily, J. Edgar. There's more."

"Come on, Kurt, what the hell did they find?"

"Cripes, you're jumpy this morning. How much coffee have you had?" Kurt Riddle was enjoying himself as he continued. "God love some Denver police officer. In the garage, they left a bag of trash filled with nothing but rotten food and really fun shit. In the middle of the spoiled bananas and soured tuna salad was a motel receipt from Glenwood Springs, that lovely mountain town right next door to Aspen. Now get this. Check-in date was two days before the Aspen lady disappeared and check-out was the day she went missing."

"Are you serious?"

"Serious as a heart attack."

"Wow!"

"OK, Whistledick, for a cold beer, I'll let you in on some top-secret stuff. Whose name do you think was on the receipt?"

"Kurt, I'm dying. Tell me."

"The name was none other than Felix Gomez, my friend. Mister Felix Gomez. Now, maybe it's just a coincidence, but that's one of the names from King Solomon's visiting list at the Virginia joint."

"Holy shit. Does Trathen know about this?"

"Oh, yeah! That young man has been a tornado in a flour factory. He started pulling people out of bed long before sunrise. The motel folks remember the room well, two guys and a woman. They particularly recalled that the last day the room was occupied, the people were adamant that they didn't want housekeeping in their room. The motel folks suspected some sort of drug activity and just stayed out of the way."

Brad interrupted. "There damned sure was something inside that room that those people didn't want anyone to see and it wasn't drugs. It was a person, Kurt, a person! This is starting to make sense now. They had Christine Reynolds in that room!

"That's exactly what Sam and I are thinking."

"Man alive."

Riddle continued, "The motel people say they drove a car and a pick-up truck. From the description they provided, it sounds like the same truck you saw yesterday and at the cabin. The motel wasn't able to confirm anything about the license plate though. They failed to get that information when your fine friends registered. Everything was paid in cash, no credit cards."

"I'm speechless." Brad whispered.

"Yeah, well, don't have your heart attack yet, Ace, 'cause I ain't finished." Kurt Riddle was absolutely having fun now. "Isn't it amazing what police can accomplish when they work all night while the Feds are sleeping?"

"I was waiting for that one, you prick."

"My, my. A bit sensitive, aren't you? Now listen, there are a couple of other things you need to know. Sam Trathen has a photo from Virginia, an image of a beautiful human being known as King Solomon. It's probably the same photo that you got from parole. The motel folks have positively identified the great King Solomon as being one of the three people registered in the room. How about them apples, Mister Hoover?"

Brad's head was spinning so fast he truly was speechless for a few seconds.

"What are you planning to do next? What about looking inside the cabin?"

"Sam and I have talked about it, and we are in agreement. In light of all that has happened overnight, we're not going to rush in just yet. Give it a few more hours at least. We got some guys in there yesterday after we talked, and they set up housekeeping in your cave. Nobody's been snooping around the cabin so far. We'll keep it under surveillance a while longer until we see where this thing is going."

"All this is incredible!"

"I agree with you for sure. There has been absolutely no sign of life at King Solomon's uncle's house. Plus, we flew an airplane over Elk Run early this morning hoping to spot the truck. No sign of it yet, but we'll keep looking. Of course, he could have parked it in a garage on the ranch, and we'll never see it."

"How about King Solomon's mother and uncle? Are you going to contact them?

"We have to find them for sure. If Phil Taylor is right, mother dear may not even know anything about her little darling King Solomon. But we've got guys out looking for her as we speak."

"Yeah, you've got to talk to Mom. May be waste of time, but you have to do it."

"What we sure as hell need to do is find King Solomon. If he gets spooked, this could blow up in our faces. And the longer this drags on, the chances of finding any kids or Mrs. Reynolds go way down and fast. We've got to be really careful."

"But, Kurt, don't you think that since the house has been searched, King Solomon is probably already spooked? It may be time to blow this open."

"I agree, but the house search still hasn't tipped our hand that we know what was inside the cabin. King Solomon doesn't know how much we know. It's a tricky call."

"That's right, it sure as hell is. I wish I had a magic answer."

"I wish somebody had a magic answer, Brad. Life would be a hell of a lot easier if we could feel safe in talking to the ranch management. But I don't see much choice here. We can't go too much longer without letting the cat out of the bag. No matter how big of an asshole the Owens kid may be, we're going to have to go public, start asking questions, and get inside the cabin. Let the chips start falling."

"I agree, Kurt," Brad said. "Something's gotta start moving." He was quiet for a moment. "It almost killed me to walk away from that search last night. I thought I was going to explode."

"Hey, I know how you feel. But you have my promise. I will keep you up on all developments as they happen today. It's the least I can do for an old friend who has gone senile long before his time."

"And I suppose you want me to say thanks?"

"Jesus, you can be an ass," Kurt said with a laugh. "Oh yeah, there's one other thing. Then I have to get back to work. That shit I gave you about the FBI sleeping all night. I take it back. Your friend, Yogi, was great. And Rick Barnes was with the Denver police all night. In fact, as we speak, Barnes is on his way to Aspen to hook up with Sam. The FBI in Phoenix has put guys with the Phoenix PD. They're pulling out all the stops to find something on Gomez and the Sanchez girl, trying to find a connection somewhere. They're looking at those phone numbers and doing every check imaginable. There are a million Felix Gomez and Maria Sanchez characters, so sorting out who is who and finding the correct people is a challenge. It may take some time, but it'll happen. At least for now, they're concentrating on the Washington, DC, and Virginia areas."

"It's about damned time the Bureau pulled the plug out of its ass. I was more than a little pissed off. Let's just hope and pray something will turn real soon. This could turn really bad, really quickly"

"I'm praying, Brad. I'm praying," Kurt said somberly.

"Thanks, Kurt. You didn't have to call me. I appreciate this more than you know."

"Not a problem. Besides, Sam threatened me with bodily harm if I didn't call you. He's missing you bad."

"I'm missing you guys too. I'm about to die. Call me when you can."

"You got it."

Brad left the flower garden and stepped back inside his house. *Lord, it's quiet in here.* He closed his eyes. He could feel the energy of the investigation that was consuming his friends. He imagined the hushed conferences, loud meetings, phones ringing, strategy planning, and prioritizing leads. It would all happen at once. How to handle the press? What to tell? What to withhold? Who should be interviewed? What information may be contained in the human trafficking investigation? It went on forever. The guys would run on adrenaline. They wouldn't eat. They wouldn't sleep. They would not call their families. They would simply work the case. Nothing else but the case.

Brad kicked at the floor as he cursed out loud. "And here I am, sitting on my ass at home while other people do the work. Jesus H. Christ!"

Brad wandered room to room. He felt trapped. His mind went back to the first night at the cabin. Three people lifting something from the trunk, carrying it through the rain. He recalled how he had walked away that night, leaving whatever or whoever inside. His stomach roiled as he whispered to his empty house, "Oh God, what should I have done? Am I responsible for what has happened? How will I ever live with myself? And how the hell do little kids figure into this? Have I even brought harm to children?"

Slumping into a chair, Brad dropped his head to his knees and squeezed his eyes shut so tightly it hurt. Perhaps he could purge the images of that night. In his mind he was there again: darkness, rain, lightning, the cabin, an opened trunk, a bundle, a ponytail. There she was, his mother, inside the cabin, waving to him. Please, come inside.

Across the room Elizabeth's photograph silently watched as her husband endured torment. Had Brad opened his eyes and looked at Elizabeth, he would have seen her pain. But he would also have seen something more. Her eyes spoke caution and warning. *This is nowhere near over for you.*

———

Evening's final glow lingered, mellow and warm. The sun gave an illusion of dipping into the Pacific Ocean as it cast a blood-red hue over the sky. Darkness finally edged twilight. On a ridge rising above the sea were vacation cottages glowing in the night. Millions of stars kept watch as a moist breeze skimmed the salty water. Lace curtains suspended behind open windowpanes fluttered like butterflies over the village below. From a distance, Latin rhythms floated in festive sounds from a cantina. The cottages offered secluded refuge, mostly to Americans on holiday in western Mexico.

No one saw the man dressed in black who silently slid a key into the door of the rented Mercedes Benz that was parked in front of one of the cottages. He easily slid a kilo of cocaine under the driver's seat.

The man quietly closed the automobile door and walked away.

———

WHITMAN LAY in the bed of his hotel room. The black broad was in the shower. She had excited him beyond words. It didn't mean a damn to him that toward the end she got angry because he slapped her tits harder than she liked. He sipped on bourbon, at ease with himself and thoughts of how he would enjoy her body again. She better calm down in the shower because he sure as hell wasn't finished with her yet.

Whitman swirled his drink, immersed in the euphoria of alcohol and a beautiful, naked woman. All Whitman needed was a phone call from Felix, reassuring him that everything had been handled. Then he would be ready for her again. She damn well better learn who was boss. What the hell, he might even take her with him when he left the country. Her mouth and tits would be a superb pleasure from time to time. With that thought, an idea began to formulate. He was about to become enormously wealthy. Why not simply buy the bitch? The fantasy solidified and his penis surged. Buy her. Fuck her. Sell her when he got tired of her. Buy another one.

Mark Whitman was fully erect.

———

JUDGE WILLIAM HOLLOWAY was well on his way to a state of inebriation. Gentle ocean breezes and soft Latin music held no interest for him. He had come to Mexico to get some ass from a young Mexican boy, and for three days he had been getting the run-around. Each night, it was the same apology, "We're so sorry. We want the best for you. We will make it up to you; you will see. You will get the best." That goddamned Whitman owed him a fucking refund.

The knock on the door was barely audible. Holloway threw the door open, an angry scowl burning across his face. His eyes took in the young girl standing at the door, an even younger boy by her side.

"It's about time. Get in the house."

He stepped aside to let the children enter. He spoke to the girl, "Take him to the bedroom and you wait out here."

Her soft eyes looked down to the floor. "Yes, I will wait," she said.

Holloway slammed shut the door to his bedroom. He was so drunk he had trouble removing his pants. In his struggle, he was oblivious to the fact that the young girl had departed from the house. He was also unaware of the backpack that she left outside the bedroom door.

What happens in the moment of death has been the subject of theological conjecture, scientific hypothesis, and general speculation for centuries. Did Judge Holloway see his last second on earth like a series of photographs passing before him in slow motion? Did he see his penis as it ripped from his body? Was his penis still in the young boy's mouth as the small skull flew across the room, before shattering into countless fragments? Did Holloway feel the shock wave of the bomb that disintegrated furniture and glass into a deadly ballistic shower?

Or was it a simple blink into unconscious, eternal blackness?

The report from the Mexican Police did not address such esoteric reflections. In a matter of hours, the US Embassy would receive notification that William Holloway, a retired federal judge, had been killed in an attack. Preliminary investigation determined that the attack was apparently related to the judge's illicit involvement in the trade and distribution of cocaine. A kilo of cocaine discovered in his automobile would be held as evidence. Mexican authorities would pursue the investigation and report findings to the embassy and to the DEA.

Mexican officials in charge of the matter were satisfied with the money they had been paid to manipulate the investigation and to conduct no further inquiry.

———————

CLIMAX WAS imminent when Whitman's phone rang. He took the call. The hotel room was silent for a few moments as he listened, then spoke in a matter-of-fact tone. "Thank you, Felix. Everything else will happen very quickly now. Are you certain that you're ready?"

Moments of silence.

"Very well. We'll speak soon."

Whitman continued with the black girl. Everything had gone perfectly.

His mind was made up, no doubt at all. He would buy this bitch.

TUESDAY, SEPTEMBER 11

TUESDAY, September 11, a day of remembrance across America, dawned over Colorado while Brad took a run. As he wove his way through a trail of ponderosa pines, he realized that autumn had made her entrance. Above him, at about ten thousand feet, aspens shimmered gold and red and soft brown washed over the meadow grasses. The surest sign of fall was a bull elk in autumn's rut. The elegant beast reared his head, thrusting his nose to the sky. Massive antlers, like small trees, extended the length of his body. Haunting and shrill, his guttural bugle proclaimed his sexual excitement, his quest for romance.

Dripping wet and starved, Brad concluded his workout with push-ups and crunches and then drove home to Willie Nelson singing with Ray Charles "Seven Spanish Angels." The previous day had been one of the longest of his life. Self-doubt continued to persist and a sense of isolation increased with passing hours. Yogi was flying back to Oklahoma today, so they were meeting for a quick coffee before his flight. Some time with his old friend would help a lot.

Brad had talked with the guys and knew that the FBI and Phoenix Police Department were doing everything imaginable. An old drug case that involved Felix Gomez and Maria Sanchez had been located under their noses, right in Phoenix. Information from that old case offered the most promising leads. Gomez and Sanchez apparently held Virginia driver's licenses but, as of yet, nothing had linked them with Colorado. Sam Trathen was going to show their photographs at the motel in Glenwood Springs. The results of what came out of that would be a big deal. In all likelihood, within hours, the case was going to take some major turns. That's why Brad wanted his run out of the way first thing. He wasn't sure what he would end up doing today, but he damned well knew he was going to do something.

After a shower and shave, Brad drove down the mountain to meet Yogi. The coffee shop was crowded, but they found a table on an outdoor patio that offered privacy. "When is your flight?" Brad asked.

"In about three hours, if you can believe the airlines anymore. Thanks for driving down to see me, Brad. We needed this chance to get together before I blow out of here."

"I wouldn't miss it for anything, Yogi. I miss your ugly face."

Yogi gave a quick smile. "Come on Brad, you know that you wish you were half as handsome as me."

"Yogi, believe me when I tell you that I've had trout in my net that had prettier faces than yours."

Yogi threw his head back and laughed. Yogi's laugh was the happiest and most infectious that Brad had ever known. It was just one of many things that he missed about his old friend.

Yogi smiled and said, "Wow! Has this ever been a whirlwind trip. No time for smoking and joking, and sure as hell no sleep."

"That's what I've gathered. What's surprising to me, though, is that you've been in town over twenty-four hours and haven't been arrested or caused an international incident. You're slowing down, Yogi. Not the same guy from our old days."

His sense of humor always brimming, Yogi laughed. "I wish I could argue the point, but you're right, my old ass is definitely slowing down. However, no matter the reasons for my good behavior, we got some big-time shit accomplished in the last day or so."

"Alright, before you leave for the hills of Oklahoma, tell me, what do you think of all that's going on here?"

Without hesitation, Yogi responded confidently, "I think there's a hell of a case here if we can just make it all come together. Since I arrived in Denver, most of my time was spent with preacher boy and searching that damned house. After we finished searching the house, we tore across town and did a toss at the uncle's place. Then we found King Solomon's mother and talked with her. Mom seems to be a straight shooter and swears she hasn't had any contact with her son."

"What about Uncle and his place?"

"He seems to have left town several days ago, and nobody knows where he is. We got a warrant for his house but found almost nothing inside—a few sticks of furniture and a coffee pot was about it. The Denver guys are digging into his background as we speak."

"Well, Yogi, you're the one who was right there in the middle of everything, but it's hard for me to believe that either his mom or his uncle, living right here in town, don't have some idea about what he's been up to."

"I agree, Brad. It seems logical, but his mother was pretty convincing. I always assume that mothers are lying about their sons, but she's either telling the truth or the best actress I've seen in a while. I really think she's over King Solomon and ready to wash her hands of him."

"I wonder if it's coincidence that his uncle left town, or did he smell something bad coming?"

"I don't know the answer to that one, Brad. Time will tell. But listen to this. Just before I got here to meet you, I was on the phone with our office in Chicago. They've turned up the true name of the asshole who was fixing the preacher up with little girls."

"That's fantastic!"

"Hell, yes, it's fantastic." Yogi put on reading glasses and pulled notes from the pocket of his jacket. "He's a guy named Melendez. Chicago said he has a long record for all kinds of stuff but dealing in prostitution and kids is his major history."

Brad shook his head. "Now isn't that a surprise!"

"He also got popped in El Paso, Texas, about a year ago. He was hooked up with some guys from Mexico who drove vans and trucks all over the country delivering illegals to various parts of the country. El Paso Police and Customs and Border Patrol worked the case but couldn't make it to court, so he got cut loose. I talked to the investigators down there to get the full story."

"I think I know what's coming."

"I'm sure you do, Brad. They told me the vans carried mostly poor, hard-working people just trying to get into the United States to find jobs. Maybe make a better life for their families. It may be illegal, but who the hell can blame them?"

Brad simply shrugged.

"The case that the El Paso Police were trying to make had to do with the fact that Melendez mixed kids in with the workers." Yogi peered over the top of his reading glasses, his eyes drilling into Brad. "I'll let you guess what he did with the kids."

Brad looked at the floor. They both knew what happened to the children.

Yogi leaned back in his chair, sipping his coffee. "Chicago is getting turned inside out today. There's half an army looking for the guy. My money says he will be in a jail cell before day's end. I sure hope so."

Brad was reflective before speaking. "What's your opinion of what was going on in the house you guys searched? After all that time you were inside, touching and smelling, what's your gut tell you?"

"Oh, hell, Brad, it stinks to high heaven. Whoever was there had gone to the trouble to clean up and wipe things down pretty good. But still, there was plenty of crap left lying around."

"Yeah, I heard about the trash bag that had some good stuff in it."

"They definitely made a mistake by leaving their trash. I don't know if they were stupid, rushed, or careless, but whatever the reason, I'm sure glad they screwed up. Man, oh man, Brad, that Denver cop deserves a medal. Believe me when I tell you there were some smelly bags of shit left behind."

Brad chuckled.

"But here's what got all of us that night. The trash bags had all kinds of stuff, food and crap. But they also had magazines, newspapers, used toiletries and so forth, all the kind of stuff that would have been used by adults. Yet, we knew that kids had been living there. But, Brad, we found not much more than scraps that were evidence of kids having been there. Some clothing and stuff were all we found. But that was it, nothing else at all for kids. There were no books, no video games or toys. There sure as hell was no school stuff, nothing at all to make a life for a kid. It painted a very ugly picture. Brad, I almost cried. The closest thing we found to anything fun for a kid was in one of the trash bags. We pulled out a pretend pearl necklace and some sort of plastic crown. They were what little girls would use to play dress-up. Jesus Christ! I sat there looking at that stuff thinking about all the horrible things that I had heard from that sick, goddamned preacher. Brad, it killed me. I thought of my daughters. I thought of your daughter."

For a moment both men were quiet.

After collecting himself, Yogi looked straight at Brad. "Sometimes, Brad, I want to tell the Bureau to kiss my smelly old ass and just go off on my own, conduct a one-man vigilante campaign against the millions of assholes that populate this earth."

"Don't go by yourself, Yogi." Brad breathed in deeply, shook his head, and spoke softly. "We'll do it together."

They both grinned. They understood each other. It was a fantasy, but a fantasy that sure as hell felt good.

Yogi spoke again. "We did a good neighborhood canvas around the house. The neighbors all said they never saw any kids outside, only a few adults around in the day. We showed photos of your King Solomon guy and got several hits. That guy spent a bunch of time there. The neighbors say that most of the activity at the house was at night, lots of cars coming and going, people in and out. At the time, the neighbors had no idea what was going on." Yogi paused, rolling his eyes. Then he stared straight at Brad. "I think we sure as hell know now what was going on."

Brad nodded but remained silent.

Hesitating again, Yogi spoke in a soft whisper, "My friend, we were a day late and a dollar fucking short."

"It sure seems that way," Brad said, tilting his head back and looking straight up.

Yogi leaned over the table, eyes burning. "This is killing me, Brad. Where in hell are the kids who were living in that house?"

The two men held their coffee, saying nothing as they took in their surroundings. They watched, felt, and listened to the people around them: chic women dressed in business suits, spiked heels and sparkling jewelry. Tennis outfits, tanned legs, and designer sunglasses were all about. Well-dressed men fresh from the gym laughed with the women as they shared expensive lattes and delicate pastries. Conversations were of new cars and winter skiing plans. Brad could read Yogi like a book. They had worked together for twenty years. Yogi was thinking exactly the same things Brad was thinking: what a screwed up world. How can some people have so much and others never even have a chance?

Brad shifted his body, set his coffee down, and interrupted their thoughts. "Yogi, the last I heard there's been no sign of King Solomon. Any ideas?"

Moving his head from side to side, Yogi responded despondently, "No, not at all. I don't have any vibes on that. He may be right here in town or he may be in Mexico. I wish I knew."

"I'm telling you, Yogi. I've felt all along that in some way this case here, with King Solomon, is connected to the other case I told you about, the missing lady from Aspen. The motel papers you guys found in the trash did a lot to confirm that hunch. Then add the fact that the motel people banged King Solomon's photo, I think I've been right all along."

"Your instincts were sure as hell spot-on about the house. None of us can predict where this is all going to end up, and it's a long way from being over. But I'm with you. I think it's all the same people swimming in one big cesspool." Removing his glasses and rubbing his brow, Yogi was quiet.

"You and I have never been much for praying, Yogi, but maybe we should start." Brad paused. "I think there are some people out there that need a little help from the big headquarters upstairs right now."

Yogi sighed. "You're right about that. Look, I've got to get to the airport and once I'm sailing along at thirty thousand feet, I'll sure as heck pray." Yogi paused and grinned. "I just hope God isn't so shocked to hear from me after all these years that he blasts my airplane right out of the sky."

Brad and Yogi stood and smiled and shook hands. They had so much history together: weddings, families, investigations, and Elizabeth's death. There was nothing to say. They each walked away.

Thirty minutes later and back in the quiet of his house, Brad sat down and reflected on his conversation with Yogi, the house that had been searched, and what had been found. He thought about what had not been found. He thought about his night in the cave. It was the same old question. *Oh, God, what should I have done?*

————

FOR ONCE, dealing with traffic actually felt good. Brad drove down the mountain for his second time that day. The interstate at least offered a temporary diversion from his second-guessing and constant wondering about what was happening. He knew he couldn't sit around his house all day. As he drove, he plotted within his mind the locations of the houses of King Solomon's uncle and mother, as well as the house that had been searched. There simply was not enough information to know why King Solomon would choose a particular part of town or where he might be at this moment. What was logical?

Upon reaching the western edge of the Denver suburbs, Brad pulled over to examine a real map. He knew the area pretty well but certainly not every little nook and cranny. Could there be other houses that King Solomon may be using? Obviously, by now King Solomon knew that the police were breathing down his neck. In all probability he would be avoiding all his former haunts. If his truck was not at Elk Run, where was it? There were hundreds of possibilities, but if Brad had to bet, he would put his money on King Solomon laying low in a motel. He wished he had some idea of other vehicles to look for. But what the hell. He should start checking. What did he have to lose?

He decided to work along Sixth Avenue, Colfax, and the interstate. Those corridors held a majority of the motels and fast food places for the area. Block by block, he methodically cruised streets and parking lots, concentrating on areas around motels. Brad wanted so badly to spot the pick-up truck, but it didn't feel right. He had no sense that he was on the right track. He certainly had no feelings of clairvoyance like he had felt when he heard about the Oklahoma preacher or when he had stood in the clearing over the Cotter estate. But he kept looking. King Solomon had to be somewhere.

When his phone rang and he saw that it was his son, Michael, Brad pulled over to answer.

"Hey, Pops, what's going on?" Michael's voice, as always, was full of life.

Brad and his son swapped some small talk before Michael broke the ice. "Dad, you sound really pooped, stressed out, or something. Everything okay?"

Brad considered how to respond. For all practical purposes, he regarded Michael as an adult, and he really did want to talk. "Well, now that you bring it up, I guess I do need to tell you about the last few days of your old man's life." Brad related to Michael what he had seen in the storm and the subsequent events that led him prowling around motel parking lots on a beautiful autumn afternoon. The only things Brad left out were the parts about Elizabeth's photograph and his inexplicable feelings that she somehow communicated with him.

"Wow, Dad! What do you think all this means? Since the police and FBI are working the case now, haven't you done enough? Can't you just, like, pass it to them and maybe go fishing?"

Brad thought about what his son said. *How much did Michael understand? How could he even suggest I walk away from this?* Was now the time for a father-son talk?

"Well, son, you just asked me a few questions. I think the best thing is to take them one at a time. First, as far as what does all of this mean, I don't suppose I know yet, at least not with absolute certainty. But I sure as heck have my intuition and gut instinct. I think that I have stumbled upon something really serious here, something that reaches far beyond Colorado."

"Really?"

"You remember when Mom was prosecuting sex crimes? You were old enough that we had some talks about what she did. Remember those times when she bounced back and forth from anger to near depression? You know how upset I would be sometimes when I came home after I had gotten involved in a case that I thought was particularly heinous?"

"Yeah, sure, Dad, I remember."

"Well, the last few days have been those very things all over again. Sometimes this stuff involves plain old prostitution and people argue for days about whether or not there really is a victim and so forth. But this is different, Michael. What we're talking about here are kids. Much of the time these kids are runaways, maybe from abuse or neglect. It can involve any number of reasons, but the bottom line is the same: the person who suffers is always a kid who is vulnerable and frightened. Then, along come despicable people who see opportunity. They prey on the victims and hurt them all over again through pornography and prostitution."

"I remember you and Mom talking about this."

"Those photos I found in the cabin are what this stuff is all about. Every time I close my eyes, I see those photos. Those are real people, real kids. We can never forget that, Son."

"I don't get it, Dad. I just don't see what can make people be like that?"

"Oh, it's lots of things but mostly it's just greed. There is a ton of money to be made. People are lined up for miles to make a buck with no regard that somewhere in the mix a real person is being destroyed. Excuse my language, Son, but it is a fucked-up world."

"That's the only way to describe it."

"Michael, let me tell you something. When it comes down to dollars versus human dignity, dollars will win almost every time. It is a hell of a sad commentary on humanity."

"Dad, I'm so sorry that you've been dragged into this. It's gotta bring back memories of your FBI days and thoughts of Mom."

"I can't deny that, Michael. But in this particular case, what causes my antennae to go up is this King Solomon guy and the guy from Chicago who was arranging kids for the preacher. Their histories indicate that they're involved not only in child prostitution, but also in trafficking kids across the border and all over the country. I think that's what we're into here."

"Dad, doesn't it seem incredible that in the twenty-first century this crap can still be happening?"

"It is absolutely incredible, Michael, absolutely incredible. People are brought across the border for everything from cheap vegetables to sex, adults and children are brought into this country for a life that is virtual slavery."

"Dad, I feel terrible. I guess I've heard this before, but I admit I have never really thought about what is actually happening."

"Michael, you're just like millions of other people who are simply not paying attention. But I can damn sure tell you we need to be paying attention. Our inattention results in horrible suffering for so many people, right under our noses, in our own country."

"Okay, Dad, I guess I've never thought this through like I should have."

"Don't be too hard on yourself. You've already thought about it more than most people."

The telephone was quiet. Brad did not rush his son. Then Brad spoke again. "Now, about the fishing," Brad said. He smiled to himself as he visualized Michael's face on the other end. He knew what his son was going to say.

"Dad, don't go fishing until you figure this out. I was dead wrong."

"You weren't wrong Michael. You just didn't understand the big picture. Now you do."

Michael was quiet again. "What are you going to do?"

"Oh, I'm not positive at the moment. Somehow talking with you has opened my eyes. I know for sure that I'm just wasting my time driving around like an idiot cruising motels. I'll probably go home, get a call in to Yogi, Kurt, or Sam and figure something out. But, Michael, I'm telling you. Somehow, some way this is all going to come together. I got a hunch."

"Dad, do you know how many times we would be waiting on you for dinner and the phone would ring? Before Mom would even answer, she would know it was you telling us to go ahead and eat because you were going be late. She would make a face and say, 'Your father is chasing a hunch again; maybe we'll see him at breakfast.' Meghan or I would tell her that you were really out fishing somewhere, and she would just shake her head."

Michael laughed and Brad thought he sounded like Michael again. Everything was fine.

"Okay, wise guy, I was going to offer you a steak dinner next time you come home. Forget it. Eat your college food."

"Hey, Pops, thanks for talking with me. I miss you. I want you to catch whoever the heck it is you have to catch. Just be careful."

"Don't worry, kid. I'm way too old and slick for any jerk named King Solomon."

"I love you, Pops."

"I love you too, Michael. Study hard. Come home when you can."

———

It was time to go home. Brad steered his truck to go back up the mountain. Something was in store for him. He didn't know what, but it wasn't driving around in circles looking at sleazy old motels.

As Brad headed his car to the west and up the mountain, he drove slowly, thinking about his conversation with his son. He thought of Yogi and the search of the house. He thought of vans filled with poor people looking for a better opportunity, children at the mercy of others. The next song on Willie's CD began to play: "Living in the Promised Land." *What providence!* This was unbelievable timing. Brad had heard the song a million times, but the words had passed over him. Now he listened, really listened.

> *Give us your tired and weak and we will make them strong*
> *Bring us your foreign songs and we will sing along*
> *Leave us your broken dreams, we'll give them time to mend*
> *There's still a lot of love, living in the Promised Land*
> *Living in the Promised Land our dreams are made of steel*
> *The prayer of every man is to know how freedom feels*
>
> ----------
>
> *Give us our daily bread, we have no shoes to wear*
> *No place to call our home, only this cross to bear*
> *We are the multitudes, lend us a helping hand*
> *Is there no love anymore*
> *Living in the Promised Land*

WEDNESDAY, SEPTEMBER 12

BERTRAM RUSSERT COULD NOT RECALL HAVING EVER experienced such pain as what now throbbed within his head. The agony had begun after watching the morning news reports, and it had grown worse with each passing minute. He wasn't sure about the cause of his suffering. It could have been either what he had just heard on the news or the scotch he had consumed the previous evening. Most likely it was due to the fact that he had stepped through the gates of hell with his visit to Whitman's office. The source of his suffering really didn't matter. He just knew that his agony was intolerable.

Following Whitman's instructions, Russert had flown to Phoenix on a privately chartered jet and had not left his hotel room since arriving. He kept his shades drawn and wallowed in scotch, self-pity, and seething anger.

He had called Brandon Reynolds to set a time to meet. It had been one of the most difficult things he had ever done, but it was over. They were scheduled to get together in less than two hours. Russert stood in front of his bathroom mirror, looking into his bloodshot eyes. Could other people see the devastation that simmered within? Russert stared hard at his image. Could he do this? He scooped water onto his face with his hands. He felt it trickle down his chest and the back of his neck. He looked at himself in the mirror and spoke with a hoarse voice, "Yes, you can do this." He had no choice. It had to be done.

In the isolation of his hotel, Russert spent much time thinking of his wife and their sham marriage. They had been passionately in love at one time. What would it take to bring that passion back? Was it even possible? He thought of his children. Russert felt sick at the thought of what their lives would be if his actions were exposed.

Russert thought about the United States Senate. He thought about Mark Whitman. He had thought about Mark Whitman a lot.

His bare feet sank into the opulent carpet. He sat down and read Whitman's letter for the hundredth time. Pouring over each word, his brain still refused to comprehend the ramification of their message. This could not possibly be happening to him. All right, this has gone on long enough, he thought. I can awaken from this horrible nightmare anytime now. Tomorrow, I will be on the floor of the Senate, business as usual, lunch with a colleague, a concert in the Kennedy Center.

Russert did not awaken.

With the letter lifted high above his face, he sliced the letter's edge across the web of skin between his fingers. Like fingernails on a chalkboard, the pain prickled his nerves. Blood appeared in the sliver of a cut. He flicked his tongue across the tacky film. He tasted his own body. The letter was not a dream, not some lingering unpleasantness to be effortlessly cleansed with a sip of scotch or morning's mug of coffee.

The horrible experience he had endured in Whitman's office would not leave him. Russert closed his eyes, seeking refuge, any refuge. His thoughts drifted, and he floated back in time. He was a boy again, hearing sweet sounds of familiar gospel hymns. Russert could see himself clearly. The young boy wore a pressed shirt. His hair was oiled and combed. He sat in attentive wonder listening to religious instruction. All souls would someday stand before God, an inescapable moment when divine judgment would be pronounced. Bertram Russert would someday be called upon to account for the life he had lived.

What was happening? He was not a young boy. He was a United States senator in an Arizona hotel room. This was not the way it was supposed to be. Nothing was as he had been taught. Judgment day was supposed to take place in the court of heaven. But his judgment had not waited for death to seal the eyes of his mortal body. His judgment had risen up from the bowels of hell, flaying his living body. He had been denied the dignity of death. He was condemned while still alive. Russert closed his eyes to pray. God, is it too late? What can I do?

With his face in his hands, Russert tried to envisage his future. Would he ever again sleep through a night? Would he ever again laugh with another? Would he ever again visit his children or hold a grandchild?

His rocked back and forth and let out a moan from deep within his chest. Was it really too late? Could Whitman be anything other than Satan himself? Another pitiful moan. What if he were to deliver Satan, bring him to a pyre before God?

Russert's cell phone lay on a table beside him. He had already looked up the numbers for the Phoenix FBI and police department. The direct office line and home telephone for the director of the FBI were in his briefcase. Should he make the call and deliver the unspeakable truth? Could he deliver Satan? Would this save his soul? Or would it only add to his already unbearable torment, a sadistic mockery orchestrated by God himself?

Would his call save the life of Christine Reynolds? Would his call insure her death?

Russert stared at the telephone and pondered the consequences at stake.

He would do it.

He would bare his soul to the FBI, the police, and the world. He would deliver Satan.

It was time.

Extending his arm, his fingers touched the smooth plastic instrument. As if his hand probed into a den of vipers, the telephone sprang to life in an ear-splitting ring. Jolted from his introspection, Russert gaped, momentarily stupefied. His heart hammered. He half expected to hear the voice of God on the line.

He answered the phone with a tentative, "Yes."

The voice of Satan assaulted his throbbing head.

"Hello, Bertram, how nice to hear you."

Russert cringed at the sound of Whitman's voice.

"My friend, Bertram the baby-fucker, have you watched the news today?" Whitman spoke loudly, sounding jovial.

"Yes," Bertram replied hesitantly. "I have watched the news shows today."

"Then surely you know of the tragedy that has befallen our mutual friend, the esteemed retired judge, His Honor Holloway."

The news of Judge Holloway being involved in narcotics trafficking was just one more nightmare. He calculated his response. "Yes, I have heard the news."

"Sounds like old Holloway got one hell of a blow job, doesn't it?" Whitman howled.

Russert was revolted and sought to block out the sounds of Whitman's gloating. He refused to respond.

"Poor Bertram. Do I need to explain to you how the world turns? His Honor had simply outlived his usefulness. What more could he possibly offer?"

"What in God's name are you talking about?" Russert wheezed.

"I'll tell you what in God's name I'm talking about. I'm talking about His Honor Holloway and Bertram the baby-fucker. The two of you have been God's gift to me. I've already explained your role in the scheme of things, Bertram. You simply follow the instructions that I have given and soon this all will be a memory. Yes, Bertram, your life can continue on. However, His Honor Holloway, I'm sorry to say, just wasn't as lucky as you."

Russert was so disturbed, he had difficulty breathing.

"You see, Bertram," Whitman continued. "In addition to periodic vacations that I arranged for His Honor Holloway, vacations that were for the sole purpose of giving him discreet opportunity to stick his dick in little boys, His Honor was the uncle of Christine Reynolds. Now, don't you see that as divine providence? Because of His Honor Holloway's relation to the Reynolds' family, I have known every word spoken inside their house since sweetie pie got taken away. His Honor called old man Reynolds two or three times a day, inquiring about what had happened, what the police were doing, and what Mr. Reynolds planned to do. This has been so easy, much easier than I expected."

Russert bowed his head and rubbed his eyes. He was unable to speak.

"His Honor thought I was interested in entering into a joint business venture with him and old man Reynolds. His Honor thought the three of us would be business partners. He loved to impress me about how intimate he was with the Reynolds family. He told me every day how easy it was to speak with one of the wealthiest men on the planet. Come on, Bertram, aren't these juicy details wonderful?"

If Whitman anticipated a response, he was to be disappointed. Silence was all he received.

Apparently unconcerned with the lack of response from Russert, Whitman continued to spew his venom. "Now, what is good for you, Bertram, is that Reynolds has repeatedly told His Honor that he is willing to pay any amount for his wife. He has no interest to pursue this matter with police and the courts. All he wants is to have communication from whoever has her and for this whole thing to go away. No mess, no fuss, that's all he wants. The cops aren't getting anywhere with this, and the FBI isn't even interested. What an unbelievable scenario, don't you agree, Bertram? "

Russert felt nauseous and faint. He was unable to respond to Satan.

"Now, surely you understand, don't you, Bertram? I could never allow Holloway to know what was really happening. He was unpredictable. He could be volatile, half crazy. He wasn't like you, analytical and practical. I had to get rid of him before your talk with Reynolds. His Honor wouldn't have cared a bit about Mrs. Reynolds, whether she lives or dies. He only cared about himself. His Honor may very well have spoiled my opportunity to collect a modest amount of money in exchange for his precious little niece. There is no telling who he may have called or what he may have done. I just couldn't take that chance. You do agree, don't you, Bertram?"

Whitman laughed his hideous laugh.

Russert had no doubt he was conversing with Satan himself. He felt himself in a surreal state, as though he were Dante being guided through hell.

"Now, Bertram, your lot in this affair is much different. You have the ability to walk away from all of this, go right on with your life. But I again warn you. If you fail to do as I have instructed, my promise to you is that you will pray for a fate as merciful as Holloway's."

As morning mist dissipates under a rising sun, a veil lifted from Russert's eyes. Everything was suddenly perfectly clear. What had he been thinking? Why had he hesitated? There were no decisions to make, no alternatives to consider. His only option was perfectly obvious.

Releasing a sigh of relief, Russert now knew that he would go through with his plan. It would not be nearly as difficult as he had imagined.

"My meeting with Reynolds is scheduled," Russert whispered. "I will see him in just over an hour. I shall call you when we have concluded our discussion. I will tell you everything that happened."

"Good man, Bertram! I feel quite certain that after this unpleasantness passes, your life will proceed in a beautiful fashion. Hell, you may even again find someone to arrange little girls for you to fuck. Life is good, Bertram. Life is good."

Satan laughed again.

Russert had heard enough. "I will speak with you soon," he said and with that he pressed the button to terminate the call.

It was amazing. No longer did he feel dazed or unable to control his own destiny. His mind stopped spinning, and he felt tranquil at last. Whitman was absolutely correct. There was but one course to take. Nothing complicated. Just do what he had to do. Get it over with. Everything truly would be fine.

Russert walked to the window. He opened the drapes and let light pour in. The streets below pulsated with life. Stark but magnificent desert beauty encircled the city of Phoenix like a necklace around the throat of a beautiful woman. At peace with himself, he began to focus on what he must do.

The hotel telephone rang. Russert ignored it. No need for more conversation. He was prepared. His cell phone rang. Russert refused to even look. It was undoubtedly Whitman, angry that someone would be so bold as to hang up on him. He probably wanted one more opportunity to twist the knife. Russert unconsciously shook his head. *Screw Whitman. Enough talk. It is time for action,* he thought. A shower would feel good. Then he would get the horrible ordeal over with.

The very marrow of his bones seemed to boil. He turned the water to cold until he stood beneath an icy spray. Russert was certain he heard the sound of hissing steam rise from his body.

After showering, Russert dressed and sat on the couch. A calmness that he had not experienced in months settled within his mind. He placed Christine Reynolds' ring on the coffee table beside Whitman's letter. Russert read the dooming words again. The diamond ring seemed to stare at him. What had it meant to Christine Reynolds? Did it embody love, a life together, the joys and tears of raising children? Had it been a symbol of status? Had it been given on a birthday or anniversary? Was it her wedding ring?

Russert closed his eyes and looked into his soul. Why were some stones and metals so precious? He fingered the diamond. At least two million dollars he estimated. Did a diamond of this size translate to a greater love? How was it that a stone, a simple rock buried in soil, could be so coveted? Why were diamonds so precisely cut, and polished, and valued? Why did some stir erotic passions while others were tossed aside for industrial use only? What if such standards were utilized to measure the worth of human life, his life? How would Bertram Russert be valued?

He chose to think about it no longer.

Russert placed the ring on top of Whitman's letter. Never taking his eyes from either, he reached into his briefcase and felt for the cold metal of his revolver. Why was the soft, yellow metal of the ring more highly valued than this hard, blue metal? Russert held the gun in his hand. It had belonged to his father. The weapon had purpose and power and with it came great responsibility. It could save a life or take a life. The ring was worth millions, while the revolver was valued at little more than the cost of its components.

Russert opened his eyes wide and closed his lips over the gun's barrel, pressing it back until it touched his throat. He wanted to feel it. How far? What angle? Would it be better if the barrel's tip pressed against the roof of his mouth or should it be angled downward? His tongue explored the cylinder within his mouth. He tasted the acrid metal just as when he was a child and had sucked on pennies.

The rasp-like surface of the trigger was abrasive against the skin of his index finger. He applied pressure. A bit more. Springs compressed. Tension increased. The hammer responded in a backward journey. Slowly. When tension on the spring became too much the hammer would fall. It would be over in an instant. This was so much easier than he had thought. Why had he not done this sooner? Serenity at last.

Russert removed the barrel from his mouth. He was ready. With slow and deliberate motions, he wrapped the ring within layers of tissue. He walked to the bathroom and dropped Christine Reynolds' diamond ring into the toilet. With a touch of his finger he flushed it away.

He would leave no note or clue.

Russert returned to his chair. Euphoric, in a near trance, he lifted the letter and held a cigarette lighter beneath it. How long for paper eight inches by eleven inches to transform into ash? That was how long he had to live. Russert looked at the letter. Only minutes earlier he had resolved to convey its heinous message to the FBI. Then he had spoken with Satan. Everything had changed.

Had not God delivered his commandments to the world through fire, etching stone with holy flame. Now he, Bertram Russert, would destroy Satan's testament to evil by fire.

A sliver of paper, less than an ounce in weight, the only lifeline to Christine Reynolds rested within his grip. Russert's thumb moved causing friction on the flint. A spark. Flame from the small cylinder. Heat, focused and intense, radiated upward. The edges of the paper shriveled in a frantic attempt to escape the ascending inferno. The words that would rescue Christine Reynolds now withered into blackened carbon, crumpled onto the floor, disappeared forever. All that remained was a wisp of smoke, grey and foul smelling—the breath of Satan.

He had just killed Christine Reynolds. Russert bowed his head, eyes closed, he whispered a prayer. "May she find peace in heaven."

Russert again reached for the revolver. Without hesitation he inserted the barrel of the gun into his mouth. This time he knew just how much pressure was necessary, exactly how hard and how long to press on the trigger. He had felt the weapon's mechanisms. He would know his final moment, the instant before his head disintegrated and eternity began.

He was so ready.

Russert was not ready for the negligible whisper of an electronic lock releasing its grip as his hotel door flung open. He was not ready for the shouting and flying bodies of a Phoenix Police Officer and FBI agent who simultaneously slammed his body, knocking him out of his chair, smothering his body onto the floor.

———

DARKNESS WAS ONCE AGAIN Christine's world. A cloth had been wrapped around her eyes and a hood cinched over her face. Her wrists were bound with a coarse rope. She could not scream. She could not cry; her tears were spent.

Once again confined within the trunk of a car, Christine's body was battered as the vehicle drove over rough streets, bouncing her unmercifully. She felt sick from the motion. The trunk was an inferno. She feared what would happen if she threw up while gagged.

The woman had said they were taking her to a different motel. How many times had she been moved? Christine had no idea; everything was a blur. She felt like she was going to pass out in the heat and blackness. She no longer prayed. Prayers from the tomb-like trunk had no way to reach heaven.

It was so hot.

———

THE HEAT WAS BECOMING OPPRESSIVE. Time in his flower garden was nothing more than a contrived distraction. Brad tried to think of next spring, make some plans, but he couldn't do it. He didn't care. The bell-flower was almost gone. Brad kicked the dirt. "Let it die," he mumbled.

So much had happened and the amount of information uncovered in the past few days was amazing. People were working like crazy all over the country. Something had to break soon. All Brad knew to do for the moment was to sit tight. If he didn't go nuts first, he hoped he would know what he needed to do when the time arrived. He kicked at the dirt of his flower garden again. Maybe, just maybe, today would be the day. Maybe today God would be on the side of the good guys.

Brad neglected to think of something that had been pounded into his head since childhood: sometimes God works in mysterious ways.

———

AFTER A SHOWER, Brad decided that maybe a drive and some music would help. Practically coasting, he steered his truck through Bear Creek Canyon, a narrow chasm of stone that held haunting beauty. Giant cliffs arched and twisted, thrust up from the earth as if grown from seeds planted millions of years ago and crafted by a master gardener. Music from one of his favorite Broadway shows, *Joseph and the Amazing Technicolor Dreamcoat,* accompanied him.

As scenery drifted, he listened to "Any Dream Will Do," recalling how his daughter, Meghan, had acted in a children's performance of the Broadway hit. He saw her face, her innocent beauty as an eleven-year-old girl. What great memories. Something inside his head told Brad that more than memories were going to be needed for the approaching hours.

His cell phone rang. Sam Trathen's deep voice sounded shaken. "Word is coming in, my friend. Major stuff is unfolding in Arizona."

Brad quickly pulled over. "Sam, are you okay? You don't sound good."

"Yeah, I'm alright. Just a bunch of stuff to tell you. You ain't gonna believe what you are about to hear."

"I'm dying to hear, but you don't sound too good. I have a feeling this is bad news."

"Well, it sure isn't great. You can tell me what you think. I've been on the phone with Arizona, and they're trying to figure out a whole bunch of craziness. Pretty darned late last night, Brandon Reynolds received a telephone call from a United States Senator, some guy named Bertram Russert. I know his face and I can hear his voice, but I can't remember what state he represents."

"Oh, yeah, I know who you mean. He's a silver-haired guy from somewhere back East. He's on the Sunday morning shows pretty frequently."

"Maybe so, Brad, but if he's a politician, I'm certain I don't like him no matter where he's from. Anyway, this senator called Reynolds from a Phoenix hotel, apparently drunk as a rat. His speech was almost incoherent, and he was sounding like a genuine fool. Brandon Reynolds knows the senator from past dealings of some sort, so he doesn't hang up on his drunk ass. He stays on the line with the idiot, trying to figure out what's going on. The senator mumbles about how he had to see Reynolds the next morning. He keeps carrying on about how sorry he was for Christine and please don't blame him for what had happened. Crazy talk! Reynolds, of course, is curious, so they set up a time to meet. But the senator won't give it up. He keeps on about the remorse he feels for the harm that has come to Reynolds and his family."

"Sam, this is lunatic stuff."

"Okay, Brad, hang on 'cause I'm just getting started. The gibberish continues for a while longer, and the senator mentions the name of William Holloway. Reynolds recognizes this name right away as Christine's uncle, a retired federal judge. So now, Brandon Reynolds is curious as the dickens and continues to listen as the senator is getting more and more screwed up. And then, the crazy-ass senator starts to cry! The goofy senator sobs into the phone, trying to talk, but becomes totally incomprehensible!"

"Jesus."

"Now, Brad, this is the part that I just can't understand. For some reason Brandon Reynolds saw no reason to call the police or FBI. Apparently, no real alarms had been set off in Reynolds' head. He thought he could meet with the senator after he had sobered up, and make some sense out of things. So, Reynolds and the senator schedule a meeting for this morning and then hang up."

"Good grief."

"Okay, as if all this ain't weird enough, Reynolds later hears on the news that Christine's uncle, the retired judge, had his ass blown to smithereens because he was mixed up in some sort of drug deal down in Mexico."

"Give me a break!" Brad breathed the words more to himself than to Sam.

"Well, anyway, after hearing news about the judge getting cremated, the coincidence was just too great, so Brandon Reynolds decides to call the police and the Bureau. So now, the people out there in Arizona gotta put all this nonsense together and figure out what's going on. Brandon Reynolds told investigators that ever since his wife's disappearance, Judge Holloway had been driving him crazy calling him multiple times a day. The guy wanted to talk business but then he also asked all kinds of questions about the progress of the case and what did Reynolds plan to do. He was asking stuff about ransom demands and what would he do to get his wife back. Reynolds told the investigators that he had been puzzled by Holloway's behavior but just figured he was a man struggling with too much time, too much money, and way too much booze. It was the news of Holloway's violent death that pushed things over the edge. Reynolds finally figured something was whacky."

Brad was stunned. He had heard a lot of wild things in his career, but this ranked right close to the top.

After taking a deep breath, Sam continued, "So, the Arizona folks interview the hell out of Reynolds, asking him all kinds of questions about the specifics of the telephone call from the senator. Now, Brad, I'm only speculating, you understand, but I think that it was probably some overeducated FBI nerd who figured out that the senator sure as hell sounded suicidal. Of course, this brings out fire trucks and the Air Force. Everyone scrambles. They try to contact the senator but he won't answer any calls, even though the hotel staff knows he's inside his room. The investigators figure something bad is happening so they get a key and go crashing into the senator's room like Geronimo on a drunk horse."

Brad had to laugh. "How did that go over? Busting through a door into a United States senator's hotel room is not exactly a routine day at the office."

"Brad, it's unbelievable. They went flying through the door, apparently only seconds before what would have been his suicide. He had a gun in his mouth when they hit him! After they finish rolling around on the floor and had him under control, the senator was loony as hell. He was dazed or crazed, who knows? The guys told me he was jabbering like a madman, slobber and spit flying everywhere, carrying on about the Devil and how Jesus would save his soul from hell. Now, Brad, please don't tell me you voted for this guy. Our tax dollars at work. My aching balls!"

"Sam, this is one of the most unhinged stories I've ever heard!"

"I hear you, but this is the absolute, damned truth. The Arizona people said they couldn't decide whether to laugh or cry."

"Is the senator talking sensibly now, or is he still crazy?"

"I guess he's calmed down and starting to make sense now. But we're gonna have to wait for details because the interview is still going on as we speak. They are busy as hell. I've spoken with an FBI agent and a Phoenix cop. Between them I got a pretty good picture of what's going on."

"I never dreamed I would hear anything like this."

"Here's more for you, Brad, and this is the part that's gonna absolutely kill you. They know that the senator definitely knew that Christine Reynolds was abducted."

Brad gasped. "I knew this part was coming," he said.

"And the senator revealed that a ransom demand was planned by some hotshot lawyer in Washington, DC. The lawyer had in some way blackmailed the senator into participating in a ransom demand. I don't know details of the blackmail."

"Lord, Sam, is there hope for this thing?"

"I don't know, Brad, but we've got problems. Apparently, only moments before they crashed the senator's room, he had destroyed a paper that contained all the information necessary to facilitate a ransom. It was some sort of document that the lawyer had written, detailing instructions for a ransom and how to arrange a release for Christine Reynolds. But it's gone, my friend, burned to a crisp. We got nothing, absolutely nothing."

Both men were quiet before Brad softly spoke. "Jesus, Sam."

"The poor investigators are moving as fast as they can. Leads are getting fired off to Washington like a damned machine gun. Your agents are trying desperately to get a handle on this lawyer, figure out what he's all about and who the hell is behind all this. Barnes has been great. He's running the FBI stuff. I'm talking to Kurt and Phoenix PD."

Brad thought before he replied. "It's a mess but at least something has finally happened."

"I know, I know. But the big problem I'm facing now is that the Washington lawyer is expecting the ransom process to take place today. I mean like right now, Brad. It seems logical to me that as soon as the lawyer smells trouble, Christine Reynolds is in extremely grave danger."

Silence. Brad searched for a response but found nothing to say.

Sam continued, "You know, Brad, a matter of seconds and that document would have been in our hands. It was all we needed to really put this together. A matter of damned seconds! Now, all I have is an abducted woman, no means to negotiate a pay-off, and no idea where she may be."

Silence again.

Sam's voice was heavy. "And if all this isn't enough, I've got one last bit of news. The senator claims that Judge Holloway's murder was in some way directed by the lawyer from his office in Washington. If that's correct, Christine Reynolds certainly is in deep trouble."

Brad still could not think of anything to say.

Sam confirmed that he had left messages for Riddle, giving him the same story. Sam's voice was strained as he spoke softly. "My old friend, we better pray for something to develop out of the Arizona interviews or from the folks in Washington. Our dance card is not looking very pretty right now."

Brad was quiet. Sam remained on the line but spoke no more.

Finally, Brad responded, "Okay, Sam. Thanks for the call. There still are missing pieces in this puzzle. Lots of things can happen. You have to hang in, Sam. You have to hang in and be ready to roll."

"Oh, I know, Brad. I'm sure as hell ready. I'll call you when I learn something."

"Thanks, Sam."

Brad could not believe what he had just heard. Short of a miracle, the worst imaginable nightmare loomed. He had been here before. It was impossible to work a case like this without knowing that in the end everyone may go home with a broken heart. Such thoughts had to be suppressed, not allowed to germinate. But after talking with Sam, Brad knew things were way past the point of germination. A poisonous weed had sprouted and was growing.

Totally heartsick, Brad turned his truck back up the canyon. He didn't even notice the beauty that he had appreciated only minutes earlier. Feelings of doom weighed on his mind. Hope seemed to have collapsed.

Brad did not know it, but the conversation he had just concluded with Sam was not even close to what would be the worst part of his day.

———

BRAD STOPPED for gasoline and heard people talking about the forecast. It called for more unseasonable heat. It was way too hot for September. But a change was on the way. A cold front was predicted. Brad breathed the miserable air. Nothing seemed right. Nature herself was out of balance.

Home again, Brad took a moment with Elizabeth. No smile, no sparkle, only sadness. He stepped outside. The flower garden reminded him of a boneyard. The few pitiful survivors looked even worse than only a few hours earlier. They drooped, wilted in defeat to the heat and neglect. Brad slammed the garden gate shut. What a horrible day. Even the flowers had given up.

Turning away from his garden he headed back to the house. His phone rang. The instant he heard Kurt's voice Brad knew something was gravely wrong. Kurt could barely speak. Usually he boomed with confidence. Now his voice was diminished to a tremor. "Brad, I need help."

"Jesus, Kurt, what's wrong?"

"I don't know what the hell is happening here and what is connected to what, but there's been a horrible twist. We've now got a homicide on our hands. Could you drive out and meet me? I sure as hell could use a little support right now."

"Of course, I can, Kurt. Where are you, what's wrong?"

As Kurt answered, nausea and a shattered heart were all that Brad could feel.

Kurt described the canyon where he was located. Brad knew it well. It was a small, rugged place, not far at all from Elk Run. He and his sons had occasionally hiked the area, taking small brookies from the crystal-clear stream that trickled through. It was not especially scenic, and there simply was nothing there to attract people, not even a trailhead or picnic tables. The only access was a dirt fire road that had been cut years earlier. Very few people knew the place existed, even fewer went there. Brad pushed his truck as hard as he dared. He had to get to Kurt.

After leaving the highway, Brad jolted over the neglected excuse of a road. He held tightly onto the wheel and tried to prepare his mind for what lay ahead. He steered his way up a severe incline and when he topped the hill, as expected, a bustle of activity came into view on the canyon floor below him. In spite of the remote location, investigators remained cautious. Yellow crime scene tape was stretched tree to tree, establishing a flimsy barricade to prevent entry into the repugnant horror that awaited those who had no choice but to cross. Brad did not go directly to the crime scene. He parked a little ways back, killed the engine, and got out. He stood beside the opened driver's door.

Waiting and watching, Brad could see Kurt on his knees, along with other investigators, focused on what had to be done. Brad squinted his eyes trying to make sense of what he saw in the distance. Reality registered. The air about the investigators appeared as a black, translucent sky and Brad's heart broke all over again. The cloud was indeed a cloud; a cloud of flies. Incessantly persistent, the creatures hovered over their opportune feast. Brad could hear their maddening drone even from where he stood.

He worked his way down the hill. With reverence in his heart and dread tightening his stomach, he stopped well before the yellow tape. He called out to Kurt, only slightly raising his voice. A shout would have been profane.

Kurt looked up and gave a subtle wave. He stood and walked toward Brad with sagging shoulders. Tragedy seemed to encumber his ability to walk. Removing his gloves as he reached the yellow tape, Kurt crossed under and grasped Brad's hand. The grip spoke of years of friendship. The men walked a distance away before sitting on a fallen tree.

"Thanks for coming out. I appreciate it."

"Any time. You know that, Kurt."

Kurt shook his head but did not speak.

Brad was silent. His friend needed time.

The scene below was surreal. Hushed sounds drifted up from the bottom of the canyon.

"It looks like four kids, three girls and a boy as best I can say at this point. The experts will figure out the technical stuff, but I've been around enough to know pretty much what happened." Kurt stopped speaking and looked up, seeking help from whomever in heaven may be watching. "Two cars, loaded with kids skipping school, drove out here to horse around, probably looking for a place to drink beer. They saw the bodies and ran like hell."

Kurt was silent again.

Brad sat with his eyes fixed on the ground, forearms over his knees, not speaking. This was not a time to rush the conversation. Kurt would talk when he was ready. Time belonged to his friend.

Kurt sighed and looked about the forest, seeking to maintain his composure. "The girls look about thirteen, give or take. I don't think the boy can possibly be over twelve. It's obvious that the bodies haven't been here very long, maybe only a day or so. It's the animals that make it tough. Could be a coyote, I suppose, but my guess is it's a bear. They're getting ready for winter already. Whatever it was, the bodies are pretty chewed up and scattered all over the place. It's taken a while to get the big picture. My guess is that each kid was shot in the head, probably at another location, before they were dumped here. That's for the crime scene experts and pathologists to figure out. No ballistics for a while yet, but the guy down there is pretty good. He's guessing a .32 caliber." Riddle's face twisted in contempt and then he said, "Typical shithead punk gun."

Riddle closed his eye, took a few deep breaths. Moisture appeared on his cheek. He gathered himself and continued, "From what's left, I think the girls are Anglo. My guess is the boy is Hispanic."

Silence.

"You know, Brad, I really can't say why I called you. Why put you through this? What are you supposed to do?"

A squirrel chattered from an overhead tree branch.

"I just knew that I needed someone from the old days. Seems like the entire department is twenty-five-years old." Kurt paused. "I don't feel old. Christ, I'm only fifty-two, but that's darned near double the age of most of these kids. I'm starting to really miss the times when you, Sam, and I could always cook up a case that got us together. We worked like no tomorrow. Our wives forgot what we looked like, but, Lord, we had fun. Put a bunch of people in jail while we were at it."

Kurt was quiet again.

"Then something like this comes along. Young kids—hell, they were just children—get shot in the head and thrown in the woods like dirty water. I don't know, Brad. Even thinking of the old days doesn't seem to do me any good today."

High pitched screeching from a red-tailed hawk pierced the narrow canyon. The bird soared. Magnificent. Glorious. A crime scene? In his canyon? The bird screeched again.

"Thanks for coming, Brad."

Brad decided it was time to speak. "Kurt, since I lost Elizabeth, about all I do is think about the old days. Whatever the hell has happened around here in the past week has really brought it home. But I've learned a few things too. People like Sam, you, and me, we're the luckiest guys in the world. Can you even imagine what it would be like if we didn't have the old days? Can you imagine the life that most people are doomed to live? Nine to five, Monday through Friday. Nice clean office. Neat, orderly desk, pretty little secretary. Retail. Wholesale. Statistics. Projections. Profit margins. Quarterly reports. What a pain in the ass."

Kurt sat without moving and listened.

"Can you imagine, Kurt? No calls in the night, no surprises, no emergencies? Can you imagine never saving a life, never locking up the rotten people who take lives? We're lucky, Kurt."

Kurt drug the toe of his boot back and forth through pine needles and dirt.

Brad took a breath before continuing, his voice soft. "I promise you one thing. Our kids sure as hell never had to wonder, what does Dad do at the office? They knew damn well. When it's time for you and me to push up daisies, we've got only one thing to take with us to the box, Kurt, and that's memories. That's it, Kurt. Memories of doing something real, making a difference, helping somebody, somewhere. We have memories of what we did and how we did it. I damn well love our memories."

The squirrel no longer chattered. The hawk had flown away.

Brad leaned to the ground, picked up a small stone, and tossed it. "I don't know where this case is going or how much this stuff is all connected. I'm pretty confused about that right now. But there is one thing I can tell you with absolute certainty. I'm glad you called me. You can call me tomorrow. I called you when I lost Elizabeth. You were there for me, and you can bet that I'll be calling you again one of these days. You're one of the best memories I've got."

Silence.

"We're always moving, Kurt. Sometimes we reach toward something, sometimes we run from something. We either grasp for what's in front of us or let go of something from the past. I think more times than not, you and I have been reaching, not running. Today is one of those days that we will try to let go, put it in the past. But you just have to keep reaching, keep grasping."

Kurt scooped a handful of dried pine needles from the ground and stood. "You're right. All you say is true. Sometimes, I guess I just need a reminder. Today is a tough one." He tossed the needles into the air. There was no breeze to carry them. They fell straight back onto the ground.

"Is it ever, Kurt. Is it ever. Today is a tough one."

"Okay, retired FBI man. I gotta go back to work." Riddle looked to the sky once again. "Thanks, Brad. I needed this."

"Nothing to it."

Kurt grinned. "I'm gonna hang up my spurs one of these days. I want to be in your ranks, an old retired guy. Keep your fly rod limbered up. I don't like to embarrass folks."

"Kurt, you couldn't keep up with me if you had a bucket of worms and an aquarium."

Kurt grinned and laughed softly. "Hey, listen, I haven't had time to tell you, but we tore the cabin up this morning. Nothing there that you didn't see the night all this crazy stuff started. I haven't yet been through what was taken. The evidence team did the hard part. I'll review everything later. The box and photos are being processed but nothing else came out of there that was a real surprise or shocker."

"What about the Owens kid?"

"We got a lucky break on that one. He was away in Texas. The assistant ranch manager was nice as could be and let us in real quiet like. We may have a little time before the cat is out of the bag on the ranch. I'm wondering if this thing here is related. My gut says it is."

"I'm with you, Kurt. Your gut and my gut are singing the same song."

Kurt shook his head in dismay. "I guess you got word from Sam about all the wild stuff that's happening in Arizona?"

"Yeah, I talked with him a little earlier. That was some unbelievable story. I'm feeling bad for Sam. He's not having the best of days either."

"Christ, Brad, is this ever a messed-up world or what?"

"Sometimes it seems that way."

Kurt breathed deeply and started walking back down the hill, back to the broken bodies and putrid flesh. He had no choice but to cross beyond the yellow tape and face the horror once more. Brad walked with him.

"Kurt, don't ask me why, but I need to walk down here with you, maybe see this straight on. Something I can't explain."

Kurt squinted and questioned with his eyes but then said, "Well, I think you're making a big mistake. But I guess you do what you have to do."

The two men proceeded. As they neared the scene, Brad stopped. Flies teemed. Kurt and Brad shook hands.

"Thanks again, Brad. You have no idea how much I appreciate you coming out here today. I'll call you as soon as I know something."

Brad barely nodded. They stood only feet from the yellow crime scene tape. Brad's eyes scanned the barbaric scene. When he saw it, he instantly knew why he had felt compelled to bring himself closer. His eyes were locked on a pile of evidence envelopes that had been neatly arranged just inside the taped boundary. As the investigators worked through the crime scene, items of value were photographed, logged, and then placed into envelopes. Brad could see what called to him.

Pointing a finger, Brad said, "Kurt, could I please take a look at that large evidence envelope?"

Without speaking, Kurt stepped back into the crime scene. He lifted the requested item and handed it to Brad. He looked directly into Brad's face and held the gaze. "You sure you want to do this?" Kurt asked.

"Yeah, Kurt, give me a little time, please. I need to do this."

With a resigned look, Kurt walked away. Brad sat on a rock and examined the clear plastic envelope, much like a freezer bag. He held it in his hands, feeling its weight and texture. The object sealed within the plastic envelope was torn, shredded, and bloodstained. But just like Elizabeth's eyes in the photograph at home, the envelope spoke to him. Brad could feel something. It was more than memory, more than thought or introspection. He had no explanation. There was no doubt. It was exactly as when he looked at Elizabeth's photograph. This was not something he would dare talk to other people about. Brad didn't know what to think about it.

Through the clear plastic, a small red T-shirt felt almost weightless. A bright yellow, smiling sun face grabbed Brad's attention. For an instant Brad thought he saw Elizabeth's face in the T-shirt. Was it her eyes he saw in the sun's face?

Moments passed. Brad held the shirt. What life had it touched before this horrendous, unspeakable violation of all that is human? Brad thought of his own children. He gazed at the red T-shirt. The smiling sun face looked back. What child had once worn this piece of cloth? Had the child ever smiled like the face on the shirt? Brad could feel the somber answer. No birthday parties, no bedtime prayers. No games of hide-and-seek. No rocking in a squeaky chair wrapped in loving arms. No first date. No school program with applause and wild cheering from friends and parents. No football. No chocolate milkshake. No hug or soft words of comfort after scraping a knee.

No loving words spoken to mend a broken heart: the heart that was broken while so small, still learning to beat.

Brad hung his head. He recalled words he had read years earlier, a passage that had remained with him throughout his career, the dying words of Crowfoot, a chief of the Blackfoot nation:

> *What is life? It is the flash of a firefly in the night.*
> *It is the breath of a buffalo in the wintertime.*
> *It is the little shadow which runs across the grass and*
> *Loses itself in the sunset.*

Brad stood up. Kurt watched him from a distance. Their eyes met and Kurt walked over to Brad and took the envelope.

No word was spoken.

Brad walked away.

———

As Brad drove home, images of the canyon crime scene traveled with him. He had never felt so totally ravaged. Once he entered his town, he picked up a hamburger to carry home. The last glimmer of sun evaporated just as he pulled into his garage. It was still hot, and he felt grimy. He tossed the hamburger onto his kitchen table and made tracks to the fridge. "A Moosehead night if ever there was one." His words echoed in the empty house. Was he dejected or angry? What was the difference? He needed at least one Moosehead for each emotion. Brad walked across the room to see Elizabeth, wondering what revelations from beyond she would have.

Brad stood only inches from her photograph, Moosehead in hand, and looked at her eyes. She smiled, looked straight back at him, but offered no message.

Brad sucked a long draw of Moosehead before speaking to the photograph. "You know, sweetheart, I could sure as hell use a little help. The past few days have been carried out on your smiles, expressions, and a bunch of supernatural hocus-pocus. If you're so damned concerned and have access to a vast, universal plan, how about letting me in on some of it, Elizabeth. Show me something real!" He stood before her photograph, staring right into her eyes.

Elizabeth looked back at Brad. Her eyes and smile were beautiful, but that was it. No change. Sure as hell no damned sign.

"This is bullshit, Elizabeth!" Brad finished his Moosehead in a final gulp, placed the empty bottle beside the untouched hamburger and left the two of them to keep company through the night. Grabbing another Moosehead out of the fridge, Brad went to his bedroom.

He did not carry Elizabeth's photograph with him.

———

THE NIGHT SEEMED to never end. Images of the crime scene and the cabin where Christine Reynolds had been held refused to allow him any peace. While Brad endured his torment, an angry Pacific Ocean churned and clouds roiled as a battle of fronts, hot versus cold, engaged in combat over the West Coast.

A storm was born.

THURSDAY, SEPTEMBER 13

A SHEEN of light nudged onto the eastern horizon. Brad sat at his father's desk, coffee brewed and grateful beyond words to see the night pass. His house felt hauntingly empty. He had heard nothing more from Sam about what was happening in Arizona or Washington, and he was concerned about how Kurt had made it through the night after the horrible events of the previous day.

Brad took great pleasure in his morning coffee ritual. Mostly, he loved the mug with which he shared each new day. It was stainless steel, inscribed with an image of the ship to which Cody was assigned. It had been Cody's gift to him before his deployment to the Persian Gulf. "Lord, he's far away," Brad whispered.

Brad gazed at photos of his children: Cody, Michael and Meghan. Cody was in his Naval uniform. Michael was in his high school cross-country uniform, and Meghan was dressed for her prom night. With a sigh, Brad walked across the room. He thought about the exasperation he had demonstrated with Elizabeth the night before and now was feeling guilty. He took a sip of coffee and muttered, "Guess I can't put this off any longer. I probably pissed her off last night." He stepped close to Elizabeth. They looked at each other, eyes entwined. Brad knew in an instant, clear as could be, Elizabeth was laughing! She could not have spoken more plainly if she were standing beside him. *You can't stay mad at me.* Brad loved her most when she laughed. He couldn't help himself. Brad laughed too.

The magical spell was abruptly halted by his ringing cell phone. Before he answered, Brad whispered, "I'll be back."

To Brad's pleasant surprise, Kurt's voice came across strong. "Good morning, J. Edgar. Did I awaken you?"

"I don't waste my time with sissy stuff like sleeping. Only people I know who sleep are wimps like you."

"Okay, Superman, whatever you say. But, my friend, here are today's headlines. Your FBI folks out in Chicago arrested preacher man's social director. I guess he is the new star in the church choir. The asshole won't stop singing. He is talking to anyone who will listen."

"Lord, that's great! What the hell is he saying?"

"It's incredible, Brad. He's laid out the whole story on Felix Gomez, Maria Sanchez, and King Solomon. They're three peas in a pod. Arizona sent the photos of Felix Gomez and Maria Sanchez out to Chicago, and the guy for sure identified them as being the people he's been working with. He says they do business in cities all over, including Denver. This is unbelievable shit, Brad. He's described a national ring that's running a huge operation of child prostitution and smuggling people, including kids, across the border. It'll take a good bit of time piece together all the details, but this is a huge break."

"I knew it. Damn, I knew it!"

"Plus, Sam got hits on photos at the motel in Glenwood Springs. Just as we suspected, it was Felix Gomez and Maria Sanchez that were right there in the room with King Solomon."

"Ain't no surprise at this point."

"We've got King Solomon's prints all over that box and the photos that you found in the cabin. Based on the information that's developed in the last few hours, Denver PD and the Feds are getting warrants for all of them. I'll probably get another warrant on King Solomon as soon as I have a second to breathe. With yesterday's discovery of the murdered kids, all of this stuff is hitting the news big time."

"I can only imagine, Kurt." Brad was afraid to ask the next question. He didn't have to. Kurt handled it for him.

"Lots of news from Sam. Not all of it is good, I'm afraid to say." Kurt gathered his thoughts. "First, I guess as big a deal as any is that the damn senator who wanted to kill himself is up to his ears in the kid sex stuff. In fact, this morning we took a closer look at the pictures that came out of the cabin, the ones you saw a few nights ago. Hell, Brad, it's obvious that some of those photos are of the damned senator! There are several photographs of that asshole having sex with kids. Can you believe that?"

"Holy shit."

"My words exactly. The next big deal is that the senator identified Maria Sanchez as the lady who delivers kids to him for his little sporting events."

Kurt was quiet for a few seconds to let his words sink in. He continued, "Get this, my friend. On several occasions, the senator has had Maria deliver little boys and girls to him in a cabin. And where, do you think this happened? None other than the Elk Run Fly Fishing Resort. Most times it was the senator and that judge, you know, the guy who got whacked in Mexico. They enjoyed their Colorado sex adventures together it seems."

Brad could think of nothing to say. He simply held the telephone.

Kurt sensed Brad's shock and continued. "It's pretty clear that the DC lawyer is the person who arranged the hit in Mexico. He set it up to look like a drug deal gone sour, but the senator claims it all revolves around the sex with kids."

Brad's mind could not process Riddle's words rapidly enough. The ramifications of what he was hearing were more than what he could take in. "Holy shit," was all he could say.

Kurt's voice was becoming more electrified and he spoke. "The DC lawyer apparently tried to blackmail the senator into brokering a ransom for Christine Reynolds. Your distinguished United States Senator claims that the lawyer told him all about how he had arranged the abduction of Reynolds. Then the lawyer gave the senator a letter of instructions and a list of cell phone numbers to make the pay-off happen. But as we learned yesterday, he burned the letter. Gonzo, everything is gonzo."

Brad was silent as he processed Kurt's rapid-fire story. So many aspects of the case were coming together from so many different places.

"So now the only way the senator has to contact Mr. Lawyer is through his Washington law firm. Surprise, surprise. Mr. Lawyer is long gone, vanished. The folks from his firm say that in the past year or so the guy was acting really irrational. Some think he had gone totally nuts. Apparently, it had gotten so bad that partners in the firm were trying to figure out a way to get rid of him."

Brad finally spoke. "This is unfrigginbelievable!" he said. "A lawyer so damned crazy that even other lawyers think he's crazy? Cripes, I'd bet on the oceans going dry first."

Kurt responded with a short laugh. "You catch on quickly, G-Man. Anyway, Mr. Senator says Mr. Lawyer planned to leave the country whether the ransom took place or not. Your guys in DC are turning the nation's capital upside down looking for him. Absolutely zero so far, but they're still trying."

Brad thought he knew the answer to his next question. "Does the senator know who the lawyer used to carry out the abduction here in Colorado?"

"Nothing he can prove, Brad, but he feels confident that Maria is in the middle somehow. The way I see it, if Maria is in the picture, then Felix Gomez and King Solomon are in the picture. They were all together in the motel in Glenwood Springs right at the time Christine Reynolds disappeared. I think all this tells the story of what you saw at the cabin. You agree?"

"Oh, hell yes!" Brad's said as he let out a torturous moan. "This whole damn thing has been right here under our noses all the time. I was less than one hundred yards from them the other night at the cabin. Jesus Christ! I watched them put her inside that horrible place. I stood outside the cabin, only a few feet from that poor woman. I stood there and did nothing. Not a damn thing. God almighty, Kurt!"

Kurt was quiet for a moment. Then he spoke softly. "That may very well be true, Brad, but what the hell were you supposed to do? Shoot them with your index finger? You had no idea what was happening. You didn't know anything about what they had done. Come on, Brad, you called me the next morning. You called Sam. We didn't know what we had either. None of us knew. Hell, Brad, if you hadn't had the balls to go back out there, go into the cabin again, we wouldn't be nearly as far down the road as we are. You should be patting yourself on the back, not beating your head on a wall."

Brad refused to be calmed. "Easy for you to say, you didn't have those people in your line of vision. You weren't a matter of yards from a kidnapped woman and the animals who took her. You didn't sit there in the dark and have those photos staring at you. I saw what those sick bastards were doing to kids. I was in that cabin literally minutes after they left. We were breathing the same damned air!"

Kurt was quiet. He searched for the right words, and he wanted to give Brad some time to settle down. When Kurt spoke again, in a soft voice he said, "I think I know how you feel, Brad. Just think this through and don't be too hard on yourself. Believe me, Brad, what I saw at that crime scene yesterday, a bunch of murdered children, was no photograph. It doesn't get any more real than that. This case has taken a big piece out of all of us. But you sure as hell can't blame yourself."

Pacing from wall to wall, Brad held the telephone in one hand and rubbed his eyes with the other; his stomach was churning. He ceased pacing and doubled over, holding his stomach.

Kurt spoke again. "There is no blame here. From the moment this horrible thing began, we have all done the best we could do. Right now, there are a bunch of damned good police officers and FBI Agents in Arizona and Washington. They haven't slept or eaten. They are doing the best they can. We've all done the best we could do. We all need a little luck and some help from upstairs maybe."

"I'm sorry, Kurt, but if I live to be a hundred, I will never stop second guessing myself over what I did or didn't do that night." Brad stood straight again.

"Take it easy, my friend. The fat lady sure as hell hasn't sung yet. Police and FBI Agents are about to turn this country upside down; a whole lot of police work is going to happen. No telling what kind of things may fall out."

"OK, Kurt, I hear you. I'll settle down."

"Alright, Brad, now listen. I'm going to be running like a madman today. Sam and Rick Barnes are holding tight in Aspen. When I get a break here, it's good for them. When they get a break in Aspen, it's good for Kurt. We're all going to come out of this in good shape."

"OK, thanks Kurt. I really do appreciate your call. I'll be fine. Call me when you can."

After his phone went silent, Brad was quiet. He wasn't anywhere close to being fine. His anger boiled, but his heart was collapsing. He had to do something. "I'm a one-dimensional idiot," he said chiding himself. "All I ever know to do is take a run."

And run he did. Brad tore into the meadow trail with fury. He wanted his legs to collapse and his lungs to explode. He needed to purge, blow every shred of exasperation through the pores of his skin, a thorough cleansing.

It didn't happen.

Even when his heart pounded to the point of rupture, when he felt his lungs seared, only one thought reverberated in his brain: What kind of day is Christine Reynolds having?

———

WITH HIS RUN BEHIND HIM, Brad found the silence of his house to be unbearable. A shower offered no relief and food held no appeal. He paced. He thought. This was horrible, how could he survive this? This was going to be the longest day of his life. Brad checked his watch and the clocks around the house. Were they even moving? He didn't think so.

The sense of suspended time triggered a memory. He recalled a church service he had attended when he was young. Even though Brad was not a believer in all of the teachings of the Old Testament, the story of that particular Sunday's lesson had remained tucked inside his head through the years. He recalled how the Book of Joshua tells of the day when the Lord delivered up the Amorites to Israel and God spoke to the universe: "Sun, stand thou still" and the sun stood still and the moon stayed until the people had avenged themselves upon their enemies, and there was no day like that before it or after it.

Brad thought about the Scripture passage and the monotonous sermon he had endured. Did the sun really stand still? Were the events those centuries ago any more profound in the struggle between heaven and hell than on the night that Christine Reynolds was plucked from life? Were the Amorites any more accomplished in the art of evil than those who destroy children today? Would the creator of the universe be any less inclined to halt the forces of nature in the aftermath of what Kurt Riddle saw in a desolate canyon only yesterday than he was on the day the Amorites were vanquished?

Brad stepped outside to look at his flower garden. It was dead. Questions and memories persisted. He looked at the remnants of the bellflower, its life withered away. He thought of Elizabeth. He thought of Christine Reynolds. Did the god, spirit, or energy that supposedly brought the sun and moon to a halt also look down upon murdered children strewn about a mountain canyon? Would the force that controls the galaxies, black holes, and supernovas have even noticed the night that Christine Reynolds was snatched away? Had it been her destiny from the beginning? Are such events merely random, galactic serendipity?

This was too much for Brad. He decided that he had become way too deep and introspective. He walked back into his house. He looked at his watch. It had not changed. Jesus! It sure as hell seemed like today was not going to pass. It appeared that the sun was standing still.

———

SON OF A BITCH. The sun was exactly where it was hours ago! Mark Whitman turned from his hotel window and went to his bed, a prisoner in a single room. He dared not step out; his photograph was all over the news. The world was looking for him. The world would not find him. He had a chartered aircraft scheduled for tomorrow morning. Thank God he had made arrangements under his new name.

He had bought the bitch. He had her, and he owned her. Life would be good. Not as good as what it might have been if Russert hadn't screwed him, but he would now destroy Russert. That was the best part of how he would conduct his new life. Incremental and hideous torture of Bertram Russert was what he had to look forward to. He had the photos and would release them periodically. Everything would be fine if he could just live through this one, last, eternal afternoon.

HAD THE SUN EVEN MOVED? Felix Gomez looked to the sky. He would swear it was exactly where it had been three hours ago. What a terrible day. He had seen his photograph on television at least a dozen times. Maria, King Solomon, the rich broad, they *were* the news. Their stories and their photographs were being broadcast almost nonstop. The bodies of the kids that King Solomon had killed had been found way too soon. King Solomon had assured him they wouldn't be found for weeks. So much for believing anything King Solomon had to say! But now that the bodies had been discovered, the news coverage would be relentless.

They had a fresh car, thanks to friends of King Solomon. Mexico was only hours away. That is, if this afternoon would ever end. If the sun would move through the sky and drop below the horizon, give him darkness, he could do what he had to do and disappear.

But the sun had to set first. Nightfall seemed years away.

———

POLICE OFFICERS and FBI agents executed their duties in what seemed a stationary solar system. They walked miles on hot concrete. They interviewed countless people, showed photographs, begged for public assistance, tracked down promising leads, and followed up on foolish leads. The hours dragged on. Records were searched. Notebooks were filled. Pens ran out of ink. Computers failed to respond. Socks soured and shirts were stained. The anticipated telephone call did not come. The prayed-for break did not come. Nothing moved and nothing changed. It was hot. Would this day ever end?

———

HOW LONG HAD she been here? Half her life? How much longer would this last? Tonight, it would be over. They would be on their way to Mexico in a few hours—that is if night ever arrived. The room was hot. Maria breathed sticky air that had already been breathed. The sun did not move. Time refused to pass.

She had spent the day trying not to see. She did not want to look at the tied hands and feet of the woman. When Maria glanced at the woman, she thought that all the tape over her mouth made her look like a damned mummy. It was easier when they had been in the house where they kept her tied in a separate bedroom. At least there had been a door to close to keep her out of sight.

This was too close. Maria could hear the woman breathe, and it gave her the creeps. But mostly it was that she had to look at the woman's face. God, her eyes were haunting. The damn woman wouldn't stop looking at her. Maria tried not to look back. She did not want to deal with those pleading eyes. The taped mouth would have to remain as it was. Maria could never risk hearing the woman's voice. Maria knew in her heart that would be a big mistake.

The pitiful eyes had bothered Maria so much that, for a while, she had even placed a pillowcase over the woman's head. But then Maria felt like she shared the room with a corpse and had to remove it.

If time would pass, she would not have to deal with the woman much longer. Maria did what she had always done: she simply turned away. She had spent her life turning away, refusing to look.

Turning away meant that she did not have to look into the mirror of her own self. Turning away had not helped today. Turning away did not make time pass.

———

THIS HAD BEEN the longest day of her captivity. Her feet and hands were bound tightly; her mouth was sealed with a horrible tape. Christine Reynolds could not make her mind wander. She could think of nothing other than her misery. *Is this what hell feels like? Is this ever going to end?*

Sleep had long abandoned Christine. Try as she might, she could not even conjure a mental image of Brandon or her children's faces. Stagnant air of the motel clung to her skin and sour juices fouled her mouth. She smelled her own body.

Christine looked at the digital clock on the table beside her bed. Was she losing her mind? The time had not changed since forever.

She knew the woman's name was Maria. She knew all of their names. Before Maria grew angry and turned off the television, news broadcasts had told Christine a great deal about the people who held her. The people who had taken her captive had names! They were human beings! Christine's hatred had intensified once she learned they had names. How could real people do this to her?

If only Maria would remove the tape, let her speak. Maria would not look at her.

Christine looked again at the clock. Nothing had changed.

———

THE STORM that had been conceived over the Pacific Coast crossed Utah and Idaho with only with light rain and gusty winds. But the storm was just teasing, having a little fun, hoarding its energy as it grew into a monster. The beast raged, its anger simmering. But first, the sun had to get out of the way. It had to be night. The storm pushed, pushed hard. The sun pushed back. It did not want to move.

The afternoon of September 13 refused to pass.

———

WHAT WOULD he do when the day did end? Just because day eventually passed into night would anything really change. Wouldn't he continue to battle the same emotions that he struggled with at this moment? Brad decided to get out of his house. Maybe an enchilada. Would that make time pass? Then the day would be gone, but after that would be an even tougher challenge. Brad had to figure a way to get through the night.

———

SINCE THE POLICE were looking for three people, the trio split up. Maria was in a motel with the broad and King Solomon was making arrangements for a car and supplies for tonight's trip to Mexico. Felix knew that if he could just get through this day, make it until night, everything would be fine. Once night arrived, he and King Solomon would dump the broad's body. Then they would meet Maria, who would have their fresh car. They would drive nonstop to the safety of Mexico. False papers for each of them were in his bag.

King Solomon had assured him that the broad's body wouldn't be found for a long time. Of course, he had said the same thing about the kids.

For the hundredth time, Felix glanced up at the sun. *Pendejo!* He had never seen anything like this. He had never lived through a day so long.

———

BRAD SECLUDED himself at an isolated table in his favorite restaurant. He ordered food and considered a Moosehead. Instead, he simply asked for an iced tea. He was moody enough already. There was no need to make things worse with alcohol. He sat alone and thought. Nothing new crossed his mind. He had already thought of every detail he knew to think about. He thought about them all again.

———

IN A DENVER MOTEL, Felix Gomez placed sunglasses on his face and buttoned a baggy long sleeve shirt over his body. He pulled a baseball cap low over his eyes and tucked his ponytail inside the collar of the shirt. He should cut the damn thing just to be safe since the news broadcasts were talking a lot about his ponytail. Fuck it. He liked his ponytail. In a few hours he would be in Mexico.

Felix drove a few blocks to a convenience store he had spotted earlier. The afternoon sun bore down. It felt like an oven. He pulled his cap lower. He didn't like being out in the open, but this had to be done. Felix told himself that he was too nervous. Hell, he looked like a hundred other people on the street. He was still nervous.

The convenience store was almost empty. Felix stood just inside the entrance, taking a moment to look around. He saw only two people: a girl, about twenty-five, stood at the counter talking with the single employee on duty. The clerk, a man about thirty, held a cigarette in his mouth and a backward ballcap on his head. His sleeveless shirt revealed tattoo-covered arms. The girl was at least thirty pounds over-weight but wore skin-tight jeans. A tank top designed for an under-weight model clung like cheap paint on her torso. Massive breasts spilled out, bulging like compressed balloons and her exposed navel gleamed with a cream-colored pearl. Felix wondered how the girl could even breathe. Making small talk, the two absent-mindedly watched a television program of ultimate fighting.

———————

THE GOLIATH STORM rumbled south and east, passing over familiar terrain. The earth's crust was an old friend. The storm knew the instant it touched Colorado. It was almost time. Wait just a bit longer before wreaking ultimate havoc. But it was time to speed up, make noise, and announce its intentions. This was not a surprise attack.

Like a freight train running open throttle, the black and grey monster screamed, accelerating to full speed on a collision course with a sun that refused to move.

————

FELIX GOMEZ MOVED through the convenience store making his selections. When finished, he stood at the counter doing his best not to look at the fat girl. His telephone rang. He listened and then spoke. "Fine, I'll meet you at the gorge at dark."

He lay cash on the counter, accepted his change, and walked out.

The man with tattooed arms and the fat girl with a pearl in her navel whispered softly to each other. The man dialed the Denver Police Department.

The afternoon that had refused to pass was over.

Earth again rotated about its axis.

The sun no longer stood still.

The storm increased its speed.

————

CHILIES GROWN under the sun of New Mexico, roasted over an open flame, and blended with beef and spices are God's gift to man. Brad had lived his life devoted to this divine treasure. Screw it. He wanted a beer with his enchilada. He asked his waiter to please take away the iced tea and bring a Moosehead.

The Moosehead arrived but it was too late. Brad was on the phone with all thoughts of food forgotten.

Kurt's voice was energized. "You knucklehead, please let your fly fishing be worth something more than a damned little trout that costs you hundreds of dollars each time you reel in one of the poor creatures."

Brad could feel the excitement in Kurt's voice, and it was instantly contagious. "What's going on?"

"Listen, Brad, the Denver PD got a call from a clerk in a convenience store and they're pretty sure it's a legit tip, a rock-solid lead on Gomez."

"Holy Mary, it's about time!" A torrent of energy surged through Brad as if floodgates had been opened.

Kurt continued, "Well, the story is this. A man comes into a store on the west side of Denver and buys some food. While the guy was checking out, the clerk on duty absolutely recognized him from the photos that have been running on TV all day. We've pulled the security camera, and by God, it's him, Brad. It's him!"

"The clerk says he overheard Felix on his cell phone saying he would meet someone at the gorge at dark. We've checked everything. There are no restaurants or businesses by that name. Nothing like that makes any sense. It's got to be somewhere in the mountains, but nobody around here knows a place called the gorge. Come on, Brad, you fly fishing fool. What or where is the gorge?"

Brad's mouth couldn't move. His brain went blank. He had heard of it, but it wouldn't come. The gorge, the gorge. Where had he heard of the place? "Oh, my God, Kurt. I don't know. It seems like I've heard of it, but I don't know. It's not clicking."

"Your brain hasn't clicked since I met you. I have to run, but think, Brad. If you have an epiphany, call me. This could be it."

"Give me some time, let me think. I'll call you right back."

Brad left his food uneaten, sprinted out the door and headed for home, half panicked and totally elated that something was finally happening. He searched his brain. The gorge had to be somewhere fairly close by. Gomez didn't know this area. He sure as hell wasn't a mountain man. In Colorado, Felix Gomez was a fish out of water. How would he know about the gorge? King Solomon, it had to be! King Solomon worked at Elk Run Resort. He would know the area well. King Solomon was setting up a meeting with Gomez at a place called the gorge!

"Oh, God, help me remember, where is the gorge?" Brad spoke the words as he screeched to a halt in his drive.

An unending stream of prayers flowed as Brad bolted into his house and made a dash straight to his desk. "Please, God, let him answer his phone" He fought to control his breathing as he dug through his desk. Where in hell was that old business card? "God forbid I should ever be one of those organized shitheads with numbers programmed into their cell phone," Brad muttered. He found it: **Clayton Price, Colorado Department of Wildlife.** Scribbled across the top of the card was Clayton's home number in his Florida retirement. Brad punched the numbers. "Oh, God, Clayton. Please answer, please answer."

Clayton Price answered his telephone.

Brad spoke rapidly, gushing out the story.

"What the hell's wrong with you?" Clayton responded when Brad asked about the gorge. "Your brain turned to oatmeal? You used to fish the gorge. You probably called it the old bridge. That's what almost everyone in the area calls the place. It's that drainage where Lightning Creek runs down, just west of Elk Run shortly before it empties into the Platte. Come on, Brad, you remember that crumbling old bridge left over from mining days."

It hit Brad like a baseball bat upside his head. "Oh, hell, yes, I know where it is!"

"Of course you do. The only people I know who call it the gorge are the folks at Elk Run. It's not on their property. The only access is that old dirt fire trail that branches off the private road real close to the main entrance of the resort. Since it's situated just off private property, almost nobody knows about the place. That's why you used to love to fish there, dumb ass."

Clayton Price heard only the click of Brad hanging up the telephone.

Brad just knew. It all came together in a blink. His night in a cave, sitting in a storm watching three people, bolts in the floor, photographs, children's bodies scattered. *This is it,* he thought. *The gorge is where it's all going to end.*

He dialed Kurt. After four rings, he heard Kurt's recorded voice explaining that he was unavailable and to please leave a message. "Jesus, Kurt, of all times for you not to answer your damned phone," Brad screamed into Kurt's message recording. "I called Clayton Price.

The gorge is the same as the old bridge on Lightning Creek just past Elk Run. You've been there. It all makes sense. King Solomon will know the place. This is it, Kurt. I feel it. Call me as soon as you get this message."

Next, he called sheriff's dispatch for Kurt. The lady promised to relay Brad's message. Who else to call? Sam and Rick Barnes were four hours away in Aspen. No point in calling them.

Brad paced as his mind spun. He recalled his night in the rain when he had sat in a cave and watched a crime unfold before his eyes. He thought of the moments that he had stood outside the cabin's door, Christine Reynolds only feet away. He had been cautious, conservative, followed the rules. How much suffering had resulted as a consequence?

Brad stood in his study and looked out the window. What to do? What to do? *What in the name of God is wrong with me? Can I be so stupid again?* Everything crystallized for Brad. He would go. It was an easy decision. The apprehension and self-doubt that had plagued him since the night in the storm vanished. He was a new man. Alert and electrified, his mind focused in icy calm. Brad walked from his office to do what had to be done.

In minutes he had gathered his gear and tossed it into the truck. He pulled from his house and drove southwest, toward the sunset.

————

THE DOOR FLEW open in a sudden rush, and Felix Gomez hurled into the room. He stood for a moment and turned his head. His gaze finally fell onto Christine. His eyes were open too wide, exaggerated but focused. Christine felt his power from across the room.

It stole the breath from her lungs.

Never altering his intense gaze from Christine, Felix spoke over his shoulder to Maria. Ice carried in his voice. "Let's do it."

I'm about to die, Christine's eyes closed with the thought.

Felix leaned his body over Christine, his ponytail dangling in her face. Christine's eyes swelled in fear and begged for mercy. Felix's dark eyes stared back. He may as well have looked at a stone.

In a matter of seconds, Felix and Maria covered Christine in a blanket. It was the same one that had rubbed her face raw on the night she had been taken. Terrifying memories flashed in her mind. It was all happening again. She felt her body being thrown. She could not move her arms or legs. It was black again. She could scarcely breathe. Christine knew she was being carried outside. Her arms and shoulders hurt when she was carelessly tossed. It was a car trunk again. The lid slammed shut.

Brandon. My children. How will he kill me? What will it feel like?

Felix walked to the driver's side door and sat behind the wheel. He turned and looked at Maria. With urgency in his manner and expectation in his eyes he said, "This won't take long. Be ready."

Tires spinning, the vehicle sped off.

Maria turned away. She would not watch.

———

DUSK WAS APPROACHING and Brad drove hard. He desperately wanted to reach his destination before dark. He was confident that if he arrived before nightfall, he would be ahead of his adversaries. Brad called Kurt again. No response. Brad could feel it as surely as anything in his life. It was predestined, somewhere in the stars; Kurt Riddle, his longtime friend, would not be with him tonight.

Leaving another message Brad told Kurt he was on his way to the gorge and then he calmly placed his cell phone in the seat beside him. No need to call again. He glanced at the sky. The clouds blackened the western horizon like an evil specter. Things were about to change.

Daylight faded and night raced. Brad turned from the highway and urged his truck up a neglected and steep track that twisted through the dense forest. His memory of this place came back as he crested the ridge and looked down into the canyon. This was one remote place.

He had beat darkness by a hair. Brad's instinct told him he didn't have long to prepare. He followed the dirt road that descended steeply to a clearing beside the creek. An old footbridge, rotting in disrepair, drooped over the water. Brad knew exactly where to go. He had to get away from the clearing and the bridge and get under cover. Just as he remembered, the road led to a secluded area in the woods. Brad parked his truck and turned his engine off. Resting his head on the seat back, he forced himself to take deep breaths. It was dark. He had made it.

Brad could feel the atmosphere changing. He lowered his windows and gripped the wheel. Brad could hear everything. He could hear the river rushing over stones. He could hear trout holding in riffles, their gills sucking life-giving oxygen from the icy water. Brad felt the ominous energy that amassed in the black clouds and heard every particle of life around him.

The first streak of lightning emblazoned the sky. Then the wind began.

Brad reluctantly closed the windows of his car. Gusts descended into the gorge. Pine needles and dirt flew through the air. He could sense that this was only the beginning. The storm had shoulders.

Brad didn't know who, or how many, were coming. But he knew they could not be far away. He had no specific plan. He simply would do what he had to do.

The wind grew stronger.

Lights of an approaching pick-up truck appeared as bobbing lanterns on a ship at sea. It crept its way down the hill, descending toward Brad. The pick-up truck cautiously pulled into the clearing and parked. It was too dark to see who occupied the vehicle. Lightning lashed like a whip tearing skin from the bones of the sky. In the eerie light Brad saw the vehicle's single occupant: King Solomon.

How long before the next vehicle arrived?

Removing the bulb from the dome of his truck before opening the door, Brad stepped into nature's fury. Creeping through inky blackness, he approached the pick-up truck from behind, keeping low and out of

King Solomon's sight. The wind was now screaming. He was no more than ten feet from King Solomon. Brad knew that King Solomon was afraid, but his fear was of nature not of a man creeping from behind. Brad did not think that the driver's door would be locked. He carried the tire jack from his truck just in case. He would enjoy smashing the window.

Crouching behind the truck, Brad calculated his next move. Lightning exploded in a flash of blue. The wind roared through the canyon and rocked the truck. *Now!* Brad flung the driver's door open. King Solomon was on the ground in little more than a second. Brad's body flattened over the stunned man, pressing his face into the earth. Brad could feel sand and gravel gouging the face of King Solomon, dirt filling his mouth and clogging his throat. King Solomon could not move. Brad pressed down with all his strength, knowing this was exactly what had happened to Christine Reynolds. He pressed harder.

King Solomon knew that he had been taken captive when he heard the familiar sound of steel-jawed cuffs ratchet about his wrists. But he had no idea who it was or what was happening.

King Solomon felt his body being dragged over rough ground. When the dragging ended, searching hands methodically slid over his body. This was also a routine that King Solomon had experienced before. His heart sank when the searching hands touched the .32 caliber pistol he had concealed inside his pants.

Brad pulled the gun from King Solomon's clothing.

A typical shithead punk gun.

King Solomon had never felt so powerless as he was hoisted to his feet and found himself looking into the face of a man he had never seen. King Solomon choked out, "Who the fuck are you? You're no goddamned cop."

"I'm from the ACLU, King Solomon. I'm here to help you."

"Fuck you."

King Solomon knew instantly that he had made a mistake. The words had been spoken automatically, what he always said to a cop.

In less time than it had taken for him to be pulled from his truck, King Solomon was again on his back, flat on the ground.

Brad stood over King Solomon, his chest heaving. Looking down upon the despicable creature, twenty years of courtesy and civility flooded through Brad's mind. He had fleeting visions of people he had arrested for all types of crimes, the hours he had spent with them in interview rooms. Yes, Mr. Robber, of course you can have coffee. Yes, Mr. Rapist, I will be happy to get you a sandwich. Certainly, Mr. Murderer, you can call an attorney. In fact, you don't even have to pay. You deserve one for free.

Without thinking, Brad fired his leg like a piston into the groin of King Solomon. The sickening thud was audible as the thunder that rolled through the canyon. King Solomon's testicles crushed like little onions.

Brad stood motionless over King Solomon, every nerve of his body on fire. *Jesus, that felt good.*

Brad thought about kicking King Solomon again. He didn't do it. Lightning flashed. Brad saw terror in King Solomon's eyes.

Spitting and swallowing vomit, tears now covered King Solomon's face. Brad lifted the limp body from the ground and jammed it into his truck.

As wind howled and lightning flashed, Brad Walker and King Solomon had a talk.

Now it was time to wait. He left his truck and walked to King Solomon's pick-up truck. Perfectly calm, Brad felt more alive than ever before in his life. After King Solomon had told the story of abducting Christine Reynolds, Brad had tied King Solomon with flex cuffs so securely that the contemptible man could scarcely move. Felix Gomez would arrive at any moment with Christine Reynolds. They planned to shoot her, dump her in the creek, cover her body with stones and then drive to meet Maria. They would then head for Mexico.

Brad seated himself behind the steering wheel of the truck. He lowered the windows all the way. He wanted to feel the storm on his skin. He wanted the energy of the storm in his body when Felix Gomez arrived.

Come on, Felix Gomez. Come on, shithead.

Brad figured the temperature must have dropped thirty degrees since he had pulled King Solomon from his truck. He watched the storm. Lightning gouged the sky. Thunder pulsated through the canyon, tremor upon tremor. Ice cold rain fired through the opened windows of the pick-up truck. It felt great.

Then, in a matter of seconds, the rain halted. A death-like quiet blanketed the canyon as the wind ceased. Nothing stirred. Absolute calm descended and the night stood still. Suddenly, in a single, horrific explosion, the sky commenced its full assault upon the earth. Hail replaced rain. Continuous lightning ricocheted from mountains to trees to boulders. Sizzling veins of fire cast a strobe effect, altering the equilibrium of the mountains. Canyon walls of ancient stone shuddered like a rag doll in the mouth of a rabid beast.

Earth lost its gyroscope.

The storm arrived.

————

HAIL BATTERING the body of King Solomon's pick-up truck sounded like the end of the world. Through the rearview mirror of the truck, Brad watched Felix Gomez's car creep down the hill. Sleet and ice flying through the beam of the vehicle's approaching headlights created a blinding illusion of white meteorites. Brad could feel the terror that clutched Gomez. He could feel it through the storm. He could hear the pounding of Felix's heart. Sticky sweat was oozing from the palms of the man who approached.

Brad smiled.

Come on, Felix Gomez. Come on.

The pick-up truck trembled in the wind's furor. Brad thought of Christine Reynolds. What must these sounds be like to her, sealed in a trunk, knowing she is about to meet her end?

Felix Gomez inched closer. Brad knew that within seconds he would be fully illuminated by the vehicle's lights. He also knew that Gomez understood survival on city streets but not in this environment. Gomez would be lost in such a storm. Vertigo would diminish his senses, and he would feel the universe spin backwards. Felix Gomez would see a person sitting in the truck. It wouldn't look like King Solomon, but Gomez would doubt himself. He wouldn't know for sure. He wouldn't know what to do. Felix Gomez breathed fear.

Brad smiled.

The wind screamed. Ice hammered on metal, threatening to shatter glass. Pounding the canyon without mercy, hail transformed the ground into white slush.

Brad's eyes fought the blinding glare of Felix's headlights as they came closer. The stench of evil was merely feet away.

Come on, shithead.

It was time. Brad felt himself on center stage, alone, within a glaring spotlight, audience in anticipation, no lines memorized.

Not a problem.

Felix Gomez stopped the car. He had survived for years in his treacherous world by trusting keen instincts. Gomez knew when something wasn't right. The figure behind the wheel of the truck didn't look right. But who could it be? It had to be King Solomon.

It sure as hell didn't look like King Solomon.

Opening his door, Gomez stepped out. He had never felt this kind of fear. Fear from what fell through the sky. Fear from what or who sat in the truck. He took one step toward the pick-up. Gomez strained his eyes to see. He took a second step.

Brad opened the truck door and stepped into the blinding lights. The moment had come. It was time to face Felix Gomez.

Out of the truck, Brad turned toward Gomez.

The sky exploded in lightning. Brad saw Felix's face, the eyes of his adversary, eyes that knew for certain it was not King Solomon who stood in the night, eyes that in an instant realized the world was about to change.

Felix Gomez ran for his life.

Brad Walker ran for his life.

Brad Walker ran for the life of Christine Reynolds

Two silhouettes tore through the frigid night, oblivious to the ice and fire over their heads. Thunder roared and wind screamed as if the gods were in celestial applause, cheering for the human contest below.

Gomez felt his life about to end. He kept running.

Brad felt new life surge. He kept running.

Between blasts of lightning, absolute darkness consumed the canyon. Brad could feel and hear Gomez only inches away but could not see his enemy. Lightning flashed and Brad again saw the profile, the strong jaw line, the ponytail. He remembered the night at the cave and the three people outside the cabin.

They ran. Lungs on fire, legs thrashing, wheezing, gasping.

In the darkness, Brad strained to see the figure only inches away. His brain screamed for oxygen as pressure pounded inside his eyes. He saw the ponytail and thought of the violated children, white rope, and bolts in the floor.

The ponytail was closer.

Murdered children in a canyon, broken bodies discarded. Garbage. Scraps fed to animals.

Inches away, the ponytail bounced.

Lungs seared. Ice water mingled with hot, salty sweat.

Almost in his grasp, Brad reached out and his fingers brushed the bound hair.

A red T-shirt. The smiling, yellow sun face.

Fingers closing.

Elizabeth's eyes.

Ponytail in hand. Ponytail snared.

From his body's core, Brad pulled the ponytail with all of his weight and strength. Time seemed to slow as the bodies of Brad Walker and Felix Gomez floated in unison, as astronauts in space, tumbling through animated suspension. As they fell, Brad concentrated with all that was within him. With every fiber in his soul, Brad Walker intended to crush the skull of Felix Gomez.

Time resumed. Their bodies collided onto the ground. Brad was on top with ponytail in hand. Felix Gomez lay face down in icy sludge. Using the ponytail for leverage, Brad jerked Gomez's head up before slamming it into the ground. He did it again, and again and again, like a piston within a cylinder.

Gomez did not move. Lightning illuminated the sky. Thunder shook the canyon; the earth's crust rattled. Wind tore through the trees. It was a celestial applause. Encore!

Brad lay on top of Gomez's inert body, gasping. Every muscle was on fire. He desperately sucked air into his lungs. Gradually, his burning muscles cooled.

I got you, shithead.

Brad lifted himself off the body and cinched flex-cuffs about Gomez's hands and feet. Now, in sheer desperation for Christine Reynolds, he grasped Gomez by his bound ankles and dragged the unconscious body back toward the vehicles. At the trunk of Felix's car, Brad dropped Gomez like a rolled carpet.

With his heart thundering still, Brad extracted the keys from the vehicle's ignition and opened the trunk. His eyes refused to adjust to even the dim light of the opened lid. Extending his hands into the trunk, he groped blindly. Something soft, a bundle. Was he touching human flesh?

"Mrs. Reynolds. It's okay, it's okay. I'm not going to hurt you. Are you alright?" Brad struggled to speak calmly, his breathing coming in desperate gasps.

The bundle moved slightly, but it moved.

Brad's eyes had begun to adjust, and he saw flesh buried within the blankets. "Mrs. Reynolds, everything is fine. I'm going to help you. There is no more danger. Can you hear me?"

More movement.

His hands trembling, Brad was on the verge of exploding. He lifted the fabric wrapped about her body. "It's okay, Mrs. Reynolds. You'll be fine now. It's all over." Finally, he unwrapped the blanket from around Christine's face. Tape covered her mouth. Gently, the bond was lifted.

Christine moved. Her eyes shifted as her lips opened. She blinked and then licked her cracked lips.

Looking up at the wet, mud-covered creature that hovered over her, Christine evaluated the situation. Was this death? Where did the gentle touch come from? The glow of light was soft, not harsh. She felt warmth. A hand stroked her hair. That gentle voice sounded far away. Where was it coming from?

"Mrs. Reynolds, everything is fine. Everything is fine. No one is going to hurt you. I promise."

Christine's mind began to clear. Sensations of life caressed her skin, eased into her brain. She was alive.

A flicker of a smile appeared.

Brad placed his arms under Christine and raised her to him in an embrace. Tears that had been dried now gushed. Her body trembled, but for the first time in days the trembling was not in fear.

Brad held her, and they cried together before he lifted her out of the trunk and into the car. Brad made a telephone call. "Mr. Reynolds, I have someone here who wants to talk with you."

———————

WHEN KURT and the patrol cars arrived, Felix Gomez had regained consciousness and was able to speak. He and King Solomon were placed into separate vehicles and Brad watched as the patrol cars drove away. He took comfort in the sight, knowing that the interview process would last for days, revealing sordid stories from cities and neighborhoods across the continent; stories about humanity, heart-wrenching stories about the lives of children.

Brad closed his eyes. "Thank you, God."

With patrol cars and investigators gone, Brad was alone. He steered his truck from the canyon and stopped and rolled his windows down. He needed to feel the night, to savor how cold it had become. The wind had ceased. The hail and rain were gone. Lightning was a memory. The fractured heavens had already healed and the night was still. Brad collapsed into his seat. With cold air across his face, he finally felt his body relax.

Several moments passed before Brad realized what was happening. It was snowing. White flakes drifted through the black night, gently touching the earth as if to heal the wounds from the evil that had intruded. Brad peered into the deserted canyon, the darkened void where he had confronted King Solomon and Felix Gomez. Brad peered into the darkened void where he had confronted himself.

It was now so quiet.

———

THE MOTEL WAS ONLY a few blocks away, but it seemed like another world and a lifetime ago. Maria had never been so glad to leave a place. But her nervousness grew as she waited. Felix and King Solomon should have been here by now. She hoped it was only the weather that had delayed them. The car was fueled and packed with food and water. She had all they needed for escape. Mexico and refuge were only hours away.

Still, images of the woman's face would not leave her. She could not rid herself of the memory of those pleading eyes. Would that horrible vision be with her for life? What of the other visions that haunted her? Could she ever forget what she had seen men do to children? It was over now, and yes, she could forget. She would make herself forget. She would never have to turn away again.

Maria sat in her darkened vehicle. Rain pounded the streets. It seemed to be turning into snow. She spoke to herself, "Please hurry, Felix. I want to be away from this place. Please hurry!"

Soon there was no question. Rain had definitely changed into snow and it flew sideways through the air. Maria could hardly see across the street. It would be so good to let Felix or King Solomon drive. She wanted to close her eyes and begin the process of forgetting. A car approached, slowing as it came near. Maria whispered silent thanks. Felix and King Solomon had finally arrived. Everything would be all right now. They would leave their car and take the one Maria was driving, the new vehicle arranged by King Solomon. There was no chance of the police having any idea what they drove.

Something was terribly wrong. Why did Felix pull in front of her?

Maria's world collapsed. It was not Felix. It was not King Solomon. Her survival instincts kicked in, and Maria's mind no longer directed her body. Pressing the accelerator to the floor, she tore through water and slush as she pulled around the car in front of her. Careening into the street, Maria's world became a blur of snow, water and flashing red lights. Wailing sirens battered her skull. The car propelled like a launched rocket, friction and gravity were her enemies.

Maria steered the speeding missile, blasting straight through an intersection. As if directed by the gods, a garbage truck lumbered its way into a perfect interception of Maria's flight path.

When Maria's face collided with the windshield, bones split, flesh ripped, and teeth shattered. Her beauty forever vanished. Slivers of glass sliced her eyes.

Maria would never again need to turn her head in order not to see.

––––––––

A BEAUTIFUL BLACK WOMAN CRIED, her face so brutally beaten that her eyes swelled, and blood crusted her lips. She called a number, a number that in her years as a call girl she could never have imagined she would need: the FBI.

He was going to fly away on a chartered jet. He had tied and beaten her, telling her that she was his property. She was to fly away with him, his sex object for as long as he wanted. She could be sold at any time. The black woman had run through the hotel lobby after she escaped, totally nude and pleading for help.

Through her tears, she spoke to the person on the telephone. She described the car Whitman drove and where it was parked. She provided details about his hotel, his chartered flight, and where he intended to go.

TWO WEEKS LATER

Brad walked with his fly rod. No other person was within miles, he had Stone Creek to himself. It was a good day. Today was Cody's birthday. In only one month, he was scheduled to return home from the Persian Gulf. Brad would be there, standing with hundreds of other people longing to see their loved one. He would cheer as his son walked from his ship, dressed in his crisp, white naval uniform. Brad longed for the embrace.

His journey to the river had been therapeutic. Driving the road that they had traveled so many times together, Brad felt Elizabeth riding with him. The feelings were not disturbing at all. Quite the contrary, they had been enjoyable, most peaceful. As Brad put on his waders and laced his boots, he could have sworn he heard her laughing. The sound was nearby. He just couldn't pinpoint its exact source.

As Brad approached the creek, the sun felt warm on his skin. Anticipation of feeling the river's current was pleasant. In the water, Brad moved his feet over submerged boulders, easing his way into the middle of the stream. This was what he needed. The water felt familiar, like an old friend. His first casts were delicate. The fly floated, almost weightless, softer than a shadow, before touching the water. Within minutes he had landed two trout. He released them, marveling in their beauty as they darted back into the cold depth.

A stone in the middle of the river offered Brad a comfortable place to sit for awhile and simply enjoy his surroundings. What a perfect day. The sky was an intense blue, and the white clouds were absolutely brilliant. Brad absorbed the sky. He would never tire of its enchantment.

When he first noticed the leaf, its mystery escaped him. Brad watched as a single golden aspen leaf drifted, fluttering, each twist catching the sun in a new angle, a different shimmer. Then it hit him. This valley was all evergreen. There was not an aspen forest for miles!

How far had the leaf drifted? *Amazing!* The leaf settled onto the river, just in front of a giant boulder. Brad sat quietly, allowing his mind to wander.

It happened again, another aspen leaf. Once again Brad marveled as it floated, swaying gently, brushing the boulder before easing its way onto the water, exactly where the first leaf had landed. Where could these leaves possibly have come from?

Brad contemplated the events of the past few days. Could he now enjoy some peace? Maybe some time with his children? Time would tell. Brad stood, preparing to cast, but another aspen leaf drifted. He watched it frolicking, carefree, on its way to the boulder.

Had he missed it before? Just in front of the boulder, where the leaves had settled, a trout arched its back in momentary suspension between water and air.

Brad's heart skipped a beat as he calculated the necessary cast. In a thousand years, he could not have made it more perfectly. The fly whispered, touching the water with the grace of a shy princess. There was no explosion of strength. The trout did not launch its body from the water. It was simply a subtle rise, a timid kiss. The fish took the fly. With a gentle roll, the creature eased into deep water and Brad felt pressure. He instinctively raised the tip of his rod, prepared for battle.

Battle did not come.

The only sensation that flowed through the rod, the only thing that reached Brad's hand and arm was a caress. The trout slid its body across the river, bank to bank, tantalizingly close. Then, the fish slipped away, tugging his line, hidden in the current.

Brad's body tingled as realization of the moment crystallized. This was not a battle. It was a waltz.

How many aspen leaves had to appear, falling into the exact same spot, before he saw what they were showing him, before he heard what they said?

The waltz continued. The fish tugged, a ripple through the water. When the light was perfect, Brad could see inches beneath the surface and, in fleeting glimpses, a special beauty that was there just for him.

Brad brought the fish closer.

A wind stirred. The air filled with aspen leaves, countless droplets of gold descended, brushing his face, touching his hair and arms. As the leaves settled onto the river, they drifted about his feet, weightless on the current.

With a single, nimble motion, the fish was suddenly directly before Brad. He watched as its silver body ascended to the surface. Brad could not believe his eyes; the tiny fly was no longer in its mouth, the trout was free, holding, close enough to touch. Then it was a shadow. All too quickly, its beauty vanished, disappearing into the water, stone, and sand.

Brad was stunned. The leaves had fallen from the air and the water had carried them away.

The leaves were gone. There was nothing but blue sky overhead. Then he saw it drift into view, just over his head. One final leaf swayed in the air. Brad stood without moving as the leaf rippled, lazily descending to him. The golden teardrop winked past his face and settled on his neck. The kiss was warm, wet, and seductive.

The leaf fell to the water and disappeared.

Brad waited for his chills to subside and then, for the first time since her death, a sense of calm entered his heart. He looked at the gently rippling river, late afternoon sun shimmered with the glow of amber.

It happened so suddenly. She was there. Reflecting above the water he saw her photograph. Elizabeth's eyes twinkled. Her smile, her beautiful smile. Her beautiful face.

Brad Walker sat. Stone Creek meandered.

EPILOGUE
SIX MONTHS LATER

Night sounds.

Like a river, night sounds ebb and flow at day's end, twisting their way through the corridors of a darkened prison. They are sounds like no others. Cage doors slam. Metal locks seal. Each night the river brings sounds to the condemned men who have no alternative but to listen. They are not the sounds of a cricket, an owl, wind through the trees, or the wail of a passing train. Rumbling thunder or the soothing song of rain is never heard. The sounds that drift on this river are always the same: a scream, an obscene laugh, a whispered prayer. A plea for mother. Sounds of intimacy.

The night sounds are a prophecy of life for tomorrow, prophecy of a world where the strong own the weak: own them to buy, sell, or trade. Lives are bought and sold for cigarettes or a gram of smuggled narcotic. Traded for sport.

The sounds are there each night, carried on currents that relentlessly drift through cold canyons of steel and concrete; a building crafted for oppression.

Those who have been there say that the night sounds never cease to haunt.

AUTHOR'S NOTE

Brad Walker, Kurt Riddle, and Sam Trathen and all of the persons depicted in the preceding pages are fictional characters. The story that has been told is fiction. However, the brutal aspects of humanity that are related herein and the efforts of so many people who combat such inhumanity are not fiction. Sadly, the issues are very real.

Each day, the men and women of the National Center for Missing and Exploited Children rise from their beds, greet their families, and go to work where they face as reality the evils portrayed in this story. On a daily basis, law enforcement officers from all jurisdictions—local, state, and federal—miss ball games, birthdays and school plays of their own children as they struggle in frontline combat against crimes that are unspeakable in our polite society. Across the United States, countless attorneys, mental health professionals, and social workers devote endless hours to help mend lives that have been shattered and to restore dignity to those who have been robbed of the most fundamental rights that God intended all humans to enjoy.

Without exception, the people mentioned above are overworked, underappreciated, and underpaid. Thank God we have them.

The Mirror in the River is a story that is intended to recognize the people who serve our children and our society. As we enjoy the lavish lifestyle that is prevalent in the United States, we will do well to remember that many among us, usually because of birthplace, skin color, or misfortune in who conceived them, bear the curse of the shameful ignominy portrayed in this story. This is a scar on our country and society.

These words sung by Willie Nelson:

The prayer of every man is to know
how freedom feels
Give us our daily bread; we have no shoes to wear
No place to call our home, only this cross to bear
We are the multitudes; lend us a helping hand
Is there no love anymore
Living in the Promised Land

ABOUT THE AUTHOR

Dale spent twenty-five years as an FBI agent investigating violent crimes and concluded his law enforcement career by helping establish the Federal Air Marshal Service. He then turned his energy to writing. Dale lives in Colorado where fly-fishing, mountains, and the grandeur of nature have been integral to him, his wife, and their three children.